# A Rogue in Twilight

The Whisky Rogues, Book 2

Previously published as Laird of Twilight / ePublishing Works
And originally as To Wed a Highland Bride / Sarah Gabriel / Avon

## Susan King

## ARE YOU SIGNED UP FOR DRAGONBLADE'S BLOG?

You'll get the latest news and information on exclusive giveaways, exclusive excerpts, coming releases, sales, free books, cover reveals and more.

Check out our complete list of authors, too!

No spam, no junk. That's a promise!

### Sign Up Here

www.dragonbladepublishing.com

*Dearest Reader;*

*Thank you for your support of a small press. At Dragonblade Publishing, we strive to bring you the highest quality Historical Romance from some of the best authors in the business. Without your support, there is no 'us', so we sincerely hope you adore these stories and find some new favorite authors along the way.*

*Happy Reading!*

*CEO, Dragonblade Publishing*

Additional Dragonblade books by
Author Susan King

**The Whisky Rogues Series**
A Rogue in Firelight (Book 1)
A Rogue in Twilight (Book 2)

**Highland Secrets Series**
The Scottish Bride (Book 1)
The Forest Bride (Book 2)
The Guardian's Bride (Book 3)

**Celtic Hearts Series**
The Hawk Laird (Book 1)
The Falcon Laird (Book 2)
The Swan Laird (Book 3)

**The Lyon's Den Series**
Lyon of Scotland

*For Jennifer, who knows all about fairy stones*

# **Prologue**



B UFFETED BY WIND gusts, Donal MacArthur climbed a rocky hill in moonlight, his plaid billowing and snapping against his trousered legs. He walked up the slope toward a tall black crevice in the rock, and reached up to a natural shelf, groping with his hand.

There, he had it—the bit of crystal he had tucked there years ago. Fitting the palm of his hand, it was pale blue under the moon, variegated and crystalline. Pressing it into a small niche in the rock wall, he felt the massive rock slide with a chink and a settle.

The wind whipped around him as he turned the crystal, which was a key. He pulled his plaidie close, clamped a hand to his bonnet, and waited. Though this was not the appointed time for him to come here, they would expect him this particular night.

Every seven years since his youth, he had come to this place according to the agreement. Seven years, and seven again, until seven-times-seven was reached. By then, he would be an old man. Only a year and a day had passed since his last visit, but he had a reason to return so soon.

*She* always came to greet him, welcoming him into her arms, taking him into her world. For a while, he would lose his sense of time, of himself, his home, his dear ones at Kilcrennan. Inside the hill, he would revel in the pleasures offered, golden wines and ripe fruits, sweet crystalline music, dancing like joyful madness, laughter like angels, like devils. Some did say the Fey were fallen angels. He could believe it, knowing their sweetness and their cruelty.

And then the private pleasures with her—sinful, graceful passions, her perfect body never aging, fitting exquisitely to his own, still hard and fit despite the years. That lush sensual feverishness lured him here too. The craving that pulsed through blood and soul slowed his aging. He could not resist her, nor did she deny him the powerful blend of touch, thrust, and magic.

Inevitably, she would release him and he would find himself standing outside the rock again in moonlight or at dawn: just Donal the weaver, tall and handsome though aging, blessed in his friends, fortunate in his business; Donal MacArthur, who as a young man had made a dark bargain with a queen of the fairy ilk.

The rock wall shifted and opened like a door. Beyond the glow of light within, he heard pipes and laughter. Oh, how he wanted to go inside. *No*, he told himself.

"Donal, dearest!" She stood before him. He did not dare say or think her name for its power. Standing inside the threshold, slim and elegant, she glowed like a moonbeam. Her garments were gossamer, her face and form beautiful. He caught his breath, feeling the lure and the lust.

"I am here," he said, "a year a day from the last time we met, as agreed. I am here for the return of my son. We had a bargain."

"Did we?" She laughed, silver music. Glancing over her shoulder, she beckoned. The sound of merriment, the fragrances of wine, apples, and cakes wafted toward the entrance. Donal drew breath, tempted, and stood still.

Then his son appeared, Niall, a dark-haired and beautiful young man. With him stood the one who had lured him inside, a lass of uncommon beauty, black glossy hair and silvery eyes. Sensing sadness in her, Donal hoped it was because Niall was leaving.

"Niall, my own, are you well?" he asked, careful to stay outside the entrance.

"Very well, and happier than any man ever was."

"You must break their power over you," Donal said, but Niall shook his head.

"The Fey have won, what's done is done," the queen of the hillside said. "Your son has found true love's enchantment here, which all humans long for. He reminds me of you, my Donal." Her eyes gleamed, and lust darkened her lips to rose. "Come."

"Not this time," Donal growled.

She laughed. "Oh, come inside forever, my love, with me." She opened her arms.

It took effort, but Donal ignored her to look at his son. "Come out, Niall."

But he shook his head. "I cannot cross the threshold now. I gave my promise and I must remain." He pulled the black-haired beauty close. "But I am happy, Da. I would gladly stay forever with my bride."

Donal's heart sank. "*Och*, my Niall."

The queen, his lover, reached out. "Forever would be our bliss too. Come to me, my bonny weaver."

He loved her, he did, but he stepped back. "It is not time. I will return as I promised long ago. Every seven years." He stepped back.

"Fine, then. Wait, the gift! I keep my promises too." She turned as a girl appeared beside her, holding a bundle. Niall's black-haired lover reached out, but the queen snatched it up, pulling down the blanket. "Here Donal, take this home with you."

He saw an infant swathed in glittering fairy cloth. The small, perfect creature had dark hair and big eyes and was so lovely and impish that his heart melted then and there.

"What is this? A changeling who will not be so lovely when I reach home?"

"No changeling. She is half our kind and half yours." His lover touched the child's brow, and a glow like a moonbeam sparked and vanished. She offered the infant to Donal. "I have given her a gift. She will see what cannot be seen."

"The Second Sight." Such a gift was by the fairies, though at a hidden cost, so it was said. Donal accepted the feathery weight in his arms, studied the infant, and knew. He looked at his son. "Yours? I see a resemblance."

"Aye. Your granddaughter. We lend her into your keeping." His bride bowed her head, and Donal understood her sadness. The Fey had good hearts for their ilk, and for humans, too, sometimes.

His granddaughter, and so perfect! His heart filled with new love. "Mine to take?" he asked.

"In exchange for your son," the queen said. "That is our bargain now. She is called Eilidh"—*Ai-lish*, she pronounced. "It is her fairy name, and holds great power. Take care not to say it aloud very often."

"Then I will call her Elspeth, after my late wife, her grandmother. And I will give her a home and love her as if she were my own child." He moved back quickly, before they could change their capricious minds about the babe. The wee squirming bundle was dear to him already. Tears stung his eyes. "Niall, come with me—"

"Not now. We will meet again, Da. Take care of her, please. She has Fey blood, and will feel the lure of it sometimes. But she will live with you until we call her back."

"Let her stay with me always," Donal protested. He looked at the queen. "I have lost my son to your ilk. Give her to me and she will thrive and be happy."

"When she is grown, she must return to us."

"Is there no other way? I cannot lose her, too." He felt near tears.

"If you would find the treasure stolen from us long ago, perhaps she could stay longer. Return our treasure and we can make a new agreement."

"The fairy treasure is gone. No one knows if the legend is

even true." The Fey were prone to exaggeration, Donal knew. *Daoine Sith*, they were called in the Gaelic—people of peace. Yet they were not peaceful if crossed. He must be cautious.

"It is true. A MacArthur of your ilk stole our treasure long ago." Her voice turned icy cold. "Until it is returned, we will claim sons and daughters from this glen. You are in our thrall. Your son is with us now. You are fortunate to have this little one for a time."

He held the babe close. "I have looked for the treasure. I do not know where it is."

"It lies somewhere in these hills, or in some earthly hall. We cannot retrieve it, but you can. Two keys will open it. You have one, the blue stone." Donal knew she meant the crystal that he used to open the rock. "The second key lies in your arms."

"The child? I do not understand."

"You will." Her smile twitched, either humor or scheming.

"Tell me where to look for the treasure."

"If we knew that, we would not need your help. Either find it or bring the girl to us when she is grown. I will set a binding spell around her." She raised her arms high.

Sensing her power about to ignite, Donal moved back. "This is a wicked bargain. Let the lass choose what she wants. There must be another way."

"Love," Niall said suddenly. "Da, listen. Love can break a fairy spell. It is the strongest magic in any realm."

"Stop," the queen told Niall.

He shook his head. "If our wee daughter finds true love, the spell that binds her to this realm will dissolve."

"Stop," said the queen.

"Our daughter must never fall in love," said Niall's fey bride. "She must come back to us!" She sounded heartbroken.

Donal held the child close, knowing he must take her now and leave his son behind. "Niall, farewell," he forced out. The young man lifted a hand, his eyes sad.

Shielding the infant with his plaidie, Donal walked backward, aware he must not turn his back on the beautiful ones or their shining world inside the dark hill. Only when the rock had closed did he turn, his heart heavy, his spirit determined.

If he could help it, his granddaughter would never set foot inside that realm, he thought as he hurried away. He would keep Elspeth safe as any treasure. Though he was obliged to visit the hillside portal regularly, he would keep the lass away from the glamour of the Seelie court and its allure and enchantment.

Yet if she were to find true love, she would be safe from the spell. Without that, the Seelie Court would take her just as they had taken Niall. He could not lose both of them. Returning the treasure could release the hold on the MacArthurs of this glen, but Donal had searched for years. He did not know where else to look.

But he would do all he could to keep this precious lass free of their realm.

*The Highlands, 1808*

ELSPETH SAT BESIDE her grandfather in one of two green brocade chairs flanking the fire. She watched small blue flames lick around peat bricks and traced her fingers over the worn brocade. Sitting proper and straight, as their housekeeper Mrs. Graham always admonished her, she smoothed her blue dress, patted her dark curls, crossed her feet in white stockings and black slippers, and watched her grandfather.

He studied a page in the small leather book where he kept his notes and the criss-cross drawings for his weavings. He wrote something with pencil, *scritch-scratch.*

"Grandda, will you teach me the weaving?"

"Someday," he murmured, distracted.

She swung her feet like the clapper of a bell. "Tell me about the Fey again."

He smiled, and looked up. "So beautiful, like you, hey. Quick-witted and joyful, like you. But fickle, which you would never be." She laughed, and he continued. "Remember, if the *Daoine Sìth* like us and love us, good fortune is ours."

"If they are pleased," she prodded.

"Aye, if they become annoyed, they will turn their hearts and their backs to us, and their blessings and gifts will become curses. And we must never look back if we walk away from them, or we will be in their thrall forever."

"Never look back," she repeated dutifully, nodding. "My father looked back."

He nodded sadly. "He did. They love and live joyfully, but they have hidden powers, and they do not forgive easily, if ever. That's the Fey."

"What do they look like?" She had heard the stories often and delighted in them. She wanted to know more about the realm where her father lived. Her grandfather had a storyteller's way about him that made every repeated tale sound new.

"Some are golden as sunshine, some dark as midnight. You are like the dark ones." He reached over to tap her knee. "Hair like jet, eyes like moonlight in that small and perfect wee face. You take after your fairy mother. But you have your father's stubborn chin and his temperament. You do not always do as Mrs. Graham and I ask." He looked stern for a moment.

"I try to listen, but sometimes I want to do as I please."

"Just like your father. Willful and smart, with a mind of your own."

"I wish my parents were here with us," she said wistfully. "Grandda, let's try the guessing game again. I will tell you what page you are looking at in the book."

"Very well." He turned a page and covered it with his hand.

She closed her eyes. She liked this game well. "It says, *blue, blue, green, green, and five threads of yellow for the weft threads.* It is the MacArthur tartan! You are looking at the weaving pattern for our own plaidie!" She opened her eyes and he showed her the page.

"True! One of my cousins wants a length of wool for a new

waistcoat."

She smiled. "Peggy Graham says I have the Sight."

"And so you do. The fairies gave it to you."

"Someday perhaps I will see where their fairy gold is hidden so we can return it to them. And then they will be grateful and happy, and send my father back to us."

Donal MacArthur sighed. "Niall and the fairy treasure may be lost forever. But anything is possible, aye?" He returned to his notes. *Scritch, scratch.*

Elspeth looked into the leaping, delicate flames, and wished she could see the fairies too, as Grandda sometimes did. She squeezed her eyes shut. Nothing came to her.

Sometimes she had lovely dreams where a handsome young man and a beautiful dark-haired lady came to her, laughed with her, hugged her. She thought they were fairy people, but was not sure. She wondered if they were her own parents.

*Someday she would see them,* she promised herself.

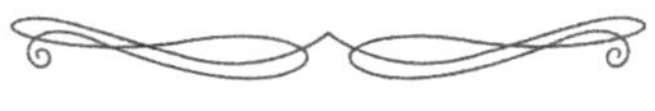

# Chapter One



*Scotland, Edinburgh*
*July, 1822*

"FAIRIES! YOU CANNOT possibly mean, sir," Patrick MacCarran leaned forward, knuckles pressed on the lawyer's desk, "that a parcel of blasted fairies stands between us and our inheritance!" He glanced at his three siblings, while the men behind the oak desk, one seated, the other standing, remained silent.

"We need not assume ruination." James MacCarran, Viscount Struan gave a nonchalant shrug of his shoulders in good black serge as he spoke quietly. He deliberately maintained an unruffled demeanor and casual pose as he leaned against the doorframe of the lawyer's study, though he felt as stunned as the others. "Let Mr. Browne and Sir Walter finish before we decide that we are done for."

His siblings looked grim—his sister Fiona pale but composed, their younger brothers, William and Patrick, scowling. James preferred distance in most things, actual and emotional. That was serving him well today with the revelation of the will.

Scarcely a farthing would come to any of them from their grandmother unless the astonishing conditions of her will and testament were met. Ruination could be in store for all of them, James thought.

"What could make this worse?" Patrick shoved a hand through his dark hair.

"A few elves might complement the situation nicely," William drawled.

James huffed a laugh. William, his next youngest brother, was a quiet-spoken physician who had hoped to be able to open a hospital with his share of the inheritance; Fiona, their sister, was an independent, serene woman with an academic bent for the study of fossil rock that made her any scholar's equal, and a bit of inheritance would help her research. Fiona stood now, stretching out a hand to calm Patrick, a Signet clerk with a strong temperament and an ambition to rise through the law courts.

As for himself, James was content as a professor of geology. He had few real needs. But what Grandmother posthumously asked of all of them was untenable.

"Lady Struan's fortune will be divided, with conditions," Mr. Browne repeated. "Apart from your grandfather's estate at his death a few years ago, which left a modest sum after his considerable expenditures."

"He helped ease the suffering of displaced Highlanders during the clearances of so many from their homes," Fiona said. "None of us begrudge his decisions."

Browne nodded. "Lady Struan acquired a personal fortune through publications and properties. She allowed Lord Eldin, her advisor in those matters, to sell off some of her properties in the last few years. Struan House remains, and will go to Lord Struan, who inherited his grandfather's title two years ago."

James leaned in the doorway, silent. As the eldest grandson, he had assumed the title; their father had died when he and Fiona had been nine, their brothers younger. As a titled but not particularly wealthy peer, James had a modest bank account and earned his daily living as a professor of natural philosophy at the University of Edinburgh. He had no aspirations of higher circumstances, enjoying his work and a peaceful academic life.

He had mourned his grandmother privately, concealing his grief as was natural to him, having learned it at an early age. He had hoped that her fortune would ensure the future of his siblings, especially his sister. As a penniless viscount, he could not adequately do for his twin or his brothers, though he would if he could.

But—fairies? James felt as bewildered as the rest. He glanced at Patrick, who still seethed; Fiona's air of serenity hid a fiery temper; and William, brow furrowed beneath golden hair, was as skilled as James at hiding his thoughts.

As a boy, James had kept himself to himself after the deaths of his parents had separated him and his siblings into different homes for fostering. William and Patrick had gone to uncles; James and Fiona to a great-aunt. He had never entirely emerged from that emotional exile, as Fiona sometimes pointed out. But his twin saw what others might not.

William cleared his throat. "I know Grandmother was fond of fairy tales and scribbled some of her own. But I did not realize she took it quite it so seriously."

Fiona sat beside William in a graceful swirl of black satin, her bonnet's curved rim highlighting her pretty face and wispy brown curls. Gazing at his twin sister, James suddenly knew her next words. *A kerfuffle*—

"It's a kerfuffle," she said, "but we shall resolve it." She smiled tightly.

Did he often guess her words from simple logic, knowing her so well, or was it the mysterious bond of twinship? James leaned toward scientific reason, which reigned cool and supreme in his thinking.

"More than a kerfuffle," he said. "This is a disaster."

"I do wonder if Grandmother was fully capable when she decided these conditions," Patrick said. "I doubt anyone influenced her, for she was smart and stubborn. But she was very ill at the last. William, as a physician, what say you?"

"Her condition made her increasingly frail, but her mind seemed balanced. I saw her often enough and noticed no diminished faculties. James saw her often too when she was in the house on Charlotte Square and he was at the university and living nearby."

"Grandmother always knew her mind. I never doubted her faculties," James said. "She mentioned the will, but never a hint of this." During the last months of her illness, he had grown closer to his grandmother. Yet he felt dismayed now, having no idea of her intentions recorded in her last will and testament.

"I knew of Lady Struan's plans," Sir Walter Scott said then. "And I regret that I was not able to confide in any of you." He smiled sadly.

The MacCarrans looked at him in unison. The poet had been Lady Struan's good friend, and though James did not know him well, he had always admired Sir Walter's genius, integrity, his loyalty to his friends, and his great love of Scotland.

"Grandmother so enjoyed your visits, Sir Walter," Fiona said. "We very much appreciate your attention to her. She looked forward to King George's arrival in Edinburgh, too. It is tragic that she died before the event could take place."

Scott nodded. "She was enthusiastic in her suggestions for the upcoming festivities. I know she will be there in spirit for the king's jaunt next month."

"And we will all be there in her honor," James said.

"Now that the will has been read," Mr. Browne said after a pause, "there are some points to discuss. Each of you has individual conditions." He turned a few pages. "Your obligations must be fulfilled or you will be considered to have failed."

"What if we cannot meet the conditions?" Patrick asked.

"Then most of the inheritance will go to another party." Mr. Brown took up a stack of folded and sealed letters and handed them around. Sir Walter assisted, leaning on his cane as he limped across the room to present a packet to Fiona, while James, Patrick, and William received theirs as well.

"The conditions are explained in the letters. Once the stipulations are met," Mr. Browne continued, "you will each be entitled to an equal share of Lady Struan's fortune, approximately fifty thousand pounds apiece. However, the portions will be reduced to five thousand pounds if you cannot, or will not, meet the conditions of the will."

In the dumbstruck silence that followed, James examined his envelope. *The Right Hon. The Viscount Struan*, it read in some cleric's hand. His grandmother, had she addressed it herself, might have written James Arthur MacCarran. He smiled ruefully.

"Share the contents among yourselves if you want, but keep it private otherwise," Browne said. "Adhere closely to the requests or the inheritance reverts to the lesser amount."

"I will not wait," Patrick peeled open the seal, unfolded the page, and read quickly and silently. "Ah. I am to help win back Duncrieff Castle, lost to debts ten years past. But—what the devil! I must make a love match for myself, with someone of…fairy blood." He looked at the others in disbelief. "This is absurd."

"Lady Struan asked me to advise you on fairy lore and such if you wish," Sir Walter offered. "She was quite the expert herself, as you know, having written several books on folklore and superstition, and even published under her own name. She had a fine reputation among the literary set."

William scanned his letter, folded it, and slipped it into a pocket. "I've been asked to do something similar," he said without elaboration. "James?"

Frowning, James held the envelope. He did not want to open it. He wanted to leave this meeting and return to his geological studies; he had a journal article to complete on evidence of ancient heat at the earth's core and a lecture to prepare for his university classes in natural philosophy and geology. He was reluctant to discuss the matter of this preposterous will any further. But he had no choice.

After what he had witnessed and endured at Waterloo a few years earlier, he had chosen to create as dull a life as possible— numbingly boring, lacking risk, involvement, or emotion to the best of his ability. He had seen enough drama and excess for a lifetime. Safe, dull—he appreciated the merit of it and tried to enjoy it.

But if his grandmother had requested that he too find a

fairy—let alone marry one or some such—that did not suit. Marrying anyone just now did not suit the bachelor existence he kept for himself. Besides, this was pure madness, and he was pure logic.

Fiona slipped her letter into her black net reticule. "This says I am to continue the charitable work that I've been doing, teaching English to Gaelic-speaking Highlanders," she said. "And I am expected to marry a Highland gentleman with fortune and breeding. Nothing to dispute there," she said with a brief smile.

"Is that all?" Patrick tipped his head.

"And I must draw fairy portraits from life. That's unlikely." She laughed. "And I am to give my drawings to James. Why is that?" She looked at her twin.

Everyone looked at him now. Sighing, James opened his letter and skimmed its contents. A muscle began to bounce in his jaw. "I am expected to stay at Struan House as its viscount—and complete any book that Grandmother left unfinished. She was working on another book about fairy lore. But I know little of fairy tales," he added.

"Grandmother's big book of fairies?" Patrick chuckled. "No topic for Professor MacCarran, who writes thick tomes about geographic strata."

"What else does it say?" Fiona, as usual, knew he was holding back something.

"I am, uh, to marry a Highland bride of fairy descent," James admitted. "A Highland wife is possible someday. Fairy? It is simply impossible."

"Good Lord, is it so for all of us? Was Grandmother truly mad?" Patrick asked.

"If we cannot meet these requirements, Mr. Browne," Fiona said, "who would inherit the bulk of Grandmother's accounts?"

Mr. Browne glanced at the page. "Nicholas MacCarran, the Earl of Eldin."

"Cousin Nick," Patrick growled, "that damnable, rotten, scheming scoundrel! Sorry, Fiona. I wonder if he influenced

Grandmother in this madness."

"That lying rogue," William agreed. "He stole our clan seat, Duncrieff Castle, away from our own cousin after he died at Waterloo. Even now, Nicholas enjoys the profits of that estate, while we—" He stopped, glancing at Fiona.

James saw his sister glance away. He knew she still felt keen heartbreak over their distant cousin's death; the young chief, Archibald MacCarran, had been Fiona's betrothed. James had felt the heartbreak of it too, for his sister's sake.

"Nick called it a good business arrangement," Patrick said, scowling.

"So if we do not comply, Eldin inherits all," James said, low and flat.

"But for the lesser funds apportioned to each of you, yes," Mr. Browne said.

"Why would Grandmother do this?" Fiona asked.

"To force us to meet her conditions," James replied.

"Your grandmother was working on a book about Highland fairy lore," Sir Walter said. He had remained quiet, but stepped forward now. "She hoped to restore the legendary fairy luck of the MacCarrans that she feared had become cursed over generations."

"We have never been a particularly fortunate sort, I will grant," William said. "But if I found a lass I could fancy and called her part fairy—who's to know?"

"Lady Struan wanted all of you to approach this in serious fashion, as she did," Sir Walter said. "Else it all goes to Lord Eldin. She hoped that would be your incentive."

James exhaled sharply. Write a damned fairy book and find a fairy bride? He had other books to write, and he was not interested in a wife just yet. The inheritance meant little to him, but his siblings had scant resources. But they would all want to protect their grandmother's funds from Lord Eldin—the only man James had ever truly despised.

He should have shot the blackguard when he had the chance.

"I must go," he said abruptly, standing away from the door where he leaned. "A meeting at the university. And it seems I shall have to request a sabbatical for a length of time." He gave them a brief wave, snatched up his cane, and limped out the door.

# Chapter Two

*Edinburgh, Scotland*
*August, 1822*

L IFTING THE FLOUNCED satin of her silvery blue court dress in one gloved hand, Elspeth MacArthur surged ahead in the crowd of elaborately dressed, perfumed women. The long train required of a lady's dress for this occasion was cumbersome, and she twisted to tug on it once again. Mr. Scott's booklet containing hints and advice for those attending the functions associated with King George's visit to Scotland specified a train at least four yards in length.

Easy enough for a man to declare, as they did not have to fuss with them, she thought wryly, as she reached down to twitch the part of the fabric train that was draped over her wrist. Slippery satin, she thought, as she glanced around for Lucie.

She had lost sight of her cousin, Lucie Graham, in the sea of ladies bedecked in satin, silk, damask, lace, jewels, feathers, and Highland tartan. The feathers in her hair—nine, another specification for the event—were held fast in her dark hair by pearled pins. She lifted a hand to her carefully arranged curls—she was not used to the fussy style—and looked around.

The press of the crowd was unbearably warm and close. Perhaps she should flee entirely, Elspeth thought, like Lady Graham, Lucie's mother, who not long ago had pleaded faintness and was escorted out by Lucie's brother, Sir John. Following them, Lucie had been swallowed in the spectacle. Over two thousand ladies and gentlemen were crammed into a few rooms and corridors in Holyroodhouse while each Scottish lady awaited a chance to be presented to King George the Fourth, lately arrived in Scotland.

With Lady Graham taken ill, Elspeth wondered how she and Lucie could be introduced to the king, since only those who had met King George previously had the right to introduce ladies to him at today's reception.

For a moment she wished she could just vanish, like one of her supposed fairy ancestors, and flee this crowd. Her grandfather had always claimed that the purest fairy blood ran in her veins, and that it bestowed wonderful abilities. But Elspeth doubted that. To be sure, she had more than a touch of Second Sight, which proved more inconvenient than magical. Besides, The Sight was common enough in the Highlands, fairies or none.

Her intuition had not warned her to keep clear of the palace on this long, hot day, where the waiting was interminable, and the reason for attending—greeting the king—might be impossible for Elspeth and Lucie now.

Her grandfather's business meeting had kept him away, leaving her in the care of her cousins, although he would have relished the event. He would have dressed spectacularly in tartan too, as the Highland laird and weaver he was, and would have enjoyed spinning exuberant tales of his early smuggling days and personal encounters with fairies. And in so doing, he would have soundly embarrassed their Edinburgh cousins. Donal MacArthur was like strong whisky, best in small quantities.

He had insisted that Elspeth go in the company of her cousins. "What other chance will you have to meet Fat Geordie?" he had boomed, using the name so many Highlanders favored for the king. With such blunt ways about him, Elspeth thought, best her grandfather stayed away from Edinburgh altogether just now.

No chance at all to be introduced to the king now, she realized, as she edged through clusters of women gusseted up like colorful, plumed, chattering birds, all waiting to meet the king. Many Scotsmen accompanying ladies today wore full Highland dress, from belted plaids to tartan vests, coats, stockings, and carried weapons too. Others wore austere black and white, though some had adhered to the suggested dress for men of blue frock coat, white vest and breeches, intended to reflect the colors of the St. Andrew's cross. Not a flattering costume; Elspeth had heard many had forgone the suggestion.

Most ignored her as she wound her way through the crowd. Everyone was so intent on reaching the doors of the royal audience room that they thought of little else.

Sidling among the throng as she looked for her cousins, she found herself close to the enormous set of doors closing off the reception room designated for the royal introductions taking place today. The doors were guarded by Royal Archers in dark green, while inside, as she understood, King George was greeting a long line of hundreds of Scottish ladies, each with their escort parties.

Surely this would take until doomsday, she thought, sighing, longing for fresh air amid the gathering heat and the press of the crowd. She wished the king would just greet all of them at once and have done with it.

Bumping against the lush satin-draped curves of a rather large woman, she stumbled in her slippers, clutching the flounces of her gown to keep from tripping on her long train. The gown, a confection of sheer silk gauze over pale blue satin embroidered with silvery buds, had been remade from one of Lucie Graham's gowns. Avoiding yet another woman, Elspeth turned again, connecting with the angular jut of a male elbow.

"I do beg your pardon, Miss," came a deep, murmured apology. A solid arm clothed in black superfine brushed her bare shoulder, and a hand came swiftly to her elbow in support, while she tilted inadvertently against him.

She looked up. A broad chest, wide shoulders clothed in black, a cream brocade waistcoat, a snowy neckcloth. A tall and muscular man, lean and firm. Afternoon sunlight cascading from tall windows added gilt to his brown hair. She glimpsed a handsome jaw, straight nose, modest sideburns. His brief touch through her ivory elbow glove was warm, strong. Her heart jumped a little.

"Pardon," he repeated.

"Quite all right, sir," she answered. "It is very crowded here."

"So true. Enchanted," he murmured in farewell and moved past her in the crowd. The mingled scents of spicy soap, of green and outdoors, wafted after him. Elspeth closed her eyes, feeling her senses heighten suddenly.

For a moment she felt lightheaded, felt the odd and unwelcome sensation—especially here and now—that sometimes preceded a knowing. The Sight had a way of inconveniently showing her images in her mind or whispering a truth about someone. Touch sometimes triggered it, and the gentleman had lightly grasped her arm.

*Please, not now,* she thought. When the Sight came over her, her tongue often loosened with it, and she could speak her mind too freely. Please no—she must not make a fool of herself here. Rising on her toes, anxious, she felt relief to spy Lucie in the crowd. She hurried toward her cousin.

"At last," she said, reaching her side. "How is Lady Graham feeling?"

"There you are!" Lucie linked arms with her. "Mother is better now that she's out of the crowd. John left her with friends and came back with me. But he did not attend the Gentleman's Assembly the other day, and so cannot introduce us today at the Ladies' Assembly. We might ask the Lord in Waiting, but that gentleman is simply drowning in requests. Luckily, John has found us a substitute, so we may proceed after all. Elspeth, you look darling, like Cinderella at the ball," she added. "Perhaps we will find you a prince today!"

"Not in this crowd! Though if I were Cinderella, I would run home before midnight," Elspeth half-laughed. "Grandfather wants me to marry a Lowland gentleman now, not a Highlander. He has become devoted to the idea. I think that is why he brought me to Edinburgh for the royal visit—not to meet the king, but to find a husband willing to take me away from the Highlands. But I do not want that." She wrinkled her nose.

Lucie laughed. "I hope you find a prince to please you, my dear. Come, John said he could arrange for his friend Lord Struan to introduce us."

"Struan?" Elspeth was surprised at the familiar name. "A Highland man? Struan House sits at the head of our glen."

"He lives in Edinburgh, but inherited a viscountcy." Lucie leaned toward her. "And he would be a fairytale prince if he wasn't a scowler. Even John says so. Struan teaches at the university, and John says he is quite knowledgeable but rather somber. Still, he is a catch with a title and property and a very nice income, or so it is rumored. He does not attend many social events. It is surprising to find him here actually."

"I am not fishing for a catch. I would be a spinster if it meant I could stay in the Highlands always." Her grandfather wanted her to make a good marriage in the South, even though it went against her dreams. Her home and her heart were in the north.

"You, my dear, are not suited to spinsterhood," Lucie said, hugging her arm. "And you will never find a good match if you stay in the Highlands weaving tartan and hardly ever coming to the city. A few years have passed since we made our debut together in Edinburgh, and you have hardly been here since. I've gone to many a party that you would have enjoyed attending, and I have had a few suitors. But no one pleases, quite. Oh, look, there is that truculent fellow Lord Struan now, standing with John."

"A truculent prince," Elspeth said, laughing as she turned. Then she stopped.

Cousin John, blond and handsome, near angelic in his black frock coat and white vest, stood with a tall dark gentleman—the same man who had brushed against her earlier and made her heart flutter madly. But her response had nothing to do with the gentleman, she told herself crossly. Just the close crowd, the

August heat, and too few open windows to offset perfumes and odors.

She went forward tentatively beside Lucie. The man beside Cousin John was tall and healthy, with a classic, well-balanced profile, slightly arched nose, dark brows over long-lidded eyes. A sweep of thick, wavy brown hair gleamed with gold. But his jaw had a stern set and his expression was dour despite a striking masculine beauty.

But Elspeth was no romantic ninny. "He is indeed a scowler," she told Lucie.

"But so handsome, quietly powerful. The frown rather suits him," Lucie said.

"The room is full of handsome gentlemen, John included. But all of them seem able to smile," Elspeth replied.

The strange feeling was returning. She felt lightheaded, even breathless, and felt as if a knowing was about to come over her. Either that, or the oppressive air in the room was too much. She flapped her painted paper-and-ivory fan frantically.

Lucie, despite the feathers in her blond hair and a flounced pale pink gown, was not the delicate porcelain doll she appeared to be. She pulled Elspeth forward through clusters of women so fast that shawls slipped from smooth shoulders, pearls and jewels flashed, and the hooped skirts peculiar to court dress swung gently as they passed.

"Ah, ladies," John said as they approached. "Lord Struan, may I introduce my sister, Miss Lucie Graham, and our cousin, Miss Elspeth MacArthur of Kilcrennan."

"Charmed," Struan said, taking Lucie's gloved hand first. He turned to Elspeth and she offered her gloved fingers and looked up.

For an instant, she felt as if she faced a warrior angel come to life. The man standing in a shaft of sunlight was simply compelling, his lean features classically shaped, his chestnut hair liberally threaded with gold. Under a slash of dark brows, lightly frowning, his eyes were summer blue, cool and reserved—under the scowl.

"Miss MacArthur." His deep voice, a quiet comfort in the noisy room, contrasted his somber expression. "Kilcrennan? It sounds familiar."

"Miss MacArthur's grandfather, Donal MacArthur, owns Kilcrennan Weavers," John supplied.

"I know the name, though I have not met the man. Excellent cloth. Sir, I would be delighted to include your cousin and your sister in my party while you look after your mother—that is, if the ladies do not mind," Lord Struan added, inclining his head. "I hope Lady Graham feels better soon."

"Thank you, Struan," John said, and took polite leave of them.

"We appreciate it so much, Lord Struan," Lucie said. "We are so excited to be here. King George is the first British monarch to visit Scotland since Charles the Second, they say," she continued in an overly bright manner. "I wonder how long it will take before we can be admitted to the reception room."

"Not long, Miss Graham," Struan answered. "The crowd has gone forward an entire inch in the past hour."

Elspeth smiled at that. "We have been waiting simply hours," she said.

"Hours," Lucie agreed, "first in that awful line of carriages—miles long, it was—and then these dreadful crowds in the palace rooms. It is taking so long, but soon we shall have our introductions and our kiss."

"Kiss?" Elspeth glanced at Struan, could not help it, and saw the viscount watching her with those cool blue eyes.

"Every lady here receives a kiss of courtesy from the king," Lucie said.

"Are we expected to swoon when that happens?" Elspeth said without thinking.

"Some might feel moved to do so, but I am sure you two can resist." Struan looked amused as he offered an arm to each of them. Elspeth took his left arm, noticing that he carried a cane, as did many fashionable men, in his right hand, now hooked above his elbow. As they walked, she sensed he favored his left leg. Unlike many, he required the cane's assistance. She frowned, wondering at the cause of it.

Suddenly she knew. As her hand lightly touched his arm, she saw in her mind an image of men running, falling, saw smoke drifting over a field as explosions sounded in the distance. She gasped, and it faded. "Oh—the war!"

Struan looked down. "Miss MacArthur? Pardon, I did not hear what you said."

"Nothing," she said, flushed with embarrassment. Lucie looked at her, puzzled, and Elspeth glanced away. Her city cousin knew little about her gift of Sight. Lucie had a good heart and a practical head and was skeptical about such things.

Struan guided them toward an elderly woman standing with two young women, all silk and feathers, elegance and hauteur. Two gentlemen stood with them, one in somber black, the other in a red plaid Highland kilt, jacket, bonnet, sporran, and socks.

Struan made quick introductions, and Elspeth barely caught the names. "My great-aunt, Lady Rankin of Kelso. My sister, Miss Fiona MacCarran, and Miss Charlotte Sinclair," he said of the women. He then indicated a tall blond man beside him. "This is my brother, Dr. William MacCarran. And this is Sir Philip Rankin. May I introduce Miss Elspeth MacArthur and Miss Lucie Graham."

"Pleased," Lady Rankin said, not sounding so. She was tall and buxom in cream silk trimmed in chocolate brown flounces, the skirt filled out by the hoops court dress used to require, and some still satisfied in their dress. Her white-plumed headdress made the lady look like an eight-foot-tall ostrich, Elspeth thought. Feeling a pale mouse beside her in silver blue, Elspeth lifted her chin and smiled.

Struan and his brother were impeccably and severely dressed in black cutaway coats and trousers, with waistcoat and neck-cloths of white and cream. They had no hint of thistle, heather, or plaid about them. Sir Philip, on the other hand, wore a blazingly red tartan plaid and stockings with a black jacket. The ladies were in formal court dress too, although Fiona's dress of muted plum satin trimmed in black appeared to be in mourning colors. Elspeth tilted her head, wondering who had passed away to affect the MacCarran siblings; perhaps the brothers wore somber formal outfits for that reason too.

*Ah, Lady Struan,* she remembered then. The elderly lady who had held that estate had passed away earlier in the summer. She had been an acquaintance of Donal MacArthur, and must be related to the young Lord Struan and his siblings.

*Grandmother.* The word came to her then. She wondered if that was so.

"Where is Kilcrennan located, Miss MacArthur?" Lady Rankin asked.

"Near the Trossach Mountains, madam, in the Highlands," she replied.

"Oh yes! We plan to travel there to visit my nephew at his new estate," Lady Rankin said. "We wish to tour Loch Katrine and the other sights described in Sir Walter Scott's marvelous poetry. They say the views are magnificent."

"It truly is beautiful there," Elspeth agreed.

"I was not aware you plan to travel north, Aunt," Struan said.

"Did I neglect to mention it? It is quite exciting. The Highlands are marvelous to behold in the autumn. I have persuaded Miss Sinclair to accompany me, with perhaps Sir Philip or your cousin Nicholas as our traveling companions."

"Fiona," Struan said to his sister, "if our lady aunt travels north, you must come with her." Elspeth detected a note in his voice, as if something was understood between the siblings.

"I shall certainly try," Fiona MacCarran replied.

"Do you know the area well, Miss MacArthur?" Struan asked then.

"Quite well. Loch Katrine is not far from Kilcrennan, where I live with my grandfather."

"Then you are not far from Struan House," he replied.

"Struan is a few miles up the glen. My grandfather knew the late viscountess, and I met her myself. We were very sorry to hear of her passing. She was a kind lady."

"Thank you." Struan inclined his head. "She was our grandmother." He indicated his siblings in his answer. Fiona smiled and Dr. MacCarran nodded.

"Lord Struan holds the estate and title," Charlotte Sinclair said, and slipped her arm through his. "But he has so little time to visit there. Perhaps for an occasional hunting party, isn't that right, James? He is quite busy as a professor of natural philosophy at the university."

Elspeth nodded, smiled, and understood she was being warned away. Miss Sinclair practically glared at her above the rim of her delicate painted fan.

"Recently I arranged to take a brief absence from my lectures in order to spend some time on the estate," Struan explained.

"I hope you enjoy it," Elspeth said. No one seemed to hear, but a smile touched his lips and he glanced at her.

"What sort of philosophy do you teach?" Lucie asked. "There is so much *of* it."

"Natural philosophy, Miss Graham. Geology, some call it now. Rocks. Earth."

"There is rather a lot of rock in the Trossachs," Elspeth said.

He inclined his head. "That sounds very intriguing, Miss MacCarran."

"Miss MacArthur, forgive me," Lady Rankin said. "I do not recall your debut."

"A quiet debut, my lady," Elspeth said. "A few years ago I attended a hunt ball in honor of the Lord Provost, as well as concerts in Edinburgh with my cousins, the Grahams of Lincraig."

"I recall that," Charlotte Sinclair said. "I was there with the family of the Deputy Lord Provost, Sir Hector Graham, and his two elder daughters. Miss Ellison Graham is a friend. I remember meeting Sir John Graham and Miss Lucie Graham there, but I do not remember you, Miss." She frowned at Elspeth.

"Oh," was all Elspeth could think to say.

Miss Sinclair turned a coy smile on the viscount. "Struan was not there either. He can hardly attend every ball for every new girl, no eligible bachelor could. He only recently inherited a title and is known here for his work at the university. And now he is in demand at parties and outings. But I believe he turns down more invitations than he accepts, is it so, sir?" She smiled up at him. "Perhaps not as eligible as people hope."

Struan cleared his throat. "I am not one for social functions," he said, and seemed to lean away from Charlotte Sinclair. "Had I known Miss MacArthur and Miss Graham then, I would have made the effort." He smiled at Elspeth, though fleeting, and looked away—and she saw Miss Sinclair frown. "Ah, we are advancing toward the doors again."

He extended an arm to Lady Rankin and offered his elbow to Elspeth, who tucked her hand in the crook of his arm again, aware of the taut muscle beneath. Behind them, his brother and Sir Philip escorted Lucie, Fiona, and Charlotte. Feeling a gaze like daggers along her back, Elspeth felt sure Miss Sinclair watched her.

They approached the doorway where the Royal Archers stood, bows crossed. Seeing their invitations, the guards opened the doors and waved them through. Looking ahead at the crowd preceding them into the vast room, Elspeth glimpsed the king. He was taller than most men there, resplendent in black and white with a red plaid Stuart sash. Elspeth smiled to herself, aware that the plaid the king had been given that week was of Kilcrennan make, woven by her grandfather with a little fairy craft.

Glancing at Lord Struan, she wondered what he might make of that. He seemed a somber gentleman who would think fairies utter nonsense, yet she felt a wayward urge to confide in him. Instead she pressed her lips together in silence and glided into the receiving room on his arm as if she were a princess, and he indeed a prince.

JAMES NOTICED THAT the girl tightened her hold on his arm as they moved forward. He glanced down at Miss MacArthur. "Nervous?"

"A bit. I hope my manners are adequate for this."

"Of course they are." He watched her, entranced by her beautiful eyes—gray-green, almost silver. Her oval face was framed by dark, nearly black curls fine and glossy as silk. He wanted to touch it. She was a lovely creature with a natural allure, and he could not help glancing down at her as if he could take sustenance from her pure, innocent beauty. She had a fragile quality with a little touch of fire that made him feel protective and intrigued all at once. "Your manners are better than many, I promise you."

"I am a native Gaelic, you see, and so my English is not refined. Nor am I accustomed to such gatherings. We live a simple life in the Highlands."

"Your accent is very pleasant," he murmured. "It is soft and graceful, and rather refreshing here. You would shine in any gathering. Do not worry. Here we go, then."

She blinked up at him, and he would have smiled, but in that moment they were announced by a footman. Their party was led forward, heels tapping and skirts swishing on the parquet floor.

King George was tall and portly in black with a white waistcoat and military touches on his costume in badges, epaulettes, and a touch of Scottishness in a red plaid sash, newly designated the Stuart plaid belonging to royalty. James was not certain, truly, there was much authenticity to it, but such things pleased many these days. King George, after all, was king of Scots, odd as it seemed. James had repeatedly heard that George did not show much interest in Scotland other than a marked preference for Highland whisky.

Coming closer, he noted clear traces of excess in the king's jowly face and doughy complexion. The royal voice was robust, deep, and surprisingly pleasant.

James quietly introduced the ladies in his party, and as each was presented, King George gave each lady a quick kiss on the cheek, barely touching skin but quite audible.

"Pleased," the king said to Lady Rankin, repeating it to the next, and the next, lady. "Enchanted. Charmed." The women, as the occasion required, curtsied and then backed away, facing the king while trying to manage their voluminous trains.

"Miss Elspeth MacArthur of Kilcrennan," James then said. She let go of his arm and stepped forward to make a pretty curtsy, bowing her head, dark curls teasing her slender neck, the nine requisite feathers bobbing. On some ladies here, they looked ridiculous. On this girl, simply swan-like. When she rose, King George leaned to kiss her cheek. James heard the moist smack of it from where he stood.

"Pleased," the king said, his gaze traveling down, then up to her face. "Lovely."

"Your Grace," she murmured, bowing her head. When she backed away, blue satin train swirling around her, she glided elegantly.

James turned to introduce the others. Then he managed to gather them together and led Miss MacArthur and Lady Rankin toward a man waiting in the receiving line farther along, several persons away from the king. Sir Walter Scott, a tall man with graying blond hair who leaned on a cane, greeted James with a nimble smile and sparkling blue eyes.

"Struan, excellent to see you here!"

"And you, sir," James said. "Sir Walter Scott, you know Lady Rankin and my sister Miss Fiona MacCarran. And Miss Sinclair. May I also present Miss Graham, and Miss MacArthur of Kilcrennan."

"Sir, I am so pleased to meet you!" Elspeth MacArthur seemed genuinely delighted. "I so admire your poetry and your collection of ballads too. I especially love *The Lady of the Lake*. I live not far from Loch Katrine and you make it seem so very romantical." She blushed as she spoke.

"I am honored to have the good opinion of a true Highland lady." Scott took her gloved hand in his. Then James saw Miss

MacArthur turn pale and gasp.

"Oh, and the Waverley novels," she blurted. "They are all yours, Sir Walter. So wonderful!"

"Miss MacArthur, I do not claim to be the author of those books. I write poetry and, ah, some scholarly studies."

"The novels are yours too, and soon the world will know and be glad of it. Your next story about…Nigel…and aye, Quentin," she said, "I think that is the name. Those will be some of your best work—oh I, beg your pardon!" She tried to pull her gloved hand away, but Sir Walter held her fingers tightly and leaned toward her. "I have spoken out of turn. I sometimes do that," she added in a soft voice.

"Miss, how did you know about the books and the new manuscripts?" Scott murmured, bending toward her. "I do not claim them as my own."

"Sir, truly, I did not mean to offend." She looked distressed.

Concerned and bewildered, James pressed the girl's elbow, uncertain what was happening, but sensing she might need a sign of support. Her arm fairly trembled under his hand. Beside him, Lady Rankin gasped in horror, while Charlotte flapped her fan and looked mortified.

"What did she say to Sir Walter?" the lady demanded.

"What is going on over there?" the king boomed to an aide, looking toward them.

"Your Majesty, only a visit among friends," Sir Walter answered with a friendly smile. The king turned away, and Scott leaned toward Elspeth MacArthur. "My dear," he whispered fervently, "am I to understand that you have the Highland Sight?"

"Sir, I—" She looked flustered, and her gaze caught James. "May we go?"

"Of course. Sir Walter, Miss MacArthur may need to sit. I'll find her a spot."

"Certainly," the poet said.

"Farewell, Sir Walter. I am—I do apologize." She sounded and looked miserable, and released James's arm to take up her skirts and hurry ahead.

"Struan, if I were you," Scott murmured, "I'd pursue that lass. She's a rare one."

"She does seem a rare bird," James agreed. He meant to pursue her, to be sure, but only to find out what the devil was going on.

Handing his great-aunt over to William, he stepped ahead to follow the girl. She had slipped through the press of chattering people to flee into the corridor beyond, but he followed the silver gown, the bobbing white feathers and that jet gloss of hair. Closing in on her, he took her arm firmly and guided her toward an anteroom just off the corridor.

"Come with me," he said sternly, marching beside her, his cane tapping as they walked. The smaller room was quieter than the other areas. Tall ferns, potted rhododendrons, and large vases of fragrant roses were arranged around the room. The air was thick with a mingled, natural perfume.

James tugged the girl behind some rhododendrons and roses, and glared down at her. "What was that all about?" he demanded.

She stared up at him. "What?"

Glowering, waiting for her to relent or apologize for embarrassing his esteemed friend, he felt surprisingly disappointed. She was lovely, delectable really, yet was not the innocent she seemed. She had done a scheming thing back there. Her beautiful eyes distracted him, but he refused to look away. "Miss MacArthur, Sir Walter keeps his identity as a novelist a close secret. I happen to be aware of it as a family friend. Now, I do not know your game here, but—"

"No game. The knowledge just came to me. I did not mean to offend anyone."

"Sir Walter is convinced that you have The Sight. It is a poor joke to play on a gentleman who cherishes such things as part of Highland lore he loves and protects."

"I do have the Sight," she said.

"It may amuse you to fool others, but I will not tolerate a

mockery of my friends."

"But I do have it! Sometimes I just know things. And then I just say them. It is not always the best thing to do, I admit." She looked distressed, and her remarkable eyes flashed silver. "And you, sir, are rude to accuse me and confront me so."

Scowling, forming his answer, he glanced over his shoulder as others entered the room. "There you are, James!" Fiona said, coming toward him.

"I am shocked!" Charlotte said, strolling in with Lady Rankin. "Outraged!"

Elspeth MacArthur glanced at James. "I suppose I am ruined now."

"Nonsense," he said. "I scarcely touched you."

"I mean for insulting Sir Walter Scott."

"Nonsense," he said more softly. "He seemed amused."

"Are you sorry, then, for scolding me?" she asked sweetly.

"I did not scold. All is well," he said more loudly, as the others approached.

"What is this?" Lady Rankin asked. She and Charlotte came toward them first, headdress feathers waving, silk and satin trains sliding like plumed tails.

"Yes, what is this?" Charlotte demanded.

"She was feeling faint," James said.

"Lord Struan was concerned for me," she added quickly.

"Ah," Lady Rankin said, narrowing her eyes.

"If that is all," Charlotte said impatiently. "That was no proper kiss at all from the king," she complained to the others. "I expected something more memorable."

"You cannot expect something romantical from King George," Lucie reasoned.

"Struan!" Sir Philip came along behind the others, and peered through the rhododendron leaves. "And Miss MacArthur! What are you doing back there? Miss Sinclair, we fellows must make up the deficit for the ladies. Like so!" Leaning toward Charlotte, he kissed her quickly on the lips.

"Oh!" Charlotte swatted him with her fan, and giggled.

"And one for you, Lady Fiona." Sir Philip said, and Fiona offered her cheek demurely, even as William bent toward Lucie, who dimpled and smiled as he kissed her cheek. Lady Rankin huffed indignantly but laughed when William kissed her cheek too.

Standing beside Miss MacArthur, wrapped in the sweet scent of flowers, James chuckled as others streamed into the room from the crowded corridor, many voicing the same complaint about the king's kisses. More and more the young men and women flirted with fresh kisses, the women coyly pouting, the men obliging with a proper cheek kiss or a bolder kiss on the lips, all amid good-natured laughter.

"It seems no one is satisfied with the royal kiss," Lady Rankin said.

"No Scottish women," Charlotte said as Fiona and Lucie laughed.

"What of the Highland lass in our party?" Sir Philip asked. "Let me do the honors, since I am dressed in proper Highland fashion." He came around the potted plants toward Elspeth MacArthur to give her a moist, smacking kiss on the lips. Grinning, pleased with himself, he stepped back.

James went still, seeing the girl's awkward smile, and told himself not to take this silliness seriously. Elspeth MacArthur managed to laugh it off; so would he.

"Look," Charlotte said, "the Countess of Argyll has accepted a kiss from the Earl of Huntly. And the Earl of Kintrie is kissing his wife—they are such a lovely couple! And Ellison Graham is over there—she is Lady Darrach now, just married, you know, to the very handsome Highlander with her."

"The laird who provided Highland whisky for the king and was shown royal favor?" Sir Philip asked. "They say Glenbrae whisky will be in great demand now."

"Oh, look, everyone is playing the kissing game now," Lucie Graham said to the others as they moved off to watch the fun.

That left James alone with Miss MacArthur behind the screen of rhododendrons and roses. "Sorry," he said curtly. "That was no proper kiss Sir Philip gave you."

"No, but let him think so." She shrugged. "I am no judge of kissing. Well, there was the draw-lad when I was a girl."

"What in blazes is a draw-lad?" He felt unaccountably irritated.

"The boy who pulls the yarn on the big looms. We have large looms and hand-looms at Kilcrennan, and he helps. But those kisses were not proper either, I suppose. Look, they are all kissing now." She laughed. Her eyes were large, silver, crinkled with amusement. "Did you want to play their kissing game? Miss Sinclair might expect it."

"She might." He made no move to pursue Charlotte, whose interest in him was more substantial than his in her.

"They are enjoying it." Elspeth MacArthur tipped her head, watching the others laugh and exchange kisses. "What is a proper kiss, I wonder?"

He gazed down at the dark-haired Highland girl as an unusual urge welled in him—he wanted to see her smile. He wanted to enjoy this moment with her. Leaning toward her, he took her chin in his fingers.

"This." He touched his lips to hers, astonishing himself.

The kiss was surprising too. Tender. Breathtaking and heart-breaking all at once, just for an instant, so that something spun inside him like a whirligig. A simple, proper kiss, and it took him like a storm. He drew back, felt her quivering hand on his forearm.

"Oh," she gasped, and tilted her face upward as if for more. "That was lovely."

"Aye," he breathed, leaning closer. Her lips met his and his lingered, warm and firm over hers. He took her by the small of her waist through the yardage of silks and satin and pulled her closer. The big flowering plants shielded them from view as the girl grabbed his coat sleeve and made a soft, willing little sound in her throat.

He felt as if he had stepped off a cliff.

He drew her deep into his embrace and she sighed against his lips, pressed her body to his, the moment wildly enticing. Her sensed her soft moan as he slid his hand upward, his fingers skimming her shoulder. She caught her breath, and his body surged.

"Dear God." He came to his senses and dropped his hands away. "I beg your pardon. That was thoughtless."

"Oh! I—I rather liked that." She stepped away. "Thank you, Lord Struan, for your—kindness today," she said in a rush. "For the royal introduction, and the—the proper kiss. I should go."

"Miss MacArthur," he murmured, craving the girl even as he stepped back, his body pulsing in answer to her sweet response. But he should never have let the kisses progress. What had come over him? He inclined his head. "Good day—"

She swept away, that silvery blue froth of a gown and its satiny train curling like a wave of the sea. She glanced back at him, her eyes simply haunting, unforgettable.

Then she vanished into a glittering sea of people and he turned away.

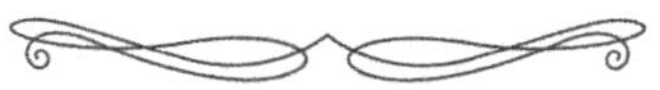

# Chapter Three

J AMES HEARD THE shriek as he stepped over the threshold of the
foyer. Unexpected and unnerving, the sound came from
somewhere overhead. Distantly in the large, drafty old house, a
dog howled as if in answer. He set down his leather satchel,
straightened, and looked up. Was the cry a creaking door, old
floorboards, or hinges needing repair? There was work to be
done, if so.

The moan sounded again, eldritch, ending on a shrill note
that shivered down his neck. Again the dog howled, and a second
one barked. James looked around the dim, quiet foyer. "What in
blazes," he muttered. "Hallooo!"

No answer. His entrance as Struan House's viscount was not
particularly promising. Ghostly shrieks, baying dogs, and no one
at the door to greet him. He stood alone, drenched by a chill
September rain. With luck, if the work awaiting him here
proceeded smoothly, he'd need be here only a few weeks.

Once again, and often of late, he wondered if he would see
Elspeth MacArthur while he was at Struan House. She had
mentioned living in the glen, and try as he might, he had not
forgotten her. She lingered in his thoughts, even in his dreams.

The memory of those simple kisses still haunted him, and so
did her sparkling, seductive eyes. He recalled the taste of her lips
under his, the feel of her in his arms—but of course, he had not
fallen in love like a damn fool. Not at all. The memories were

persistent though, and he was sometimes distracted with the desire to see her again.

Nor had Sir Walter helped the matter. "Miss MacArthur is an intriguing young lady. When you go to Struan House, seek her out. Find her, James. That is my advice."

But he had come to Struan House for other reasons, with no time to visit Kilcrennan, wherever it was. Drawing off his gloves, he crammed them into a pocket, brushed the rain from his coat shoulders, removed his hat, and shook the moisture from it. Too damned much rain lately, he thought.

Eyes gray as rain—his mind did it again, made that little leap when his thoughts were not on the girl. He was obsessed. He disliked it.

"Halloo the house!" he called. Nothing.

Perhaps he should find her, he thought, and ask what mad spell she had put on him, and why she had pulled that silly ruse on his friend Scott. He still was not satisfied in that matter. The poet was the one obsessed with finding her—not James. There. Seeing her in ordinary circumstances, when she was not done up like some sparkling fairy princess, would help dissolve his mind's damnable obsession.

"Halloo!" The echoing foyer was spacious, floored in slate and lined in dark wood paneling, with a stairway along one wall balanced by a marble fireplace on the other, carved with angels and topped by mounted stag heads. The walls were hung with antique weapons and small paintings of landscapes and portraits of dogs as well as people.

It was all familiar, racing back to him. He had not been here since childhood. He thought of the beasts howling upon his arrival today and remembered enjoying stories of ghosts and monstrous creatures when he had been as a boy. He had almost forgotten how spooky Struan House could seem. He had visited a few times as a boy, but now he was a grown man, a thorough skeptic, a calm and unruffled soul who allowed nothing to make him anxious. Not even this place.

"Anyone here?" he called again, his voice echoing.

He walked forward as a bloodcurdling shriek sounded, lifting the fine hairs along his neck. He spun around. What the devil was that?

Fatigue did not help his calm or his patience. Three days ago, he had headed north by landau, entering the foothills of the Highlands to stop at an inn at Callander; after a night's rest, he dispatched his driver back to Edinburgh and spent a solitary day walking the sunny hills, finding interesting formations of mica schist, which answered to the bite of the small hammer he carried with him. He made notes on his geological finds and had a quiet evening enjoying the peace and simple beauty of the Highlands, and wishing he could take time to do so more often. Next morning, the ghillie from Struan House had arrived to fetch him in an old carriage pulled by a pair of sturdy bays.

Angus MacKimmie was a grizzled, bearded fellow in an ancient red kilt and a threadbare brown jacket and bonnet. When he had turned to the task of tending the horses, James had gone to the door. When no butler appeared, he had simply let himself inside.

"Where the devil is everyone," he muttered now.

A door creaked in the shadows beyond the staircase, and a huge gray wolfhound padded toward him on rangy legs. Its throaty woof belied its age as the dog approached calmly to sniff the newcomer, as if not bothered to defend the house against a stranger. James patted the dog's head.

"Not just screeching banshees but fairy hounds too, hey?" James asked.

The dog pushed his head under his hand for more petting. Somewhere above, the eerie sound echoed again, miserable and faint. The hound whimpered. A creaking floor, a madwoman trapped somewhere?

"'Kirk-Alloway is drawing nigh...where ghaists and houlets nightly cry,'" James murmured, quoting Burns as he rubbed the dog's ears.

Then the front door opened behind him and Angus MacKimmie stepped inside. "No one about, sir?" He picked up James's leather case. "Upstairs I'll be taking this, then. You must make yourself heard in this place. My wife is a bit deaf. Mrs. MacKimmie!" he thundered as he went up the stairs, boots pounding. "Mary MacKimmie, where are thee?"

The door beyond the stairs opened again, and a woman came down the hall followed by two terriers, one black and one white. Stocky and middle-aged, the woman wore a plain dark dress, her gray hair wisping beneath a white cap. "Oh, sir! Lord Struan, is it! I'm Mary MacKimmie," she said, dropping a slight curtsey. "Welcome to Struan House. I hope you did not wait long. I was in the kitchen. I'm that surprised to find you here so early in the day—"

"*MacKimmie!*" thundered the ghillie above stairs.

"I'm here, ye loon!" she yelled, and turned back to James. "He's a wee bit deaf. So you've met my husband, and these are the dogs. Osgar," she said, patting the wolfhound, "is a big lad but gentle and old now. The black one is Taran and the white one is Nellie. They're good wee pups, though do they see a fox or a rabbit they'll be gone after it and stay out until they feel like returning."

As she spoke, the shriek came yet again. James felt a sharp chill with it, as if an outside door blew open. Osgar howled plaintively and the terriers made low, gruff barks. Mrs MacKimmie glanced calmly upward, smiling.

"We expected you later today, with the roads so muddy from the rains. But MacKimmie drives like the de'il sometimes, to be sure."

"An interesting ride indeed. Mrs. MacKimmie, I must ask. What is that sound?"

"Oh, that? It's our banshee. She's glad to see the new laird, I suppose."

"I came to Struan as a boy, but never heard about a banshee."

"You weren't the new laird then, were you. That's why. I'll

take you to your rooms." She led the way up the stairs.

On the top landing, Angus MacKimmie met them. "So you've brought out our *ban-sith* with you, then."

"Either that, or there are hinges or floorboards need repair," James said. He spoke loudly enough that both MacKimmies might hear him.

"Aye, could be," Mrs. MacKimmie said.

The upper corridor turned a corner at the far end, with several closed doors along cream-colored walls hung with paintings. A worn Oriental carpet ran the length of the hall, with a table here, a bench there. He had visited his grandparents here only a few times, for his guardian in boyhood, Lady Rankin, felt boys should be schooled and busy, not allowed to run about like Highland savages, so she had claimed.

He had rather wanted to run wild about the Highland hills. But that was long ago.

"It's a very nice house," he ventured.

"Aye, it is. I take care of repairs when I can, sir," MacKimmie said. "I am your factor, caretaker, head groomsman and coachman, and your ghillie too, do you care to hunt or fish. Come find me for all of it."

"I will, thank you. Struan House is quite impressive. A banshee is an old ghostly hag that prophecies death and disaster, is it not?"

"Some are," Mary MacKimmie replied. "The Struan banshee is the sort that belongs to a house and a family. A fairy spirit who makes herself known over deaths, births and important things in the family. Today she marked the arrival of the laird, so she may go silent for a while." She smiled. "Unless you should marry and have a child, and so on."

"A sort of weather glass for the family," James said. "I thought fairies were pleasant, harmless wee sorts. Small wings, delicate beings perched on flowers and such."

"There are many kinds of fairies in Scotland. You will learn more when you read Lady Struan's pages. You came here to do that, I think?"

"I did," he said.

Angus departed down the stairs, and the housekeeper led James to the laird's rooms, which included a bedroom, sitting room, dressing room, and bathing room. He walked past the large, carved bed with its embroidered hangings to look at the view from the windows of mountain crests against a vast, rainy sky.

"Handsome view. And excellent rooms," he pronounced.

"You'll want to explore the rest of the house of course. Downstairs is a library and the study where Lady Struan worked. The parlor is on that level too, along with the dining room. Kitchens are below stairs and lead out to the back gardens. Normally high tea is at half-five, and serves for supper too, unless you request otherwise." Mrs. MacKimmie went to the door. "If you like, I will set a midday tea for you in the parlor in a few minutes, since it is past luncheon."

"Thank you, Mrs. MacKimmie. That would be excellent. Oh, I am expecting guests from Edinburgh in a fortnight or so. They plan a Highland tour, and will stay for a few days as guests here."

"I will ready the rooms, then." She smiled, nodded. She seemed a patient and easygoing sort. He felt a sense of relief, not knowing what to expect.

He had planned to work on his grandmother's manuscript until Lady Rankin and the others arrived. Once they departed, he intended to finish the work and return to Edinburgh to resume teaching. He had little time to waste.

The housekeeper paused at the door. "Sir, there is summat you should know. Just now, we have few staff. Only myself and Angus, a groom, and two housemaids, local girls. Last week two girls arrived by post-chaise from Edinburgh, sent here by Lady Rankin." She stiffened a little.

"My aunt sent them to be helpful." Last week James had assured Lady Rankin that the Highland staff at Struan House were surely capable. But she did not trust Highland servants to keep a house the way she liked. "Is that sufficient staff for Struan House?" He had no idea.

"Normally, aye, but…well, 'tis near time for the Fairy Riding. A local tradition," she explained. "The fairies go riding this time of year. They ride over the lands of Struan because these lands once belonged to them, so legend says."

"Why would the household staff be reduced because of this, uh, festival?"

"Not a festival, sir. It is a time when we keep away from the hills to allow the fairy riding to take place. Your grandmother and grandfather would close up the house then, and would not allow hunting parties to hire it in later years. Already some fairies have been sighted, I hear."

"Sighted?" he asked, confused.

"Oh aye, some see them. But 'tis unlucky to be about when the Good Folk ride over Struan lands. You do not want to see them, sir."

"Ah." He felt bewildered, as if he had stepped into a foreign land. "You stay inside your homes because of fairies?" *What on earth,* he thought.

"We do. Our staff will return after the fairies go back to their world."

"Remarkable," James said. He would have to record that odd custom in his grandmother's book. "My needs are simple, so a large staff is unnecessary. Whatever you have done in the past for your local holiday, please continue."

"It is no holiday, sir. No one risks going out during a fairy riding, not with them sort about. We prefer to close the house for a few days. There is a good hotel in the next town. You would be comfortable there for a bit, as would your guests."

The housekeeper seemed too sensible a woman for this nonsense, he thought. "If you and the others want to leave, I am perfectly content to stay here. I have a good deal of work to do and the solitude would be useful. My guests will not arrive for a while yet."

"Lord Struan, you do not want solitude. 'Tis best we all leave."

"Nonsense. I'm a capable bachelor, so long as there is food in the larder and a few simple comforts. Please follow your usual custom. I will not disrupt local tradition."

"Very well, sir, but be warned. You must always beware the fairy ilk when you walk about on Struan lands at any time of year, but especially now." Her glance flickered to the cane he had set against a chair.

"I take long walks when I can," he said quietly, "but I will heed your advice."

When she left to prepare tea, James turned toward the window to gaze. The view was spectacular even in poor weather. Mist drifted over the hills and draped the treetops like veils. He thought again of Elspeth MacArthur, who lived somewhere in this glen, and wondered if she remembered that Struan's new laird would be arriving.

He left in search of the parlor and tea, half-expecting to hear the shriek again. Mr. MacKimmie must have found and silenced the squeaking door.

ELSPETH STEPPED AWAY from the shuttle loom, pausing to stretch, arching her back a little to ease the strain collected there. With one length of weaving nearly done on the loom, she was thinking about the next pattern. Preoccupied, she left the weaving cottage and strolled across the yard past two cottages that also held looms. Another building was used to store yarns and finished plaids, its limewashed stone walls and flagstone floors protection against molds and moisture.

Entering that cottage, Elspeth perused the shelves, racks, and baskets filled with yarns and cloth, colorful skeins looped on pegs, clustered in baskets on the floor, and spilling in rainbows on a worktable. The single window was shuttered today to prevent too much sunlight from fading the yarns and fabrics. She pulled her plaid shawl closer about her shoulders, for the room was chilly as well as dim. A small brazier kept the cold and damp away; smoke from a hearth or candles could discolor the wool. Grandfather did not even smoke his tobacco pipe in here.

The table held a large book of patterns that she often consulted. But she had an original design in mind today, not a commissioned length like most of their weavings, but a tartan she wanted to weave for herself. Opening a writing box, she set out paper, quill, and an ink bottle and sketched a grid of crisscrossing lines. Then, counting out the warp and weft lines in dotted lines, she began to choose and label the colors she had in mind. While she looked through the yarns to see what dyes were on hand, she looked up as the cottage door opened and her grandfather entered.

"Supper, Elspeth! Did you not hear Mrs. Graham calling you?"

"I did not. I was planning a new thread pattern."

"Aye then. Come ahead, there's lamb pie and boiled potatoes, and Peggy Graham's apple tart that she made just for you."

Elspeth left her apron on a hook by the door and walked with her grandfather across the yard. The buildings outside the main house contained Kilcrennan's four handlooms, the storage cottage, another where wool and yarns were prepared, and yet another building where finished tartan lengths were wrapped and prepared for sending to patrons and shops. The smallest building, where Elspeth preferred to do her weaving, was the original weaver's cottage used by generations of MacArthurs, the weavers of Kilcrennan. She loved the old stone cottage and the ancient shuttle loom that her great-grandfather had used. It was as if that old loom knew how to do the work on its own, having produced tartan cloth for so long.

Kilcrennan House, alongside the cluster of cottages, was a large fieldstone manse of three floors, a simple facade with rows of windows and a lower wing that housed the kitchen and servant quarters. Clustered behind the larger house was a laundry house, smithy, and brewhouse.

"I mean to weave a lady's arisaid shawl for my next sett on the loom," Elspeth told her grandfather as they walked. "We have plenty of the cream-colored yarn for the ground color, and I will use some purple with pale brown and a bit of indigo. That last is expensive, but what we have left is just enough for this."

"I several color batches from Margaret," Donal said. "Orders have increased with customers wanting to show their Highland colors of late. Most of the yarns are ready now. Margaret's eldest son brought some along earlier today."

"I can fetch the rest in the next few days while you are away in Edinburgh."

"Come with me to meet with the Edinburgh tailors."

"To see your friend Mr. MacDowell? I know you want him to court me, but I will not marry him or any Lowland man, even though you want that. I told you so, Grandda."

"But you would be happy. He's a good man. You could learn to love him."

She glanced up. Donal MacArthur was tall and spare, still a handsome man even approaching eighty, though he looked twenty years younger. His brown eyes sparkled, his dark hair was scarcely gray. Most never suspected his true age, and those who knew attributed it to healthy habits. Only Elspeth and Mrs. Graham knew his youthfulness included a touch of magic.

"I will not fall in love with a man just because you decide I should. I am happy here. And I am too busy to bother with that. I have a good bit of weaving to do since we have so many new orders," she went on. "I'll work on our tartan orders while you travel."

"The royal visit was good for weavers of tartan." Donal's eyes twinkled. "We have had fine luck of late, but it is tiring for us. Come to Edinburgh for a little holiday."

"Auld rascal," she said affectionately. "You love having so much work. You love producing it faster and better than any other weaver could."

"I'm grateful for our luck." His mood turned sober. "Elspeth, if you go to Margaret's, do not cross the glen alone. Take a cart and bring a maid and a draw-boy to help you. It is almost time for the fairy riding."

"I will be fine. Let the fairies ride their cavalcade over the glen. I won't see them and they won't see me. Do not worry, I will not be stolen away," she reassured him, tucking her arm in his. "I intend to stay here with you for a long time to come."

"Lass, you must marry soon, and may that man watch out for you as well as I have done. And may he take you south and far away from this glen. That is what I pray."

"I need no watching over and I need not leave."

"This Mr. MacDowell is a good man, and successful—"

"And keen on inheriting Kilcrennan's weaving business through me. He would not be so keen if he knew the truth about me," she added.

"Then we will not tell him," he replied.

"He will never know if he does not court me."

"He would be well suited to manage this place after I am gone. I will not be here forever, and I must think about your future."

"I can run Kilcrennan Weavers myself someday. There are not many who would believe the truth about me and you. They would never understand why you must go off to the fairies every seven years, and that I..." She stopped, shrugged.

"That you are half fairy, and may be called back someday? That is why I want you to marry and leave this glen—or you might disappear from here. I will give Mr. MacDowell permission to court you. I should have done so earlier."

"Grandda, please do not! I will not leave Kilcrennan."

"Stubborn lass! But leaving is best for you." He looked at her sharply. "Unless...is there someone else? You mentioned meeting the new Lord Struan at the king's ball in Edinburgh. What a match that would be!" He grinned. "Lady Struan!"

"*Och*, stop it." She smiled, but would never admit that ever since August, she had yearned for a man she might never see again, and should not dream about. His tender kisses had been too brief and had meant far too much to her—and likely nothing to him.

"I hear he's returning to Struan House to look after his grandmother's affairs. Reverend Buchanan heard it from Mrs. MacKimmie."

Elspeth caught her breath. "I expect he would only stay a few days. Likely he would never live at Struan, being an Edinburgh man. There is no match there, Grandda. A grand laird would never marry a weaver girl."

"Why not? Your grandfather is a wealthy weaver." He shrugged. "Truly I hoped you would marry and be gone from Kilcrennan by now. It worries me that your birthday approaches and you are still here and unmarried."

"A spinster already, am I?" She wanted to tease him into his usual bright mood, but she knew he was convinced she was in danger. She knew Donal's stories of meeting the Fey and his claim that he regularly visited them. She liked the notion that she was part fairy, but privately she thought Donal MacArthur had invented the tale to please his lonely, orphaned wee granddaughter—that her mother was a fairy and her father, Donal's son, was trapped in that realm with her.

Mrs. Graham, on the other hand, had told Elspeth that her mother had died and her father had run off. Still, Elspeth knew that local rumor said both Donal and Niall had gone over to the fairies, with Donal returning and Niall lost. Donal insisted it was true. More, he insisted that she had a binding spell that would come due on her twenty-first birthday in October. The Fey would take her back to their realm then, unless she found love before that day.

Truth? Or just a charming fairy tale from a charming man? She thought the latter.

A few years ago, she had secretly followed Donal to a hillside above Struan House, and had watched him set a pretty stone in a rock wall. He seemed to disappear into an opening that suddenly appeared, but the day had been misty, after all.

She had run home frightened. Donal had been gone for two weeks, and Mrs. Graham had little to say about it. Traveling, she said. On his return, he said he had been in the city, but after Elspeth questioned him, he had confessed where he had been, and then told her that his weaving talent was a gift from the fairies, and so he owed them.

Nearly seven years had passed since then without incident. Donal MacArthur was a storyteller, but she could not believe this tale. She did believe that fairies existed—few raised in this glen failed to believe, with so many traditions, legends, and strange occurrences permeating the area for generations.

Yet despite Donal's warning, she felt no reason to fear the fairies.

Now she took his arm. "You worry too much about me, Grandda."

"Because you do not worry enough."

"I believe in the fairy ilk, but I wish I knew truth from fancy."

"Listen to your heart and you will know what is true."

"Grandda, will you go back to the fairies again, as you said? When you say you are going to Edinburgh, do you mean you are going into their realm?" She meant to tease him into a smile. But he looked too serious.

"When I go, I always come back. When they finally take you, you will stay."

"I have no agreement with them and so have nothing to fear."

"Be wary, lass. And never look back if you see them. Never. Remember that."

She sighed. All her life she had accepted the Sight and loved the fairy stories, but the older she got, the more she wanted proof. "Grandda, what became of the special blue stone that you said was a key for entering the fairy realm?"

"It stays in its rightful place, hidden in the hill above Struan House."

"With the gardens enlarged at Struan House in the last few years, I wonder if it is still there. Now the stone wall runs up the hill behind the house."

"The stone should still be there, but perhaps you are right. I will make sure of it when I return from the city."

"You must find it before Lord Struan arrives. Mrs. MacKimmie will let me look. I will tell her I dropped something in the gardens the last time I brought her a plate of Mrs. Graham's clootie dumplings. I will stop there when I fetch the yarns from Margaret."

"Not yet. The fairies go riding through there. You keep away."

Elspeth frowned. She thought then that if she had the blue stone, she would go into the hills and set the stone in the rock as she had seen old Donal do. When nothing happened, she would know the truth. If she did see the fairy realm, she would know to take care. Besides, that stone was very special to Donal, and must be recovered from Struan's gardens, where he thought he had lost it.

What if she tried the stone and discovered that the magic, and Donal's bargain with the Fey, were indeed real? She shivered.

# Chapter Four

*T*HESE SPRITELY CREATURES *often inhabit the lush wooded groves of Scotland, particularly in the Highlands, found in caves and hillsides....fairies prefer to reside in hills, mountains, caves, and near natural wells and springs....*

What a load of nonsense, James thought. He dipped his pen in fresh ink to make notes on the paper, and read on.

When a knock sounded at the study door, he looked up, glad of an interruption after working all afternoon. Mrs. MacKimmie peered inside and entered. "My lord, beg your pardon, but Mary the downstairs maid has just quit your service."

"Another one?" He set down the pen. "The banshee again? That sent the other girl screaming from here last week." The creature, or was it the door hinge, sometimes shrieked through the whole of the night since the first day he had arrived.

"That, and the haunts and fairies too. She says she canna stay in a household plagued by strange things. She is returning to Edinburgh."

He frowned. "That's all the housemaids gone in two weeks."

"Aye, sir." She stood with hands folded, wearing a long tweed coat and bonnet.

"Are you ready to leave my service too?" he asked gently.

"Not me, sir. I am used to it."

"Used to a place infested with fairies as well as banshees, ghosts, boggles, brownies, nesting doves, and a few mice?"

"The fairy ilk will soon ride, as I told you. Some in the glen are ready for it."

"It is a charming local tradition. What did the maid see? A moth flitting from lamp to lamp?"

"She saw a fairy in the garden today, a beautiful creature that turned and saw her, and vanished among the bushes. Poor Mary was so upset she could not stay another day. The city maids Lady Rankin sent have no head for a good fright, being Southron. Begging your pardon, sir."

"I am Highland in origin and Southron in residence, so I take no offense. Truly I am surprised the girl saw anything in the garden with all this rain," James remarked. "Not even the bravest duck would be out in such a downpour. Not that I believe in phantasms, fairies, and whatnot." He dipped his pen in the ink again, to resume writing about exactly such whatnot.

"Struan House is a favorite place for the fairies, sir. Used to belong to them, so they say. There is more of the Otherworld in our world than we realize."

"Well, if I see a fairy in the garden, I will invite her inside to dry off and have tea." As he spoke, he turned a page in the manuscript and took a few notes, inked nib whispering over paper. *Fairy riding*, he wrote. *Local custom in autumn. Find out more.*

"Sir, I came to say that I do mean to leave, but only for a few days."

He looked up. "I was hoping the fairies had not frightened you away as well."

"Not at all. I always leave the house around the time of the fairy riding. But my daughter just had another child and I would visit them."

"Certainly! As I said before, I am happy to have some time to myself here."

"If you feel comfortable, sir. Mr. MacKimmie will drive me, and he will also take the housemaids to catch the post-chaise in Callander to return to Edinburgh. I will be gone just a few days. Beg your pardon to leave you thus."

"Not at all." *Locals avoid the Fairy Riding at all costs*, he wrote.

"There's food in the larder, sir, and soup in the kettle today. The groom will come by to see to the horses, cows, and chickens. I also sent word to a local family to ask if their daughter could come round to see to the housekeeping for you until I return."

"I will be fine with or without. Thank you."

"Oh, I nearly forgot," she said. "The mail arrived just now, very late. The postman said the roads are that muddy, he does not expect to be back for a week or more." She set three letters on the corner of the desk. "I'll just leave, shall I?"

"Good day, and safe journey."

When she had shut the door, he sat back to open the letters. One was from the lawyer, Mr. Browne, another from Lady Rankin, the last from his brother, Patrick. He scanned each one. His great-aunt wrote to inform him again of her travel plans, fretting if Struan House was acceptable for sophisticated city guests. James snorted a little at that, wondering if they could manage shabbiness and banshees, and realized he did not care.

Patrick reported he would travel to the area with Sir John Graham, who was interested in a business venture in the north, though they had declined Lady Rankin's invitation to join her party. James chuckled, knowing his brother had no tolerance for Lady Rankin and her so-called sophisticated friends. The lawyer's terse note only made him frown, and he set it aside; it required no response at the moment.

Reaching for one of the books stacked haphazardly on the desk, a volume of Sir Walter Scott's work on ballads and legends, James flipped until he found a section on fairy lore.

"Fairies and elves," he read aloud, "are interchangeable terms in the Highlands. Ah. So the elven sort are the fey sort. Right, then." He scribbled that in his notes.

*The most formidable attribute of the elves*, Sir Walter Scott had written, *was their practice of carrying away, and exchanging, children; and that of stealing human souls from their bodies....the power of the fairies extended to full-grown persons, especially those found asleep under a rock or on a green hill belonging to the fairies...*

"Even Sir Walter believes this nonsense," James muttered. He flipped pages, skimming the essay. A farmer, he read, had gone out to wait for a procession of fairies, then heard "the ringing of the fairy bridles, and the wild unearthly sound that accompanied the cavalcade."

The fairy riding? James sat up, thinking of the local tradition Mrs. MacKimmie had mentioned. He wanted to be sure these details were included in his grandmother's book. Flipping pages, he came to the old Scots ballad of Tam Lin. Tam had been lured by the irresistible charms of the queen of fairies; appearing to his true love, Janet, he asked her to meet him when the fairies rode in procession. Janet had to grab him and hold fast no matter what, so that he could be free.

*Betwixt the hours of twelve and one*
*A north wind tore the bent*
*And straight she heard strange eldritch sounds*
*Upon that wind which went.*

Outside, the wind and rain picked up fiercely, rattling the windows. He glanced up, hoping Mrs. MacKimmie and the others traveled in safety now that they were on their way. Taking up a stack of handwritten pages from Lady Struan's thick manuscript, he placed his own notes neatly beside it. The pages were piling up right and left, and stacks of books teetered on the desk and the floor by now. The work was well under way.

Standing, he fetched another book from a high shelf, reaching for it, then limped back to the desk. He moved around easily enough without his cane in a close space, though he needed it for distances. Lately, he had used it often due to the cold and rain, as dreary weather made his leg ache. He settled in the desk chair to read again.

"Fairy rings…fairy phosphorous…now that is interesting," he said.

The study walls were lined with books behind mesh-fronted shelves, and the small, cozy library beyond, with sofa, chairs, and fireplace, held a considerable assortment of books collected by his grandparents and previous generations of the lairds of Struan. His great-grandfather had purchased the property and had been elevated to a peerage for bravery in the military, making James the third Viscount Struan. A shiny new title, as such things went.

He picked up a sheaf of his grandmother's handwritten manuscript, its topmost pages curling at the edges. Her handwriting was small and certain, every page densely covered, some sentences crisscrossing. She had left at least six hundred such pages, he had estimated. He had spent nearly a fortnight reading her written pages along with various books on fairy lore and Scottish traditions. All the while he took notes, so that the pile of pages grew daily.

The scope of the thing was more than he had expected. Lady Struan's book was a scholarly study of Highland fairy lore, and some of it was fascinating, he had to admit. The material captured his interest for the most part, and though he applied himself diligently to the work, he took care to go for walks to stretch his muscles, clear his head, and search for rocks to support his ongoing geological studies.

Now he rose and went to the window that overlooked the back of the house. Gazing at the vast garden, with its back section sloping upward to include a grotto cut into the hillside, he watched the rain. Then he spotted something moving on the slope.

For an instant, he thought of the fairy the maid had claimed to see. No doubt that was an illusion of mist and flowers. In the rain and twilight, the shape moved again.

A girl. Wraith, ghost, human, or mist, someone was there.

He saw her move again. Definitely a girl. Dark hair, pale face. She paused, then disappeared behind wet shrubbery. Fairy indeed. Someone was in the garden.

He frowned. Rain trickled in muddy rivulets down the hillside. If someone was there, they might slip on the unstable hill.

A flash of lightning showed the girl again. His grandmother had written in her manuscript that the grotto, completed just before Lady Struan's death, was a fairy portal. More nonsense. But there was no doubt it was a precipitous slope in heavy rain.

If a local girl was mucking about on the hill in this torrent, he meant to stop her before disaster occurred. Turning, snatching up his cane, he marched out into the corridor. Osgar the wolfhound, resting in the hallway outside the door, rose and loped after him.

*BEST HURRY,* ELSPETH reminded herself. She had seen the MacKimmies and others leaving by coach so the house might be empty; since they had left, then Lord Struan was likely not there either. Now was the time. She would look for the stone and slip away quickly, for the storm had not held off as she had hoped.

Soon everyone at Struan would leave to avoid the days of the fairy riding. She could come back then, but today she was nearby and so it had seemed a good time to look for her grandfather's blue stone. In good weather, someone might come outside.

She had told Mrs. Graham she intended to stay with Margaret Lamont if the weather turned poorly. Elspeth enjoyed any chance to visit Margaret and her husband and children, and she liked lending a hand in the process of combing, dyeing, spinning, and twisting the new wools. But she had decided to stop at Struan House first. Now, in this awful rain, she regretted the detour.

Well, she was here now and may as well search. According to legend and to Donal too, a fairy portal existed somewhere on this hill. She was curious to know if Donal's tales were true, but the rain and mud, not to mention lightning, had interfered.

She stopped, suddenly wondering if the *Daoine Sìth* had influenced the weather to protect the entrance to their realm. Some said they had such power, and they might sense her intention.

Feeling uneasy, she hesitated by the rock wall high on the hill.

Huge rocks had once crested the hill, but men had broken some of it away to create the grotto. The slope was changed now. Where had Donal stood when he had come here years ago, the day she had followed him? He had set the stone in a niche and seemed to disappear into the fairy world—or had he only stepped aside in the mist that day?

Drawing her plaid shawl higher against the rain, she was aware that her green woolen gown and her leather boots were already soaked from the slanting downpour. She had to hurry. If she was discovered, she could hardly explain that she had come here to find a magical crystal stone that was a key to the fairy realm. That would sound like pure madness. The late Lady Struan would have been eager to know more, for she had been keenly interested in local lore and very knowledgeable. But she was gone now, and others would not be so curious or accepting.

Lady Struan had often invited Donal to Struan House for tea to talk about fairy legends, as he knew so many tales. Sometimes Elspeth had been included in their meetings, and she recalled her grandfather cautioning Lady Struan to keep some of his stories to herself, as adding them to her books might anger the fairy ilk. The lady had graciously promised, and Donal shared more as their friendship grew. But Elspeth did not know how much Donal had shared about his experiences.

The rain increased as she climbed the slope, and she slipped a bit, pressing her hand in the mud. Even the fairies would have enough sense to stay out of such a rain, she told herself. Shivering, she gathered her shawl closer. Her arisaid, the Highland plaid often worn by women, woven in paler colors than a clan tartan, gave her some protection from the elements. But even that wool, closely woven and protected by natural oils, would soon soak through.

The sky was darkening already and she had to reach Margaret's before evening. Climbing carefully, the earth mucky under her boots, she jumped as thunder boomed overhead. Then a dog barked and a man called out somewhere in the garden below.

Elspeth whirled. Peering through sheeting rain, she took a step, and her heel hit a sluice of muddy water. As her feet went out from under her, she slid downward, unable to stop on a slide of muck. Bumping and rolling, grasping for a hold, she landed with a lurch at the bottom of the slope, skirts tangled and muddied, legs sprawled. Sitting up, she pushed the plaid off of her face and shoved her hair back, her bonnet slipping back.

Black boots stood an inch deep in mud just in front of her. Looking up, she saw brown trousers, a walking stick, gray gloves, a brown jacket, a damp neckcloth—

Lord Struan stared down at her.

NEITHER FAIRY NOR eldritch hag sprawled at his feet, James saw, but a wet, bedraggled girl in a muddy dress and plaid shawl. Her face was obscured by dripping dark hair, but he noticed she was young, slim, and well-shaped from neat ankles and calves to her slender, curvy frame wrapped in sopping fabric. She looked young, pretty—and rather miserable.

"Miss." He leaned down to extend a hand. "Let me help you."

The girl gasped and shoved her skirts to cover her legs, then pushed back the plaid and looked up. Her heart-shaped face was haloed by wet tendrils of nearly black hair, and two large eyes looked up at him, silvery-green in the low light.

"Why, Miss MacArthur," he said nonchalantly. "How nice to see you again. What the devil are you doing in my garden?"

"Lord Struan! You need not swear," she added, struggling to rise.

"Apologies. I plead the shock of the moment." He offered his hand again. She ignored it and stood, wincing. "Are you hurt?"

"I am fine." She waved away his extended hand.

He doubted that, for she hopped about, favoring one foot. "Well, what can I do for you?" Water ran from the brim of his hat. He was drenched and so was she, and the rain continued to pound as they stood there. Thunder rumbled overhead.

"Welcome to Struan, my lord," she said. "Have you just arrived? I hope you are enjoying your visit." She wiped a hand across her face, leaving a muddy trail.

James inclined his head. "I'm quite enjoying it now."

"Oh dear, I must go. Please excuse my intrusion." Turning, she stepped to the side, gasped, and flailed her arms as one foot faltered. James grabbed her elbow before she could topple.

"Come along," he said firmly. "I am not going to let you walk out in a thunderstorm, and you seem to be hobbled. Into the house we go." He turned with her.

She did not protest as he guided her down another incline to the stone pathway. Leading her through the wet, raggedy garden, he realized she was sincerely limping. Heavy rain lashed nearly sideways as he set an arm about her shoulders to support her.

Lightning cracked overhead and the wind whirled through the garden. James felt an eerie sense of danger in the air, even beyond the storm.

"Best hurry." He picked her up in his arms then, taking the path in long strides. He hardly noticed that his weaker leg did not hinder him as he rushed along a path lined with leggy marigolds and late pansies toward the kitchen door. The girl clung to his neck riding in his arms.

Thunder pounded again, and for an instant his mind flashed on the nightmare sounds on the field of Quatre Bras, where he and a Highland Watch regiment had defended ground against an onrush of French *cuirassiers*—the booming thunder was too similar. Hurrying to the door, he wrenched at the handle and hurtled inside with the girl.

In the dim corridor, the wolfhound and terriers waited, shuffling out of the way with a woof and a few terse barks. James kicked the door shut and rushed down the hall, carrying the girl past the kitchen and up the short flight of steps that opened to the main hallway. He turned toward the parlor, the dogs trotting close and curious on his heels.

The MacArthur girl, though wet, fit in his arms like sin itself—the wayward thought came to him as he crossed the parlor threshold. Her curled body eased against him, her face rested close to his, her breath soft upon his cheek. An arm rested around his shoulders, a hand on his chest. She felt as if she belonged.

His heart slammed, though he was not out of breath. He was too aware of the girl snuggled so warm and wet against him. No doubt she was ruining his shirt, he told himself sourly, though truly he did not care about that. He must think about getting the girl dry and safe, he told himself. Think about the ache in his left leg from the wound he'd received over seven years ago. He had dropped his cane in the garden when he had lifted her up. Blast it all, he had lost his hat, too, and likely ruined a good coat in the rain.

Mundane thoughts would keep his mind off the delicious creature in his arms who gazed at him as if he was a hero. Not that! Dull was what he had tried to become these past years. Boring, solitary, and untroubled. A mad rain-soaked adventure was out of character.

But before things returned to normal, he intended to find out why Miss MacArthur had been in his garden. Was she the so-called fairy that had scared off the housemaids and sent Mrs. MacKimmie, despite excuses, rushing away?

# Chapter Five

H E SET HER down in the drawing room and urged her to sit in one of the damask-covered wing chairs angled beside the hearth, where a fire crackled in the grate against the damp chill. He grabbed a tinderbox and lit the candles in brass holders on the mantel.

"We must get you warmed up. You are soaked," he said.

"So are you. Lord Struan, I appreciate your help, but I must leave." She stood, shifting to favor one foot. "I am too wet and muddy to sit here—I may have ruined this chair already."

"My concern is not the chair but the lass, Miss MacArthur. Sit, please. My housekeeper would have my head if I let you leave here in such weather, and injured."

She sighed. "I could stay until the rain lets up. I know Mrs. MacKimmie, and she would care about the fabric. I will move over here." She took off her damp plaid shawl and draped it over a wooden bench beside the fireplace. Brushing ineffectually at her skirt, a mud-stained gray-green wool embroidered in florals at the hem, she tried to right her sorry-looking bonnet, then finally loosened its wet ribbons and set it aside.

With her plaidie and hat removed, James noticed how the wet fabric clung to her graceful curves. He looked away. "I'll fetch you a blanket," he said, turning.

She sat, attempting to rub mud from her skirt. His own coat of superfine was fair drenched, but he could not properly go about in shirtsleeves with a girl in the room. A silly nod to polite company, but he could endure the discomfort. Being here alone with her and carrying her in his arms earlier, was damaging enough. If the MacKimmies should return unexpectedly to find them in wet disarray, things would look worse than they were. He did not want the MacArthur girl to feel embarrassed.

Looking for a blanket, he opened drawers in a highboy to find table linens, candles, papers; another contained paper, ink, quills. He was not yet familiar with things beyond the study, the library, and his own rooms. Finally he opened a low chest under a window to find a red tartan lap robe. She thanked him and tucked it around her shoulders.

He pulled a tapestry foot stool toward her and she set her left foot on it. "Where are you injured?" he asked. "If I may inquire."

"My ankle is a bit sore." She drew her skirt hem up to reveal a creamy woolen stocking, then glanced up. "Turn away, sir, or your fine manners might be offended."

"No matter. I have a little medical experience, if that helps. I studied a year of medicine in university before I took up another science. Perhaps I can be of assistance."

She nodded. James dropped to one knee, then unlaced and eased off her leather boot. He took her stockinged foot in his hand. Her pretty little ankle in its muddy stocking was swelling a bit.

"You wanted to be a doctor like your brother, the one I met in Edinburgh?"

"My brother William is well suited to it. I am better suited to natural philosophy. Geological science in particular." He did not tell her the reason for changing his mind—a bloody field the day before Waterloo, when he had done his best to help in the futile aftermath despite his own injury. His third cousin, close as a brother, had died in his arms that day. Numb to his core, James had eventually returned to Scotland, stuffed his emotions away, and took up the study of rocks. Sometimes he still thought about medicine and wished he had continued, for he cared about helping as William did—but rocks were safe. Rocks challenged the mind but did not demand much of the heart.

He cupped her heel, turned her foot. "May I?"

"Aye." She drew her skirts higher, and modestly through the wool skirt, worked her stocking down and off.

He ran his fingertips along her bare foot and up her ankle, most of it delicately contoured, but for the turgid area where the shadow of a bruise had begun. He gestured to the other foot, and she complied, untying the laces and pulling it off. It looked fine to him, and nicely shaped.

He gently rotated the injured ankle. She winced but did not cry out. He nodded. "It looks like a bad sprain," he said. "I do not think it is broken. But we will not know for certain unless a doctor looks at it." Cradling her foot in his hands, he felt a thrill go through him—physical, aye, for she was delectable, but he felt something more rush through him, crown to foot. He felt protective, compassionate. His heart pounded.

Glancing up, he saw the girl incline her head, eyes closed. "Oh," she whispered.

He set her foot on the cushioned stool. "Does it hurt?"

"Not much." She gathered the dry plaid closer, blushing furiously. "Just—something else. You have—a nice touch."

He cleared his throat and stood. "You need something to warm you and help the pain." A table held two glass decanters and a few glasses on a tray, and he lifted the decanter that held amber liquid, and poured a healthy dram into a glass. He brought it to her. "Whisky. I know ladies do not usually indulge in strong spirits, but this will help."

"Whisky is perfectly fine for Highland ladies. Thank you." She tipped the glass to her lips, swallowed, paused. Then she took more, without scarcely a cough or a tear in the eye. Pink sprang into her cheeks as she handed the glass to him. "Your turn, sir. There is a Highland custom of passing the welcome dram, even between genders."

"A welcome to Struan House, is it?" The sweet, mellow burn

of it seared his throat. Seeing her smile, all dulcet and radiant, he wondered what to do next. He was quite alone with the young beauty who had appeared in his dreams recently.

He set down the glass and knelt to take up her injured ankle again. "This ought to be wrapped."

"I feel like Cinderella about to get a slipper." She giggled, then reached for the whisky glass and downed the last drops. Then she slipped her skirt hem over her ankles, mucky folds covering his hands as well. "The ankle is just twisted. I can manage. My home is only eight miles from here. I should leave before dark."

"Eight miles!" He looked at her, incredulous. "You walked eight miles to get here?" He ought to ask why she had been in the garden at all.

"Not so far a distance in the Highlands. I was heading to my cousin's home, just three or four miles from here. I will go there instead of back home tonight."

"You should not be walking anywhere just now." He still held her foot under the hem of the gown—it felt improper and exciting—nor did she protest. "Your ankle is swollen, Miss MacArthur. Bandaging will help support it, but anyone could tell you that you must rest it and avoid walking for a while."

"Perhaps I could borrow a gig or a pony cart from you, then."

"I can drive you once the rain eases up, but just now, the landau and gig are in use by MacKimmie and the groom, who took Mrs. MacKimmie and the servants elsewhere."

"Ah. They would be going away just now," she murmured.

He frowned. So she knew about this too. "I believe there is a pony cart here, or I could take you home on horseback after the storm lifts."

She looked through the tall parlor window at the lashing rain. "If it ends, aye."

"It will end soon." He set her foot on the stool and rocked back on his heels. "Miss MacArthur, there is something you should know."

"Aye?" She tilted her head prettily, eyes sparkling, cheeks a perfect pink. Was that natural beauty, or a blush from the whisky?

"We, ah, you—we are alone in the house."

"Utterly alone?" She kept her head tilted—most young ladies would be shocked, but she only seemed curious.

"For a little while. MacKimmie will be back, I think, but the others have gone to visit kinfolk for a few days. And to be honest, some have quit my employ entirely."

"Perhaps the banshee made them anxious." Her smile was calm.

"You know about that? Mrs. MacKimmie went to see her daughter for a few days. She left the house in good order with food in the cupboard. A local girl will come in to do chores, perhaps tomorrow. But we are alone for now. I should have said so sooner."

"We were distracted. So no one will be here tonight, and perhaps tomorrow?"

"Quite possibly."

"My grandfather is away from home now, and I told our servants I was going to see my friend across the glen. But she is not expecting me. No one knows I am here."

His heart thumped hard, and a shot of excitement sank through him. He ignored it. "An unfortunate set of circumstances."

She sat up quickly. "What if it was—a perfect set of circumstances?"

Startled, he shook his head. "Perfectly awkward, you mean. Rest assured that you are safe in my company, Miss MacArthur."

"I know. But what if—" She leaned forward, silvery-green eyes twinkling, cheeks flushed high. Kneeling so near, James felt the soft whisper of her breath on his cheek, felt the allure of her nearness. "This is a rather compromising situation, you know."

"Some might think so. But it is not the case," he said firmly.

"I do not mind being compromised," she said.

He frowned. What was this? Did she think to catch a wealthy man who would feel obliged to marry her? But he was not wealthy, so she was wasting her time. "You are in no danger here."

Her smile bloomed like sunshine. Dimples, two impish indentations, flashed at either side of her mouth. Her lips were full, winsome, rosy. He knew their taste—and remembered that he had all but compromised her behind a rhododendrom in Edinburgh.

He stood. "Miss MacArthur, I apologize, but—"

"It might be convenient if a scandal resulted from this."

"What!" He said it aloud this time. Outrage, even passion, swirled like heat through him. "A rascal might compromise you in this situation. But I am not that sort," he said firmly. "Explain what in blazes you are going on about."

"You swear quite a bit. Highland gentlemen rarely curse. It is not Gaelic custom. Is it a Southron habit?"

"Pardon. It is a habit I developed among soldiers and by living a bachelor's life. Which I do not intend to change," he emphasized. "Do not play coy, pouting like a pretty child, swatting your eyelashes at me like that."

"Oh." She frowned. "What should I do, then?"

"That depends on what you want here." He nearly barked that out.

"A gentle compromise. Just that." Smile. Sunshine.

She was trying, in a clumsy and oddly innocent way, to manipulate and charm him. "Miss MacArthur, best say outright what you intended by coming to Struan House."

"I came here to see your garden. That is all. But now I am here, and all this has happened . . . I would rather enjoy being compromised."

His heart thundered. "Do you know what you are asking?"

"Gloriously *rrruined*," she went on, in a broad Scots burr. "That would suit! If you do not mind, that is." She took up the whisky glass as if to sip, then turned it upside down and smiled up at him again. "It is empty."

He stared, suspicions churning. "Ruination," he snapped,

"would lead to marriage. Both would be a mistake."

"But we are alone here. Regardless of what happens, I am already compromised."

"So you plotted, and not very well at that, to trap the local laird into marriage? This will not work, I assure you."

"I did not! It only occurred to me just now." She sat up, frowning. "Perhaps I misspoke."

"Undoubtedly."

"I only thought it could solve a problem for me, and perhaps for you too."

"The only situation to solve is how to get you safely out of here and back home."

She tilted her head, assessing him. "Something troubles you. I wonder if marriage might solve it." She frowned slightly, sympathetically.

How the devil would she know what his grandmother's will had specified? He stared down at her, thoughts racing. Her damnable suggestion had merit, he suddenly saw. He had come to Struan House to finish Lady Struan's book, and attempt to find a woman of fairy descent to marry. Those were the stipulations. With those fey and graceful looks, Elspeth MacArthur could fit that role. And Sir Walter Scott, who was to judge this profoundly irritating scheme, already liked the girl.

For an instant, he was tempted. Then he dismissed it out of hand. "This is ridiculous. Compromise has one companion—marriage."

"I know."

"So we avoid compromise."

"Or we marry."

"Do you truly understand what you are proposing?" he nearly shouted.

"I think so." She frowned, seemed to think, then nodded. "Aye."

Temptation struck again. Pass her off as one of fairy blood, marry her, finish the damned fairy book, and return to Edinburgh. *Do not be absurd,* he told himself.

He could not ruin a girl and marry her for his own ends. He lived on a level far above that. And yet such thoughts were dancing through his head. She was irresistibly alluring, a coy and darling beauty, forthright and seductive all at once. Something about her drew him in—luminous eyes, elusive dimples, the bow curve of her lips? Her graceful throat, the rise of full breasts beneath that sodden gown? He glanced away.

She sat calm and smiling. His heart and body pounded, wary and yet aroused. And he was already hatching schemes in tandem with her mad suggestion.

The idea was preposterous. But the conditions of his grandmother's will were equally preposterous. The girl was eager and all too willing.

Had she devised a trap for him—or was he about to trap her?

"Miss MacArthur." He cleared his throat. "Neither of us are thinking clearly. I must tend to your injury. I need some bandages—the kitchen—there will be something there." He turned, ready to bolt.

"Lord Struan." She rose to her feet and hobbled close, and he took her arm to steady her. She was fine-boned, his hand large on her forearm. The contrast made him feel strong and protective. Needed, that was it.

She looked up and batted her eyelashes deliberately. "My lord."

"Sand in your eyes?" he murmured.

"Sorry, is it too obvious?"

"It is."

"I am not very good at this."

"At what?" He was not very good at it either, whatever was happening here.

"Flirting, I suppose. Here, let me have this." She reached up to tug on his neck cloth. "Your cravat would make a fine bandage, if you will part with it. Then you need not search."

"Very well." He undid the knot in the cloth, his hands brushing hers as she tried to help. Her small fingers worked the soft knot under his hands. He looked down, his brow and a fall of his hair brushing the top of her head. She smelled of rain and blossoms. Just then, she looked up just as he looked down. The tips of their noses touched.

He sucked in a breath. So did she. Too vividly, he recalled wild kisses behind potted shrubberies at Holyroodhouse.

"Please," she said, breathless.

A surge went through him, hard and sudden. "Oh. The cravat." He drew it away.

Her hands brushed his, and the air upon his bared throat felt sensual as a caress, setting a fire in him that only willpower smothered.

"A man might feel at odds without his cravat. Do you?"

"I have a dozen such. I will fetch another." He sounded wooden. Her touch and nearness unsettled him, whirling his usual composure off balance. He felt like stalwart iron drawn to a curving magnet.

"Sit, Miss MacArthur." He pushed on her shoulder. She winced, sat. At least her injury was genuine, he thought, though he could not sort out if her attitude and eagerness were real or pantomime. "Let me wrap your foot."

She lifted her injured foot to the stool and pulled up her skirts again, revealing her shapely bare foot and neatly muscled calf. His body surged uncomfortably.

The sight of her advancing bruise startled him out of a haze of desire. Kneeling, he wrapped the cravat carefully around her foot and ankle, circling and crossing to provide snug support. The cloth was too long, so he tore it, tying the ragged ends to fit. He did not have a dozen cravats, but he would not admit that.

"Thank you. That does feels better." She wiggled the bare toes peeking out. "If you did not complete your medical studies, where did you learn to do this?"

"War," he said succinctly. "I helped where I could."

She watched him. "Quatre Bras was a terrible ordeal."

He looked up, startled, silent. He had not told her that.

"The Royal Highlanders," she said then. "The Black Watch. They were so brave, held their own, the day before Waterloo. But they lost so many men when the French came at them, where they held ground there."

His hands grew still on her foot. "How did you know?"

"I heard there was a battle where the Scots held the day. But sometimes I see things in my mind like a dream, and I saw this just now for you. And I heard the name. Cot—cat—Quatre Bras. You were there."

"Someone told you that."

"The knowing told me."

"Knowing?" He met her direct silvery gaze. "Miss MacArthur, do not play me for a fool. What a cruel scheme, to pretend to have a vision about my past."

"I have no scheme. I saw it just now." She leaned forward. He leaned back, tensing up. "I saw you on a battlefield, in a kilt and a red coat. Blood on your leg. I heard 'Quatre Bras.' I did not know until just now that you were there."

He tugged fiercely at the torn ends of the neckcloth, simmering with anger.

"You tried to save him!" She closed her eyes. Her cheeks went pale. "There was a flash of steel, like a blow. A horseman. A soldier jumped the line and was shot down. You were trapped—your leg—under the horse. You were injured, you could not save him. He called your name—Jamie, he said—"

"Enough!" He stood. "That nitwit Philip Rankin told you this!" He was livid. Anger burned clean through him, a ring of fire.

He preferred calm passions, the love for an excellent library collection, or a case of rock specimens neatly labeled, or for thoughts and theories expressed on the written page. Safe, solid, reliable passions. Not this muddy emotional tumult.

"No one told me. I swear I saw it in my mind."

"You could easily assume I was part of a Highland regiment,

and the Black Watch is a good guess. Very good, Miss MacArthur." He clapped three times. "But if you want me to believe you are capable of Highland divination, you need a better explanation than 'the knowing.' Is this what you did to Sir Walter Scott at the royal reception?"

She sat up swiftly, yanking her skirts over her feet. He saw tears glint in her eyes. An actress of some skill? He frowned.

"You are the cruel one, sir. Sometimes when I touch someone, or they touch me, I just suddenly know something about them. I see pictures in my mind. And sometimes I speak too quickly and say more than I should."

"Far more, and you damned well know it."

"I beg your pardon." She stood. "Who was he, the friend you lost? A kinsman?"

"You are the one with the blasted Sight, you tell me," he snapped.

"Your chief," she said quickly. "Chief of your clan."

"First you accost Sir Walter Scott with this nonsense, and then you feign a desire to be compromised. Now this. Stop this scheming now. It is done." He bowed stiffly. "Rest here, Miss MacArthur. When the weather improves, I will take you home."

She stood, hopping, fists clenched, and faced him. "For a man raised in the Highlands, I thought you would understand about the Sight."

"Who told you I was raised in the Highlands?"

"*You* told me at the ladies' assembly. I thought you would understand *Da Shealladh*, the Second Sight. But I was mistaken. Do not bother to take me home. I will go. Now." She snatched up her damp plaid and her woeful bonnet, grabbed her boots and stocking, and limped, clearly fuming, toward the door.

James stood back, arms folded. Anger fell away as he watched her. Amusement trickled through him, and he was suddenly not so convinced she was a schemer. He was wary of minxes with an eye to a man's fortune, having courted the princess of them all, Charlotte Sinclair. She was Lady Rankin's marriage choice for him, and he had fallen for her charms, being a vulnerable soldier returned home. Too soon he saw her manipulative, ambitious, haughty nature. He had not proposed nor would he, though she expected it.

Elspeth MacArthur was not cut of the same cloth, but he was confused. She lacked guile, yet she had some scheme in mind, and she was damnably alluring.

But he would not be played for a fool. "Miss MacArthur, please sit down. I am not throwing you out."

"You need not. I am throwing myself out." She hopped about, trying to push her bandaged foot into its boot.

"The man killed beside me at Quatre Bras," he said, "was my cousin. He was chief of Clan MacCarran."

She looked up in silence, hands stilled on her boot.

"Someone might have told you that, though. As for my wound, it is bloody obvious I require a cane. So I will not credit your intuition entirely. But stay, Miss MacArthur. I will not be responsible for further injury to you."

She watched him. "Trout," she said.

"What?" He straightened, frowned.

"Trout. And…pudding?" She wrinkled her nose.

"Puddin'—" Startled, he spoke quickly. "My cousin loved desserts when we were boys at school. The lads teased him mercilessly. He was a bit of a pudge then. Puddin', they called him."

"And trout?"

"Enough. I will fetch tea." He went to the door.

"Lord Struan," she called. "I am sorry."

In the corridor, he shoved a hand through his hair. *Trout!* No one knew about that but his siblings, who would not have told a stranger.

How did Elspeth MacArthur know? Was there some other scheme at hand here? The only other person who knew some of this was his cousin, Lord Eldin, who had also been at Quatre Bras. He might be low enough to tell a local girl about the devastation

James had endured if he had it in mind to ruin the new Lord Struan. But he could not credit that guileless girl with that much plotting. He could not piece it all together.

Trout had been his boyhood name for Archie MacCarran the day he fell into a stream while fishing with James and William. He emerged with a trout jumping about in his trews, and the boys had collapsed with laughter. James had laughed about it with Archie again only the day before his cousin's death.

Elspeth MacArthur could not have known that.

Sight or none, ruination or none, if he stayed alone much longer with his pretty visitor, marriage might indeed be his obligation. Finding a fairy bride, ridiculous as that was, did not compare to this real predicament.

He had wanted a dull and ordinary life, but risk had found him once again.

*Tea,* he reminded himself. That was ordinary enough. He headed for the kitchen.

# Chapter Six

*R UINATION AND COMPROMISE?* Elspeth covered her face with her hands in embarrassment. What was she thinking, to talk of that, and then mention visions, death, and battle! Either the whisky or the Sight had loosened her tongue in a most deplorable fashion. Now she must convince Struan that she was neither madwoman nor hussy.

Fairy gifts, so her grandfather said, came with a price. Her gift of Sight asked a good deal for the privilege. Sometimes she impulsively blurted out whatever came to mind. She had offended Sir Walter Scott and now Lord Struan. No wonder James MacCarran of Struan thought her a fortune hunter. She must leave. But she had not had enough time to search the grounds for her grandfather's blue fairy stone.

Donal MacArthur was in Edinburgh even now, and may have already promised her hand to MacDowell. She might be standing before a parson with the tailor soon, for her twenty-first birthday was three weeks away.

But if these hours alone with Lord Struan could compromise her reputation, she might escape marrying the tailor. If Struan felt obligated, she did not have to accept. She wanted to avoid what her grandfather seemed determined to arrange for her, and she was equally determined to remain at Kilcrennan—even if she had to do it as a disgraced spinster.

She stood, hopping on her stronger foot. The rain continued, the darkness increased, and she was chilled, for her things were still damp. Draping her plaid to dry by the fire, she threw the woolen lap robe about her shoulders and limped out into the hallway. Seeing a faint glow from the back staircase, she went toward it, supporting herself with a hand on the wall.

A faint, unsettling moan echoed distantly in the house. Surely that was the banshee of Struan House. On one visit with Grandda for tea with Lady Struan, she had heard the eerie cry and mentioned it. The lady had been delighted that Elspeth had heard it, and had told Donal MacArthur that perhaps the child had some connection with Struan House. Now, hearing it again, chills ran down her spine.

Limping down the steps and into the back corridor, she saw a light glowing in the kitchen, and moved toward it. The huge gray wolfhound emerged from the shadows. He shoved his head under her hand, pressing close as if to offer his tall shoulder for support. Walking with him to the kitchen door, she peered inside and saw Struan standing at the long work table, arranging bread and cheese on a plate.

She entered beside the dog. The scrubbed pine table held a bowl of apples, a blue-and-white porcelain teapot, delicate teacups and saucers. In the arched kitchen hearth, a steaming iron teakettle hung from a hook. A second hook held a second bubbling kettle.

"Soup," Elspeth said, sniffing the seasoned air. "It smells delicious."

"Aye. The housekeeper left soup for my supper. We can share that and have a hearty tea if you're hungry."

"Thank you, I would love that. No need to take it upstairs," she added as he reached for the tray. "We can eat in here. It is just the two of us."

She began to arrange the tea things as he fetched dishes and spoons. She grated sugar from a cone into a bowl and set it with teapot. Then she found a knife to slice into a loaf of thick brown bread while Lord Struan went to the hearth to ladle soup into bowls.

Elspeth felt tension dissipate in favor of cooperation as they worked. Struan carried the tray to a small table beneath a wide window, pulled up two wooden chairs, and held one out for her. She sat, pulling the lap plaid around her shoulders. Struan set a bowl of soup before her, another for himself, and sat across from her.

"You're shivering," he said.

"My gown is still damp," she admitted. And she wore just one boot, with her injured foot wrapped in his neckcloth. Struan wore shirtsleeves and no cravat with his brocaded gray waistcoat, having discarded his wet coat. Stifling a sigh, she reached out to pour tea into two cups and watched as he stirred sugar into the steaming liquid in his cup.

"Forgive me," he said. "I should offer you some dry clothing, but I am not very familiar with what might be available in the house. We could look."

She shook her head. "My things will dry." She sipped hot tea, grateful for it, and saw that he waited courteously for her to begin eating. She took a little bread, buttered it, then sipped a spoonful of soup. It was excellent, savory, thick, and soon he began eating too. They were silent, focused, as rain pattered the windows above the table and gusts rattled the panes. Then Elspeth glanced at the dark sky.

"Do you think anyone will return to the house tonight?"

"Honestly I doubt it. The roads will be muddy and unsafe in the dark. Likely they will arrive tomorrow. Here, you. Good lassie." Elspeth blinked, but he spoke to one of the dogs, for the terriers had come in while they had been preparing the meal.

Struan set his nearly empty soup bowl on the floor, and the two terriers rushed for it, nosing at each other. When Elspeth set hers on the floor too, the wolfhound came over to lick it clean.

"I will give them more, but it has to cool first." Struan sat back. "Miss MacArthur, we both know you should go home, but it is impossible for you to walk, and dangerous for us to ride out by cart or horse yet, for the horse's sake more than ours. I fear you may have to stay the night."

"I know." Her heart gave a little flip. She reached for the teapot and poured a little tea into both cups. They sipped in silence. Then he set his cup down.

"I must ask—why were you in the garden?"

Hot tea, swallowed too quickly, made her cough. "I was looking for something my grandfather lost there. He knew Lady Struan. Sometimes she invited us to tea," she added. "He is a weaver. Donal MacArthur of Kilcrennan."

"So I have heard. What did he lose in the garden?"

"A stone. It is very special to him. It was lost around the time that the grotto was finished. He mentioned it recently, having forgotten it. So I—I thought to look."

"Is it a valuable stone?"

"Crystal and agate. Or was it chalcedony?"

"Agate is a form of chalcedony. The banded varieties are very colorful and pretty. Chalcedony itself tends to be gray. What color is your grandfather's stone?"

"Blue."

"Agate is unusual in this region, and the blue sort is rare any-where. Did your grandfather find the stone near here?"

She nodded. "I believe he found it on that hill long ago. The property belonged to the MacArthurs when my grandfather was young, you see. He had the stone with him one day and—dropped it, I suppose. But the garden is different now and he could not find it."

"If it holds special sentiment for him, we must try to find it. On my walks around the estate, I have seen massive beds of sedimentary rock, granite and sandstone with crystalline deposits. But agate is generally found in volcanic rock."

"Volcanic?" She looked surprised. "There are no volcanoes here."

"Not currently, but there may have been thousands of years ago. My research addresses that question, as a matter of fact. Layers of volcanic rock implies tremendous heat long ago in the terrestrial past. Geologists are only beginning to investigate Scotland's mountains, and indeed much of Europe, for signs of the history of the earth. Why did you come back today to look for it?" he asked quickly.

"Grandda remembered the stone, and I wanted to find it." She could hardly explain that Donal needed the thing to open a gate to the fairy world.

"I see. Did you say Struan House once belonged to your family?"

She took a sip of tea, judging how much to tell him. "The estate and much of the glen belonged to my great-grandfather. When Grandda was young, he spent time here. Lady Struan was very interested in what he knew about the area and its—legends and such. The grotto in your garden was once a large hill with a rocky precipice."

"I remember. I came here now and then when I was younger. My grandfather had the stone wall extended up the slope to form the grotto, and some of the rock wall broken apart to encourage water flow from the burn on the hillside above. Unfortunately he died before he had time to enjoy it, and my grandmother did not live long after that."

"I do not remember meeting your grandfather, or seeing you. But Lady Struan was a wonderful person. I liked her very much."

"So did I. Miss MacArthur, why not just come the door and ask if you could look for your missing stone? I would have helped you."

"I thought no one was here. It is the time of the fairy riding."

"Mrs. MacKimmie mentioned that. So you believe it too?"

"It is a local tradition." She shrugged. "I thought to look quickly. But I did not count on the rain. I am sorry I disturbed you, Lord Struan."

He waved a hand to dismiss that and sipped tea. The cup looked small and delicate cradled in his hand. She imagined those long, nimble fingers turning a beautiful rock over and over, holding it up to sunlight…and then imagined his hands upon her, warm and agile and caressing. She shivered again, not from a chill.

"You study stones," she blurted. "You are writing a book about volcanic rock." A strange word sounded clear in her head. "Geo…nosey. What is that?"

He lifted his eyebrows. "Geognosy? It means earth knowledge—the study of the earth as a complete structure, interior and exterior. I did not realize that you were familiar with the work of Werner, who coined the term."

"I never heard of him. The word just came into my head."

He stared, teacup halfway to his lips. "Good God, how do you do that?"

"Do what?"

"Echo my thoughts. I am working on a book about geognostic science. Three years ago I studied in Freiburg with Abraham Werner, who developed the theory of geognosy, which looks at the earth as a whole. Either someone told you, or—"

"Or I just knew," she supplied softly.

About to speak, he only poured more tea in her cup and his. "While I am here at Struan, I want to explore the rock formations in these hills. If your grandfather found agate nearby, that could be meaningful for my work."

"If you wander these hills, be careful. You may encounter the *Daoine Sìth*."

"The dowin-shee?" He looked puzzled.

"It means the people of peace in Gaelic. The fairy folk. The caves and hills in this glen are their territory. Geologists should take into account that otherworldly creatures may inhabit the subterranean earth." She smiled.

"Not if they value their reputations." He sat forward. "I am also here to study my grandmother's work on fairy lore. Perhaps you can help me understand some of it."

The thought excited her, but she only smiled. "Studying the rocks here might bring some surprises. Fairies are everywhere here, or so they say." She felt a little mischievous. *Sitting here before you,* she thought, *if family lore is true.*

"I cannot believe in fairy nonsense, but I promised to work on her unfinished book, and I must honor that. Tell me about the fairy riding custom," he added.

"They ride in this season of the year especially, but might be seen at other times. The 'time-between-times' are the hours when the curtain between our world and theirs can grow very thin—dawn, twilight, midnight, mist, and some holidays too. Halloween, and so on."

He tapped fingers on the table, thoughtful. "Just when visibility is poor enough to allow for tricks of the eye and mind. I see."

"I think you do not see," she murmured. "Though you could, if you wanted to."

He quirked a brow again. "Well, the custom has frightened the living wits out of my staff. Between the banshee in the foyer, the ghosts in the house, and the fairies in the garden, the maidservants who came from Edinburgh have packed up in haste and left. They could not get away fast enough."

"Southrons." She laughed. "Highlanders do not mind such things."

"Even the Highland staff have gone because of this fairy riding business. From what I hear, everyone avoids Struan House and lands this time of year."

"Not everyone. But no one wants to be taken by the Fey, you see. Legend says they ride through this glen and across this estate at this time each year. Neither you nor I should stay here, come to that."

"I am not intimidated by legends." Then he smiled, and it was so warm and genuine that she felt herself relax. "But you are the expert, being a fairy yourself."

She nearly spit out her tea. "What do you mean?"

"One of the housemaids claimed there was a fairy in the garden, and she departed in great haste. She must have seen you out there."

"That was not me, unless it happened just before you came

outside. Perhaps it was one of the fairies of Glen Struan." She frowned, wondering what Grandda might have said about that.

"Of course, that is the explanation. Such stories are part and parcel of folklore. By the way, I saw your grandfather's name in my grandmother's manuscript. She seems to have respected his knowledge of tales and traditions. So I thought I might talk with him about some things."

"About your grandmother's book? Or about me spending the night here?"

He huffed. "Good point. I suppose—both."

Elspeth laughed too. Sitting here with him so peacefully, sharing a meal while the rain lashed the windows, she felt good. She liked him, she realized. Quite a bit, in fact. His intelligence, his stubbornness, his wit, even his skepticism was sharp and intriguing.

She stood. "The dishes need cleaning. I will do that." She carried her bowl to the work table while Struan brought the rest over and fetched warm water from a kettle to fill the wash bowl. As she cleaned the tea things, he helped, and within minutes, the dishes were cleaned, dried, and set away. Then Struan took the lamp from the big pine table.

"I'd best close up the house. There are no servants here to attend to any of it."

"A Highland laird sees to the shutting of his own house, regardless of servants," she said. "Even in fine Highland houses, it is the laird's responsibility to bolt the doors and look to be sure the fires are banked."

"Then I am a good Highland laird this night. I hope locking up is custom rather than necessity here in this glen."

"We have not had cattle raiders or feuding clans for two generations or more. There are whisky smugglers in the hills, but they keep to themselves even as they bring their goods along the lochs and rivers to the sea. We hardly see them, and if we do, we look away. The next day a keg or two might appear on the doorstep."

"I suspect we all benefit from their work by cover of night."

"The people of the glens definitely benefit from the efforts of Highland smugglers who move Highland whisky and other goods—wool, yarns, laces, hides, and such—to avoid unfair taxation and put the coin in the pockets of the folk who need it most."

"Ah," he said. "The noble smuggler."

"Here, it is more often true than not. We look after our own. Only English pockets and accounts are deprived of coin." She shrugged. "What disturbs the peace of any house in this glen is not kept out by locks, unless they be bolts and latches of iron."

"Iron keeps the fairies away." He nodded. "I read that somewhere."

"But if the wildfolk want to come in, be sure they will find a way."

He chuckled at that. She knew he thought it all harmless superstition, but she found his practical attitude intriguing. She tilted her head, watching, wondering. Standing in that cozy kitchen within arm's reach of him, she felt a sense of ease and comfort go through her. She did not want this night to end.

For a moment she recalled tender kisses shared months earlier, and she remembered his arms around her. An urge to feel that again, the kisses, the passion, the sense of cherishing with it, made her yearn suddenly and deeply.

*Love,* the thought came to her then. *Love feels like this.*

He tilted his head at her silence. "Miss MacArthur?"

"Where—where shall I sleep, Lord Struan?" she asked hastily.

"Take your pick of the guest rooms. This way." Holding a lantern, he led the way, offering a hand to her elbow as she limped along. He limped too, without his cane, but his focus on her was solicitous and touching.

A thrill went through her like small lightning. The man had a restrained sort of power, masculine and controlled, tempered by courtesy and reserve. It was compelling. She walked unevenly beside him, his hand light at her elbow, her breath catching with it.

The wolfhound followed, nudging helpfully at Elspeth, now and then setting her off balance. She stumbled against Struan, and he put his arm around her. The plaid slid from her shoulders, and he caught it. She stopped, for a moment resting her hand on his chest. His eyes were dark blue in the lamplight, and she could feel his heartbeat under her hand through his clothing. She took her hand away quickly.

"You made a friend in the wolfhound." His voice was gruff.

"We call his breed fairy hound here. They take readily to anyone with fairy blood, so it is said."

"Do you have fairy blood?" he asked sharply. She blinked.

"Oh—they say that of many here," she replied lightly. "Osgar has taken to you," she went on. "Perhaps you have fairy heritage."

"My grandmother wished it was so, I can tell you that. She claimed the MacCarrans had a fairy ancestor long ago. She was not of MacCarran blood herself, but was fascinated and hoped it carried in her husband, children, and grandchildren. She was certainly believed it. Are there such legends among your kin?"

"Oh," she said with a shrug, "there are legends in our family too. It is not uncommon in the Highlands. My grandfather liked to say that my mother had fairy blood. I never knew her, you see."

"I am sorry. But I could believe it, looking at you. Beautiful," he said softly and straightened the plaid about her shoulders, then brushed back her hair. Wonderful shivers coursed through her. His hand dropped away. "The tales are entertaining, certainly."

"But it is all nonsense? You truly disdain it."

"I am a man of science. But the legend persists. My grandmother kept it alive, I suppose. As children, we were told that long ago, a MacCarran ancestor saved a fairy woman from drowning, and married her. Supposedly her blood runs through those descended from the main branch. That includes myself and my siblings. They say some MacCarrans have strange abilities because of this mythical ancestor, but I have never seen any evidence of it. Come along, you lot," he called to the three dogs now following them. Struan took Elspeth's elbow to help her up the stairs.

"Your ancestor saved a fairy woman?" she asked, keenly interested.

"Charming Highland hogwash."

# Chapter Seven

"THERE ARE A few guest rooms on this level," James said as they reached the upper corridor. "And more above, but you do not need to climb more stairs."

He understood the concessions needed for a weak limb, and even more, he wanted her to disappear into one of the rooms just now. He was distracted and responding too keenly to this girl. The feeling was best ignored.

Until morning, he wanted some distance between them. No matter what she had said earlier about a willingness to be compromised, he would not ruin her reputation or his with some heady passion that could be easily controlled with willpower and reason.

"The rooms are freshened for use, as guests are expected next week."

"And I am unexpected," she said.

"But welcome to stay." He opened a door and stood back as Elspeth stepped inside. "The hearth is cold in here. Let me tend to it." He followed her into the room as the three dogs plopped down to arrange themselves in and around the doorway.

Limping, his leg aching, he wished he had gone back to look for his cane in the garden. He knelt by the fireplace, found peat bricks neatly stacked, and used the tinder box Elspeth found and held out for him. She lit an oil lamp while he coaxed the peats to catch. Then he sat back. "It will take some time, but the room should warm soon."

"Thank you. I could have done that. I am used to such."

"And I am the laird who looks after things here," he said, amused.

She held her hands before the small flames. James stood, his gaze flickering down her body, lush curves beneath a damp gown, nearly translucent in the firelight. When she looked up at him, he went still, sensing compassion in her eyes.

This girl—who was she? How did she know his past? That had shaken him—*she* had shaken him. Nor could he forget those lightning kisses in Edinburgh. Although that had been part of a game of flirtation, he felt its deeper impact come back to him now.

"The first time we met," she said, echoing his thoughts in that damnable way she had, "we kissed."

"Part of a merry game." Only a little fire-warmed space separated them. He could easily lean to kiss her. Was she inviting it? Her mix of innocence, coyness, and perhaps a ruse confounded him. "I must go. I planned to do some work in my study this evening."

"On the fairy lore? I could help you."

"Another time, perhaps. The less we are together now, perhaps the better."

She sighed. "If we are found alone here, it will not matter what we did, or did not do. Others will make assumptions and only we will know the truth."

"*We* will know. That is more important."

She watched him. "I have been honest with you, sir. The slightest compromise will do for me, and I will hold you to nothing."

"It is not in my character to ruin a young woman and abandon her."

"Only a hint of it will be enough. I do not expect your obligation."

He huffed. "Few men would see a difference in your request

to be ruined."

"You do."

"You," he murmured, "cannot know what I would do."

"I do know." Her eyes crinkled in a half-smile.

"You are a blithe and bonny girl." Impulsively he leaned forward and kissed her, swift and powerful, surprising himself. "There. Do you feel compromised?"

"Not quite." She slid her arms around his neck and kissed him so that his quick kiss became a slow caress of lips, feeding the flame in him.

Sliding his fingers into the dark silken mass of her hair, he cradled her head; slanting his mouth over hers, he felt her buckle against him, heard her sigh. Her lips opened to his, and he grazed his tongue over her lip. The touch shuddered through him.

He had not intended this. He had meant to kiss her for an instant, a warning of the risk she recklessly invited before he removed himself from the situation. Yet her unique allure, purposeful or not, overwhelmed him, as if he had touched a flame, wanting to be burned. He forced himself to pull away. Her eyes stayed closed, lips rosy, cheeks flushed.

"Lovely," she said in a dreamy voice. Her eyes opened. They sparkled.

"Oh no, you lass," he said, hands to her shoulders, pushing her gently away.

"You think I meant to trick you because you are a wealthy man, is that it? You are wrong."

"You are a charmer, Miss MacArthur. Let this be enough compromise and consequence, aye?" He stepped back. "Something has happened between us, and I admit my role and my guilt. Does that suffice?"

If he married her, it could be to his advantage and hers. He wanted to succumb, pull her back into his arms, wildly, wanting marriage and more.

Instead he stepped back as if he stood on a precipice despite his cautious nature.

Elspeth hopped about on one foot and grabbed a chair for support. "I did not plot to trap you, even if you think it. But the kisses were very nice."

He blinked. No face-slapping, no huffing or hysterics, no attempt to invite more and entrap him. What was she about? "Nice?"

"Wonderful," she said softly. "And we are alone. All the elements—but you need not marry me."

"Not all the elements, to be honest," he pointed out. "But you said you only wanted the compromise for your own ends, whatever those are? Or will a forced marriage come later, with the fish well and truly caught?"

"You want to know why I prefer to be disgraced," she clarified.

He folded his arms. "That would be good."

"I would rather be a ruined spinster who never marries—than marry as my grandfather chooses."

"That," he said, "is medieval. Straight out of a fairy tale."

"Well, then, that is perfect." She shrugged.

"I imagine your grandfather just wants to ensure your future." He wondered if the old fellow had sent the girl here to snare a wealthy, titled husband.

"He is determined that I must marry a Lowlander." She wrinkled her nose.

"What in thunder is wrong with a Lowland man?" he asked, offended.

"Nothing, except that I want to stay in the Highlands. Grandda wants me to leave the Highlands. But I do not want to marry the tailor he has chosen for me, a man who just wants to take over my grandfather's weaving business once he is gone. If a little disgrace will discourage him, I am content." She lifted her chin. It was a lovely chin, above a slim and elegant throat.

"Content to never marry, never be happy?"

She looked down. "I do want to be happy. But I would rather live lonely in the Highlands than unhappy in the Lowlands. But

Grandda says I must leave here."

"Why would he want that?"

"I—cannot explain why, but I will not do it. I suppose you think this is all play-acting. I suppose you scoff and suspect me of some plan to snare a rich man."

"I am of two minds on that, Miss MacArthur."

She met his gaze, and there was pure clarity in her eyes. "I have another request."

"What?" Would entrapment be next?

She pulled at her damp dress. "May I borrow something for the night?"

"Of course." Relieved, still bewildered, he went to a tall wardrobe, opened its doors, and rummaged inside, finding shelves and drawers of folded garments. "There must be something here."

She limped to join him just as James drew out a pale, translucent, lacy chemise. He felt himself going red-faced. "Er, look for what you want," he said.

Elspeth pulled out a folded white garment on a shelf, lifting its lace-trimmed sleeve and high-necked bodice. She held it up under her chin. "This is a nightrail. Whose is it? Oh dear, did this wardrobe belong to your grandmother?"

James regarded the white, billowy thing, which all but swallowed the girl. His grandmother had been a tall woman. "Perhaps."

"I could not wear this."

Elspeth in his grandmother's nightrail—perfect. That would make the girl less appealing, he thought. "Take it. I insist."

She pressed it to her, the globes of her breasts outlined beneath his grandmother's clothing. An excellent deterrent. "Thank you!"

"Good night, Miss MacArthur. Oh—one reminder." He stood with a hand on the open door. "You do realize I am a Lowland man?"

"I do. But if we married, you—would not mind if I stayed in

the Highlands." In shadows and firelight, her eyes were wide and silvery, innocent yet wanton. It was wrong to be alone with her, and he would never take advantage of that. Yet even in his grandmother's nightgown, this girl was all he desired.

"You do not want to marry. You just want a wee bit of scandal."

"I could change my mind," she said softly.

"Good night," he muttered, and backed out, rushing down the corridor as if the hounds of hell were after him. Only the terriers followed. The wolfhound stayed with her.

Fairy hounds knew their kind, James remembered.

His innate reserve was usually enough to keep him aloof and controlled in any situation. Yet when this fey and fetching creature blithely wanted to be compromised, he had very nearly acted the fool and done it.

He crossed through connecting rooms into the study, brightened an oil lamp, and sank into the leather chair to take up the pages he had set down hours ago. Before she had come to Struan House. Before his life had changed. He waved the thought away.

Soon established at the desk again, he tried to keep his mind on his grandmother's manuscript, but thoughts of a delectable girl in a quaint nightrail distracted him. Tapping his fingers on the pages, he looked through the window into the darkness where rain pattered forcefully against the glass, and winds whipped loudly.

He could not even take the girl home and put distance between them.

He was never wary of women, enjoying their character and strength, their differences, their softness. Nor did he care much about society's opinions. But he would not satisfy blatantly ungentlemanly urges. He'd had a mistress several years ago, a companion of respect and affection, and he had dallied with love before and after that, though he had never discovered what love truly was. For the past year, he had neatly avoided Miss Sinclair's affections and expectations, which had become tedious.

He thought of the others. His Belgian mistress had been the widow of an esteemed geologist, a man he had admired and respected. Meeting James, the young widow had allowed him to study her husband's scientific papers when he was on leave from the Black Watch, and she soon offered him access to her person as well. Young, hungry for passion, knowledge, adventure, and fearful that he might end on a battlefield, he had let the dalliance continue. They were both lonely, and they had parted friends more than lovers, and he returned to Scotland to dive deeply into geological research.

Wind whipped past the house then with such strength that for a moment James heard a faint shrieking. Creaking doors or the storm sailing over rooftops, he thought. Or perhaps it was that pestering banshee again.

Wondering if the noises would alarm Elspeth MacArther, he sighed, pushing fingers through his hair, and decided not to inquire about her wellbeing. She was a hearty Highland sort, used to such things. Setting aside an urge to go upstairs, he took up a stack of handwritten pages and resumed reading his grandmother's small, careful handscript.

*A local weaver, Mr. Donal MacArthur, is an abundant source of history and traditional tales for this account,* his grandmother had written. *He claims to have been abducted by the fairies when he was a young man. However, the gentleman politely refuses to elaborate on the details of his experience. He believes the fairies will show their wrath to those who speak too intimately of them and reveal their true ways. It is this author's fervent hope that the weaver will share his fascinating story of fairy abduction with the world someday. His little granddaughter, he claims, is part of his story.*

James sat up and read the passage again.

THE WOLFHOUND WAS growling.

Elspeth woke, alerted by Osgar's low rumble. The hour was

very late, she thought, the darkness quiet and deep. The noisy storm had faded. "What is it, Osgar?"

The dog padded over to the side of the bed to stare at her through the darkness. He sat on his haunches, whimpering. She reached out to pat his head.

"The door is open—go on. Go down to the kitchen, where the door has a flap to let you out, if that is what you want."

He tipped his head, stared, and whimpered.

She shooed him toward the door and lay back. The bed was soft, the pillows plump, the linens cool and fresh, and she was comfortable. Yet she could not sleep. A faint sound came through then. *Her name.*

Sitting up, she looked at the sparse light of the peat fire, flickering blue-gold, with all else in shadow. Had Lord Struan called her name?

*Eilidh...*The soft sound was her Gaelic name, whispered through the air.

Osgar whimpered again and began to pace around the room. Gasping, Elspeth drew her knees to her chest, still and silent. In a corner of the room, she saw tiny translucent lights spinning—pale green, shimmering blue, soft violet. She thought the fire's reflection danced on some surface. But the lights formed into a cluster of shapes.

Tall, graceful contours, heads and shoulders, long draped robes.

*Eilidh...*

Shivers rose along her neck, arms. "Who is there?" she whispered.

The shadows and lights moved closer. Ghosts? She felt chilled all over.

She thought a pale hand reached toward her. She scrambled off the bed, leaping away. Pain stabbed through her ankle and she cried out, staring at the corner of the room.

"Who are you?" she asked in a hoarse whisper. Snatching her drying plaid from a chair, she went to the door, heart pounding.

The dog bumped against her, as hasty as she was to escape. She took his collar and rushed out of the room into the corridor.

Thunder rolled, and mingled with a distant patter of hoofbeats.

*The fairy riding.* She shuddered.

Osgar gave a loud *woof* and stood tall and alert, ears lifted. Elspeth heard her name again. Had *they* had come for her, as Grandda had said?

"Leave me be!" she gasped, and ran, limping, down the dark corridor, anxious to get away from that room. Remembering she was not alone, she ran down the hall, wondering which door might be his. She knocked on one door after another, frantic.

A crash of thunder shook the walls. She shrieked, then remembered Struan had said he would be working in his study. She ran toward the main staircase, the dog alongside her, and hobbled down the steps. She had to find him.

She could not bear to be alone—and she feared he might be under threat as well. She had tried for years to tell herself the fairy stories were all fancy. But in her heart, she had always felt that they had the ring of truth.

But how could she explain to Lord Struan that the wildfolk had appeared in her room, that she could hear their horses' hooves outside? How could she tell him that the Fey rode out tonight, and had entered Struan House? He would never believe it.

He would think she had gone mad in the middle of the night, hearing thunder and rain. But what she had seen was not mere imagination.

Were the locks here made of true iron? Had Struan shut the house as he had promised? She reached the bottom of the long staircase, wincing as she went.

*Eilidh...*Soft as a breeze. That was her birth name, her fairy name, which Donal had said she must never use. A sudden crack of lightning made her leap and shriek. Blue-white light filled the hallway. The dog rushed ahead, pausing to look back at her.

She heard her name again. She hurried on, suddenly tempted to glance back.

*Never look behind you in a fairy-held place,* her grandfather had said, *for in that moment they will have you.*

# Chapter Eight

A SCREAM, AND a blaze of lightning through the windows had James on his feet. He ran from the study into the wide hallway, the terriers barking and running with him. That was no banshee. *Elspeth!* Alarmed, he turned for the stairs just as the wolfhound hurtled toward him. A ghostly figure in white followed.

The slender wraith leaped at him, arms looping about his neck. "What—Elspeth!"

"Oh! Oh, Struan!" She sank against him, trembling. He gathered her close as another whipcrack of lightning flickered. She felt so good, too good, in his arms. He smoothed her tousled hair, his heart beating heavily. "What is it? You are frightened."

"I am not," she protested, clinging to him like a squirrel on a tree.

"Well, I was bloody frightened," he said. He held her tightly. "I thought you were a ghost. What happened?"

"I could not sleep, and came down to find you."

"Just thunder and lightning, my dear." He had not meant to say it that way.

"I am scared of such things. I just thought—I might sit and read while you worked in the study, if you were still awake." The way she clutched the lapels of his waistcoat belied her words. He had been working in shirtsleeves for comfort, his coat still damp.

"You ran here as if demons were after you. I thought you

were the banshee herself when you came at me in that floaty white thing—"

"Hush!" Her fingers pressed his lips. "Do not call the *ban-sith!*"

"It's just the storm, or creaking hinges, or rain."

She shook her head. "It is not that—oh, James, please—"

Then, for no reason that he knew, he was kissing her. Tender and fervent, one kiss melting into another as he tilted his head to hers, caught her face in his hands, pushed his fingers through her hair. She moaned and sank against him, her mouth urgent beneath his, driving him onward when he knew—and surely she knew—this should not happen.

Yet he wanted this so keenly that his mind went foggy. Catching her by the waist, he pulled her hard against him, pressing his body to hers through thin fabric. The wanting pulsed so hard through him that he thought he might go mad with it. He was already a bit of a lunatic where she was concerned.

*Not this way. Stop.* The thought sobered him. He took her by the shoulders and put a little distance between them. "Enough, else we both regret it."

"I do not regret it," she said, breathless.

"Sorry, I was trying to comfort you—poorly done. We must be practical."

"Neither of us need be that. But we do need to—to—be careful."

"Careful, aye." He moved back, heart pounding. What was driving him? This girl was more than he had ever bargained for when he came to this place. "If you do not want to be alone upstairs, come to the study. But cover up a bit, lass, would you. I am not so strong a fellow."

"Oh, you are," she said with a little laugh.

About to answer, he just smiled. She had a sort of lucent glow standing in the dark hallway, her face a pale oval, her thick black braid slung over her shoulder, the white billow of the gown showing more than she might realize. His grandmother's gown, he told himself. Yet her eyes were as luminous as moonlight even on this dark night, and she looked frightened. He felt protective and deucedly entranced at the same time. He turned, glancing behind him, and reached for her hand.

"Never look over your shoulder at the fairy ilk," she said oddly.

"Come." He took her hand and she went with him, barefoot and limping, *slap-pat* on the floor.

"Where in botheration did the dogs go?" he asked, hoping for a distraction. He was too aware of Elspeth in a nightrail, dragging a plaid blanket over her shoulder. His hands found the warm curves of her body beneath the soft fabric. His grandmother's nightrail, he insisted to himself again. "Blast and damn," he muttered.

"Lord Struan, please do not swear," she admonished, but sounded amused.

"We hardly need a banshee in this house with you here. You've cast your lunatic spell over the laird."

"He is acting the gentleman."

"Is he? He desperately begs your pardon, Miss MacArthur."

She laughed and held his arm as formally as if they entered a ballroom. Both of them were partly clothed and in disarray, alone in the house in a fierce storm. Her lush allure and her delightful willingness, together with the passion and affection gaining equal influence in him—this had the makings of disaster.

He wondered if they could get through the night without an obligation of marriage. He was drawn to her like iron shavings to a magnet. And she seemed to like it very much. He could have used a little discouragement.

The dogs followed them into the library, and James led the girl through a connecting door to the study. The place seemed reassuringly ordinary, messy desk, papers shifting, his coat on a chair, teacup abandoned on a plate with crumbs.

He sat at his desk, but Elspeth stood with her head cocked, looking wary, as if listening for something. Thunder boomed. She jumped.

"Sit down," he said. "Read a book." He gestured toward the volumes on table surfaces, on shelves. Contrary to the restraint and control he liked in some things, he was not particularly tidy when he worked.

"I am fine here." She stood, arms folded, the plump of her breasts visible through the pale fabric, for the plaid had fallen to the floor.

"I cannot think if you stand there like that," he murmured.

She went to the cushioned seat tucked beneath a tall window that overlooked the back garden. All was darkness and whipping wind and rain. "The roads will be flooded and the bridge will wash out."

He cocked a brow. "Is that a prediction?"

"I know the glen. The old bridges sometimes crumble in bad storms and the roads go to mud. The local men make repairs, but it is difficult to keep ahead of it."

"New bridges should be built and the roads resurfaced."

"Aye. But no one can afford that here. Bridges and roads take money."

Nodding, he wondered again if she thought the laird of Struan had the generous pockets this glen needed. He scarcely had enough funds to keep his city house in order, let alone keep up with Struan House and pay for bridges and other repairs needed in the glen. Unless he finished his grandmother's book—and wed a fairy bride, he reminded himself sourly—he would inherit only a modest sum.

*Fairy bride.* He glanced toward her again. He could hardly concentrate with her curled on the seat like that, the thin gown defining the delightful shape of her body, a blush of skin showing through the fine fabric. Standing, he decided to put some books away, carrying them to a wrought iron ladder to climb up to higher shelves. His awkward gait made the process slow, but the activity was what he needed.

Again he wondered if he had been duped—had Elspeth Mac-

Arthur set this up deliberately, anticipating the weather, aware that the laird might be alone? Had she hoped to invite a quick marriage to benefit kin and community? She had been very frank about wanting to be ruined. But had she been honest about the rest of it?

He looked down to see her flipping through a book. She was lovely, a fey sort with that long dark hair, pale features, and delicate frame. Anyone might believe she had fairy blood. Even Sir Walter Scott had been intrigued by her when they first met in Edinburgh. If James did marry her, he could meet the will's conditions.

*Preposterous*, he thought.

He and his siblings should have further disputed the will rather than agree to chase will-o'-the-wisps. Still, he found it a privilege to work on his grandmother's manuscript. He felt close to Lady Struan this way, and he wanted to honor that, regardless of the fanciful subject. What seemed pure nonsense to him might greatly appeal to others.

The wolfhound loped toward the girl. She patted his great, unkempt head. "Good lad, Osgar," she said.

"That dog follows you everywhere now," James said. "You need not be frightened in this house. He could scare off anything, earthly or unearthly."

"OH NO, HE'D probably let them in."

"Them?"

"The Fey. They are out riding tonight."

"Come now, Miss MacArthur. Not even a fairy would be out in such a storm. Let us put the pretense aside."

"I would never fool you."

"A pretty promise," he answered, easing another book into place.

She looked up. "You have closed off your heart from hurt, James MacCarran," she said. "You trust no one."

His heart pounded. "Life goes more smoothly that way," he

said casually, shoving another book into place. "It eliminates complications and—" *And love.*

"And love?" She watched him from below.

He crammed another book onto a shelf. "Silly notions and sentiment."

"So you do not believe in the Sight, or fairies, or love. Why?"

He climbed down and returned to the desk. "Believing," he said, "requires accepting what we cannot see in reality. I am no fool. Give me good solid rocks to categorize. Those are real." He stamped his boot heel. "The earth beneath our feet. The air we breathe. What we touch and see. That is real. That is what makes up our world."

"You are afraid to believe." She sat up, eyes like silver in the lamplight. "Afraid that what you cannot explain might be true. Afraid to trust something unseen and powerful."

"I go to church on occasion. I was taught to trust in that." He did not, especially, but that was not under discussion here. "Few would trust unseen forces easily. Certainly not me." He picked up another stack of books.

"You are a little afraid of me, I think."

"A wee slip of a thing like you? Not at all."

"You are. I am not frightened of you, or of being alone with you. Nor am I afraid of what might happen—to us. Or to my heart." She watched him openly.

"Your heart?" He glanced at her. She did frighten him a little. She was too honest, too damned enticing. She had invaded his solitude and stirred up too much. "This situation frightens me, Miss MacArthur, on your behalf. Disgrace is not the solution to your marriage dilemma."

"It could be," she answered.

He reached for the decanter of whisky that sat on the corner of his desk, lifting it to swirl its contents. "Mrs. MacKimmie set bottles in every room," he said, changing the subject. He could use a good swallow of whisky to fortify him against the fetching little wraith in his study. Better to keep his wits about him. He set the decanter down.

"Struan House has a good supply," she said. "It is the laird's house, after all. The smugglers are generous if we look the other way. My grandfather never wants for free whisky. If you are pouring some, I will have a taste. It is a night for a few drams."

He did not disagree. Relenting, he poured a dram into a glass and brought it to her. She swallowed, gave it back. "Now you."

He sipped, set it down. "Enough. If I got foxed, you might compromise me."

"I must abandon the idea. You're too unwilling."

"I am quite willing, but too much the gentleman." Silence pulsed in the air.

The wolfhound stood then, whining, and padded toward the door. A distant, eerie shriek drifted overhead. Elspeth stood too, grabbing James's arm, and dragged him toward the door. A cracking glow of lightning split the shadows, and thunder sounded.

"The banshee—" Her fingers tightened on his arm.

"Just an old rusted weathervane." He was not convinced, yet persevered. "I'll have Mr. MacKimmie fix it."

"The banshee is warning us that something is about to happen."

"Being alone in these blasted circumstances is enough for me."

"It wants to warn us that the fairy ilk are riding across Struan grounds."

James was forming his next denial when a cacophony of thunder shook the walls. "What the devil," he muttered. "It sounds as if the horses have gone loose from their stalls. I must check. Wait here," he said. "Osgar, stay."

"I am coming with you," Elspeth said. Wasting no time on argument, James hurried toward the back corridor, then down the steps past the kitchen. The girl and the wolfhound followed him.

"No, wait here please." Snatching a coat that hung on a hook, he grabbed a wide hat from another hook and stepped out into a heavy gust.

"Struan!" she called.

He looked back. "I will be fine, lass. Stay there."

"Whatever happens, do not look back!"

He waved and walked into the storm.

*EILIDH.* HEARING HER name on the wind, Elspeth grabbed a plaidie folded on a bench and left the house. She knew Struan would find the horses safe and the stable closed. The eerie sounds had not come from there. James might be walking into the path of the Fey said to be riding that night; part of her always wondered if it was true, despite local beliefs and her grandfather's insistence.

But she could not take the chance, knowing James might be in danger. She had to find him and urge him back to the house. The fairy cavalcade was said to sometimes take those who were near, whether they believed or not.

*Eilidh! Come with us...* The voices blended with the wind and the rhythm of horse hooves. But Elspeth knew the risks. Donal MacArthur always claimed that he had fallen to their mystical lure and must pay the price still. Her father had disappeared into their thrall too, so said Grandda. On ordinary days, she found it easy to resist believing all the tales. But on a night like this, she felt the strange unearthly pull.

But James MacCarran, Lord Struan, was a solid and skeptical man—the power of the Fey might simply diminish in his presence. She had to warn him to be cautious, even as she felt that his pragmatic nature might keep him safe.

Spying his cane beside the path, she grabbed it and used its support as she hurried through the gardens and past the low stone wall leading to meadows and hills. Rushing on, nightgown and plaid and hair whipping, she searched but did not call out.

Then the tall wolfhound was beside her, shoring her side like a guardian. Relieved and reassured, she thanked him and took hold of his collar as they crossed the wet, soggy grass together.

Limping and barefoot, she was surprised that she did not feel the chill, and her ankle felt stronger than she expected. The Fey, it was said, could make a person feel good, healed, even euphoric. Certainly some kind of magic was in the very air that night.

Something moved ahead, shapes and shadows in the mist that took on a strange blue glow. She heard the faint sound of bells and hoof falls. Then a line of horses and riders emerged, light and dark moving through the night mist past a woodland. She hurried forward, then stopped, hesitant to be seen. Where was James? She looked around but saw only the several riders moving across the landscape.

This could not be real, she thought, just a vision conjured in her mind of the Fey, the *Sidhe* of old, the ones called the Seelie Court. They glided by on horseback, a sparkling group of tall men and slender women sitting their horses elegantly. They were impossibly beautiful, all glitter and spark, as if webs of starlight and fire surrounded them. Their cloaks and garments, a rainbow of color, were hemmed with gold and gems, and the horses' reins were bejeweled too. Their hair, pale and dark, was threaded with filaments of gold and silver, softly curled and beribboned. Rings flashed on their fingers, buckles glinted on belts and shoes. Their eyes glowed like crystal.

Elspeth stood in shadows, scarcely breathing. Was she dreaming? Or was this what her grandfather had seen more than once? Tiny silver bells chimed soft and clear as they approached. She recognized magical symbols embroidered in shining threads on hems and saddles.

A blonde woman in a glittering cloak rode in the lead between a man and woman with dark hair and sparkling garments. Others followed, twelve riders in all, one leading a horse with an empty saddle. They meant to bring someone back with them this night.

A chill flooded through Elspeth. They had come for her. She knew it like the certainty of stars and sunlight. She stepped back into the shadow of a huge oak and watched the cavalcade stream toward Struan House at a steady pace.

She flattened against the oak, sheltered beneath its dripping leaves, as the riders passed clean through the garden wall as if it was only made of fog. Their gait was musical: clip-clop and bell ring and the soughing of the wind.

Though Elspeth shrank against the tree trunk, the lady in the lead looked to the side, then angled her horse toward her. *There! Eilidh! Come to us, Dear One!*

They drew closer to the oak, its boughs shaking in the storm winds. The lady, beautiful in green and gold, pale hair like a stream of moonlight, reached out a beringed hand toward Elspeth, who shrank back. The Sidhe, if she was really seeing this, could steal the very soul from a human. If they took her, she might never come back.

The tug she felt was nearly irresistible, but she clung to the tree and thought of James, disbelieving, strong—he might look and never see them, and that might keep him safe. The wind whirled, high and hard now, rocking the tree branches, billowing her gown and hair and plaid, so that she reached for a lower branch of the oak to hold fast.

*Come with us,* she heard the pale-haired queen say in a melodious sing-song. Then the dark-haired lady, small and lovely, reached out to her. *My sweet one, at last, there you are!*

She felt drawn to this woman, and lifted her arm, feeling weaker against the thrall. This was their domain, the earth, the trees, the rocks, wind, rain, the very air. Out here, their power was strong. As the fairy woman reached out, she felt as if the air lifted her—

*"Elspeth!"*

James! His voice cut through the noise of the wind and she looked to the side to see him running toward her. Tearing herself away from the tree, she bolted toward him over the wet grass, aware the cavalcade advanced too. She waved the cane like a weapon, like a sword, cutting through the air, slicing through the vision. They did not vanish, and she heard hooves pounding alongside her. *Eilidh! Here!*

"Elspeth, here to me!" James held out his arms.

As she ran, the riders veered toward James, clopping hooves and singsong and bells chiming. The pale-haired lady stretched out an arm toward him.

"James, no!" Elspeth called, running. He looked up as the riders approached, hooves flying now. The wind tore at his coat, his hair, and the mist enveloped him.

"No!" She plunged into the thick mist, found James and grabbed his arm fervently. He wrapped his arms around her as the wind whirled and spun around them.

The horses were but an arm's length away, the riders stretching toward both of them now. Elspeth pushed James away, out of their path, and turned her face away from their glow, tucking her face in his shoulder, holding his head down to hers. As he held her tightly, she drew her plaid up to cover both of them, but the wind tore at it like a banner.

The Fey hovered in the mist, calling both their names. *Come, Eilidh...Seumas...*

"No!" she called into the wind and mist, toward the vision she wished she could not see. She took James's face in her hands to keep him from turning. "Do not look back. Do not look at them!" she told him desperately.

"Who?" he asked.

Then she pulled his head close and kissed him, hard and frantic, not wanting him to see them. She gasped at the touch of his warm, pliant lips, and pressed her body to his under the plaid that billowed about them. He caught her tightly to him and renewed the kiss. Beyond them, lights and shadows glittered in the bank of fog, waiting.

"You shall not have him, you!" The words spilled out of her. "He is mine and I am his!"

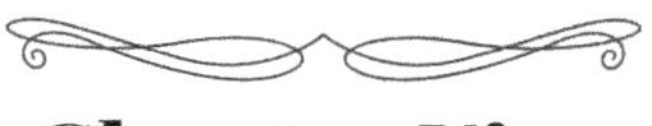

# Chapter Nine

"**Y**OU ARE MINE, I am yours," he repeated, "but if you want—"

"I want, I want. Hold me tight, do not let go," she said, and felt him take over the moment, pulling her to him at her waist, his other hand cradling her head. He kissed her, her lips opening beneath his, and she held him close, not wanting him to see the Seelie Court or the magical lady who would take both of them into her realm.

"Hold me," she whispered again. "Do not look back."

He scooped her against him, his kisses as powerful as the wind that rocked them in the long grass, nearly taking her to her knees, her limbs melting more with each kiss.

Fairy lore claimed a loved one could be saved from the pull of the Fey by a fast and hard embrace, by not looking back or letting go until the danger passed. They were fickle sorts, the Fey, and if thwarted, would move on and find another to lure away.

James kissed her again and she sank against him, feeling as if a whirlwind spun around them. Her hair bannered out, his fingers threading into the strands as she tilted her head back for kisses renewing, wild and hungry. The wind shoved them, turned them about, and Elspeth strived to keep him from looking toward the riders.

Sensing a change, she glanced through her lashes to see the riders fading into mist. The man who rode in the lead with the women looked back. He looked strangely familiar, but Elspeth could not think why. Then he vanished with the others.

*Soon you will be with us, Eilidh,* came the echo of his voice on the wind.

Now she had seen them and felt their power; now she knew what her grandfather had known all along. They did exist, if her eyes told the truth. And they wanted to take her away, just as Grandda had said.

But snug in the circle of James's arms, she felt safe. Loved, if just for the moment. Real or not, she wanted that feeling to last. She wanted to be with him.

The mist and the chime of tiny bells faded, leaving drizzle, fog, and darkness. The air was damp and ordinary and the wind had died. The danger had passed.

She had saved James; they had saved each other. He leaned to kiss her again, slow and tender this time, and he wrapped the plaid around both of them as the kisses resumed, still hungry but different now, nurturing and certain. The rain wet her face, slicked her hair, her hands, wet their lips in slippery and delicious kisses. He cupped her face, lips caressing, coaxing. She wanted only this, only him, the need, and the cleansing rain.

"Hold me," she whispered, pressing against him. "Hold fast, never let go—"

He groaned low and tightened his arms around her. She slid her hands under his overcoat to his shoulders, where fabric and muscle felt warm to her chilled fingers. She pulled at his open collar, starved for skin and warmth, still seeking wildness. He slid his hands along her arms, over her waist, up over the damp nightgown to find her breasts, and she sucked in a breath at the sweet shock of his touch.

They turned, slow and dance-like, his fingers cradling and teasing, thumb grazing. She cried out softly and found his mouth again in a deep kiss. His tongue glided now against hers as his hands teased her breasts, finding the tips. As her knees folded a bit, she sank down into the soft, wet grass. In a way, the thrall of the Fey was still with her, weakening her, driving her to act impulsively, craving without thought. James sank to his knees with her, pressing together, chest to breast, abdomens tight, so that she felt his desire for her, hard and sure. Melting within, she pressed closer, arms around his neck, lips caressing, his fingers seeking, their breathing heightening.

The mist thickened once more around them, suspending them in a place that was nowhere and everywhere, faded light, cool and heat, kiss and caress, breath and touch. She wanted this, his touch, his kiss, whatever he wanted, she craved too, anticipating with thudding heart and pulsing body the next moment and the next.

Arching as the strength of it built within her, she gasped, hungry for him, sliding her hands over him, tugging at his shirt, shaping his chest, his shoulders, the power of his torso. He pulled her deeper into his arms, rolled with her as she rocked her hips against his, intimate, daring, wanting.

He whispered softly at her ear as her nipples turned to pearls beneath his fingertips. She moaned as he dipped his head, lips seeking, hands rucking up the damp fabric of her gown, and when his lips found her breast, she gave an ecstatic gasp. His hand slid boldly down, fingers cupping, slipping, teasing. The delicate pressure, the deepest wanting, took her breath away. Shaping her hand over his breeches in silent answer, she felt his heat, his steely solidity. She felt wanton, tingling deep, wild as one of the very Fey herself.

Something powerful moved through her, a craving to be free, act as she pleased, do what she willed, a freedom and a commitment to what she was allowing, what she wanted, all this with him.

"James," she whispered as she drew his head up to kiss him again. "James."

As if in answer, he drew his hand up, away, outside the plaid. He angled on an elbow, lying with her in the wet grass under a thin blanket of fog, and pushed back her rain-slicked hair.

"Dear God," he rasped, "what is this?"

"A wild pledge on a fairy night," she whispered, breathless, and kissed him again. She felt that her pledge was true, even if this was all they would have. *Love*, her thoughts repeated. *Love*. Could it be as quick and sure as this? She was often impulsive, direct, and certain, and she felt that now. But he was pulling away.

"Not here, not like this, savage in a garden." He got to his feet, and reached down to pull her up beside him. "My God! A wild pledge on a fairy night—I could almost believe in fairies."

"Did you see them?" she asked.

"Who?" He looked around.

"The *Sidhe*," she whispered. "The Fey. They were so near, may still be about."

He stared at her. "Has the storm got to you, or did the whisky addle your brain?"

"But you must have seen them. They rode past us. The Seelie Court. They tried to lure us into going with them."

"We had best get warm and dry." He lifted the plaid, draped it over her shoulders, turned her toward the house. "On such a night as this, it is easy to imagine all manner of things."

The cane lay on the grass and she stooped to grab it. "James, what did you see?"

"Rain and mist. And you, my girl. The fog was—strange. I heard—bells. Where are the dogs?" He looked around. "It's coming down hard again. Come away, Elspeth."

She handed him his cane, and he leaned on it as they went toward the house. The pain in her ankle had returned. She wondered if James's limp had improved when the fairy riders came near, as hers did.

The dogs met them on the way, circling and barking, and they all headed into the house through the kitchen door, shaking off the rain. Elspeth laughed as the dogs bounded around them.

James removed the borrowed coat and hung it on a hook. He brushed the rain from his hair and his shoulders. His thick curls were wet, his cheeks stained uneven pink in the chill. He looked wildly handsome, Elspeth thought, liking the bit of natural disarray in this cautious and regulated man.

"What a storm," he said, taking the wet plaid from her and hung it on another hook. A red plaid, thick and dry, hung near it, and he wrapped that around her shoulders. "The trees were blowing and bending so much that I should look for damage in daylight. The horses were fine, thankfully, when I looked in on them."

"You saw only the storm?" She kept very still.

He touched her cheek. "I saw a lovely woman out there," he murmured. "And I did not act the gentleman. Elspeth—"

"We were in their thrall."

"I was in your thrall." He brushed his thumb over her cheek. "Forgive me."

"Forgive me, do—but please tell me if you saw them!"

He frowned. "I hope we were not seen out there."

"The fairy riding," she said. "They were out there tonight."

He quirked his brows and said nothing, pausing to stamp his muddy boots on the old carpet by the door.

He must think her a fool. She wondered again what had happened out there. Had it been a vision, or something real? For a moment she burned with shame at the way she had thrown herself at him. She turned for the stairs, limping. "I must go."

"Elspeth, what is wrong?"

She looked back. "If I tell you, you will call me seven kinds of lunatic. So I will not trouble you with talk of fairies. But I thank you kindly for the compromise. It was lovely, better than I could have imagined. It will do nicely."

"Compromise," he repeated. "Blast it, come back. Talk to me!"


"Wait," James said, but she was gone, footsteps rapid in the corridor, on the stairs. He grabbed his cane and went after her, the dogs eager in his wake. Pausing, he took the little black terrier by the collar before it could race ahead and trip the girl up, for her gait, though quick, was as uneven as his just now.

"Miss MacArthur! Elspeth!" he called. "Wait!"

He caught up with her in the main hallway outside the library and study. She turned when he called again, and nearly missed her footing, setting a hand on the wall.

"Careful. Tell me what the trouble is," he said.

She tipped her head, folded her arms. "Truly you saw nothing out there?"

"Rain and fog, and two foolish people kissing in a lightning storm."

"We were nearly stolen away by the fairies. We were saved by those kisses."

She was a puzzle, turning him this way and that, and he was—enchanted, intrigued. Falling in love, it came to him then. But he regretted his actions outside and was determined to compensate for them. "The wind was fierce. It nearly lifted you away. And a sort of madness came over me."

"It came over me too." She pushed at her damp, beautifully messy dark hair. "When the Fey are near, a sort of madness can come over those who see them."

"I saw you, and felt a madness indeed." He approached. "I will not blame the Fey or the stories of the riding. I accept the responsibility for what happened." He reached out to touch her shoulder, smooth the dangling curls of hair that cascaded over her shoulder.

"The thrall had both of us in its power," she said.

"Madness or magic, tomorrow morning we might see it as a disaster. What do you want to do?"

She sighed, frowned. "If you did not see them, that is fine. But you might remember suddenly. It happens that way with some. They forget for a while."

He stroked her arm. "I cannot forget what happened between us. No need for a wild story to explain this away. The truth is that I went looking for you, worried about the storm, but I went too far. You should be angry with me."

"You were worried about me?"

"You ran out into thunder and lightning in a nightgown," he said. And not even his grandmother's nightrail had deterred him. "In the rising wind, I saw you out there and feared the trees might snap. Anything else that happened was my doing."

"Mine as well. Did you see the horses in the mist?"

"The horses are in the stable. I suppose one could imagine horses and riders in such mist, but it was just trees whipping about." He frowned. "But something put a thrall over me." He tipped up her chin with a finger. "I should have resisted."

"It was magic did that."

"And you have more magic than you know. What were you doing out there?"

"I came looking for you to warn you against the storm—and the fairy riding, for I felt they were out tonight. The only way to stay safe was to hold tight to each other."

He stared. "Good lord. Are you fevered?"

"Do you know the ballad of *Tam Lin?* 'Hold me fast, let me not go,'—"

"'I'll be your bairn's father'," he finished. "Very nearly, which we must discuss. We are in extraordinary circumstances here."

"Extraordinary," she agreed. "And I do not mind being ruined. You know that."

She tensed as she spoke, as if it did bother her, shoulders tight, brows tucked. Yet she looked an angel to him—or a fine fairy beauty, come to that.

"If this suits your mad plan to be ruined but not wed, I am not entirely in favor."

"What do you mean? I will ask nothing of you."

He blew out a breath. Fairy, angel, waif—she confounded him. "I want you to ask something of me. Expect it of me."

She turned away, shaking her head. "I could not do that. I just want to stay in the Highlands with my grandfather, but he wants me to leave."

"Lady Struan wrote about your grandfather," he said then. "I came across it in her pages. He told her his story. He claims to have had some strange encounters."

"Claims! My grandfather is a storyteller, but he does not tell lies."

"She wrote that he was taken by the fairies and returns every few years."

"Every seven. You will think Donal MacArthur a daftie if I tell you the whole of it. But you do not believe, and that gives me pause, now that I have seen them. Away with you, Struan! Believe what you like."

"I do not think you are a daftie. Eccentric, perhaps. Superstitious, certainly."

"I need to rest my foot," she said suddenly, and leaned against the wall. "I do not want to go back to my room. I heard—voices."

"Ghosts, I suppose. I might believe those in this place. There is a fire still going in the library hearth and in the study too."

"I will rest in the library, then, and not disturb you."

He nodded, took her arm, and helped her toward the library door.

"My grandfather," she said then. "He says that when he was a young man, he lived with the fairies for seven years as their willing hostage."

"Seven years," he repeated slowly. Skeptically.

"Well, to be fair, it felt like seven days to him." She limped into the library.

James stared after her, dumbfounded. Osgar padded up beside him, looked at him, and then followed Elspeth.

"Go on, fairy hound. Follow your wee mistress. Keep her safe, hey?"

But that felt like his job. His responsibility. He exhaled sharply, pushed a hand through his damp hair. Tired, excited, unable to rest, not wanting to leave her alone here, he was not quite sure what to do next.

Seven years with the fairies? That gave him pause. His

grandmother's will expected him to find a fairy bride. Had fate led him straight to her?

He huffed. Anything was possible, so he was learning at Struan House.

SHE SETTLED ON a chair in the spacious, book-lined library room, wanting to rest and think. James went through to his study through the connecting door, glancing back at her for a moment with a rueful smile.

Nothing could be decided at this late hour, when both were tired and distracted by what had happened outside. She believed that she had seen the Seelie Court. It had seemed too real to deny. James insisted he had not seen them. Many did not, and she would let it go, thankful that he could remain practical and innocent—without a vision in his memory that would challenge his view of the world.

The fire was low but still bright and warm, and she held out her hands, glancing around. Rain sheeted against the windows again—what a dreadful, extraordinary night.

The library soared with polished wooden shelves crammed with thousands of books, and a wide round mahogany table filled the center of the room. Various chairs and small tables were arranged around the room, but her chair was closest to the fire.

The heat felt good, and the damp nightgown was already drying. She glanced toward the study door and outlasted an impulse to knock. Glancing about the library again, she noticed a glass case that held several objects, vases, pedestal cups, boxes, glass figures. The firelight glittered over them, bringing out the sparkle of gold, silver, and crystal.

Stones as well. She stood and went to the case to look more closely. One shelf held an assortment of colored gemstones and crystals with beautiful striations. One stone, placed on a velvet-covered pedestal, glinted blue in the low light.

Turning, she picked up a candlestick from a small table, lit its wick at the hearth, and returned to the glass case.

The blue stone was as big as her palm, round and crusted with crystals, sliced through its center to reveal concentric rings of rich layered color that ranged from indigo to palest blue.

She gasped. Could this be the blue crystal she had come to Struan House to find? Had it been in the house all this time?

Years ago, her grandfather showed her a rock very much like this one. That day was the first time he had explained his ties to the fairy realm. Another day, she had followed him to Struan lands and the back garden, where he plucked a blue crystal chunk of stone from a high crevice and had inserted it into a niche in the rock.

She jiggled the door handle on the case and saw it was locked. The other pieces inside the case looked valuable—stones, buttons, arrowheads, cups, vases, other things. If she could hold the blue stone in her hands, she might know it was the one. It was like a living thing, a powerful key to unlock the fairy world, so her grandfather had insisted.

And though Grandda only visited every seven years, he could not get through the portal without the stone. She had to get it for him.

Then she remembered something else. Grandda had mentioned that he had promised to find fairy gold that was stolen long ago. Somehow that was tied to the mysterious blue stone too. If her grandfather could fulfill the bargain, the *Daoine Síth* would be satisfied. Donal would be free of his obligation. She would be free too, never again pursued as she had been that night.

She breathed out in relief. At last she had found the stone, and now she must ask that it be returned to Granddda and the MacArthurs who had once owned Struan lands.

# Chapter Ten

HE HAD NOT seen any blasted fairies out in that storm, despite Elspeth's insistence that they had ridden through. Should he doubt her sanity—or his own?

Firelight flickered over the old canopy bed as James lay on the coverlet, still dressed but for boots. Propping an arm behind his head, he lay sleepless, staring at the embroidered fabric of the overhead canopy.

Coming to Struan House had plunged him knee-deep into fairies and whatnot, from the banshee in the foyer to Grandmother's fairy book, to a fetching girl who saw fairies riding about at night. He had seen trees whipping dangerously in the wind, and a strange mist filled with shapes he could not define. This place was full of superstitions and legends, and his grandmother had ordered him here deliberately to deal with them.

At the moment, he had more immediate concerns. Elspeth had taken over his every waking thought. Compromise or not, he wanted her desperately—and had ever since he had met her at Holyroodhouse, the day he had kissed her behind a potted plant. He was well and truly caught, and did not care if it was by her design or by fate.

Not long ago, he had nearly taken her on the grass in the middle of a storm. That was how besotted and beside himself he had become. He could not justify it, and he wanted to make it up to her. However blithely she wanted a little scandal to free her from an unwanted suitor, she could hardly have wanted that.

He rubbed a hand over his eyes. He wanted to marry the girl, and soon, but he would have to convince her. Ridiculous as it seemed, she might qualify as the Highland fairy bride that Lady Struan's will stipulated he find. That was fortunate, for this marriage seemed inevitable, practical, and necessary.

That was settled in his mind, but still he could not rest. Finally he got to his feet and headed back downstairs to read for a while. He found fairy lore a true soporific.

Walking past the guest chamber where Elspeth slept, he paused, and heard a light cough, a few footsteps. So he was not alone on this strange, restless night.

He tapped on the door. "Miss MacArthur." After a moment, he knocked again.

"Go away," she answered.

"You need not open the door. Only listen to me, please."

"Say what you will, then." Her voice sounded close.

Resting his head against the door, he tried to compose his words. "What happened tonight has consequences. I want to make that up to you."

"It is unnecessary."

"Miss MacArthur," he said, exasperated, "I want to marry you."

He waited in the ensuing silence, heart slamming. He should have planned this proposal more carefully. But fate and whatever wild magic had hold of this place had put him in this position. He felt need and emotion swamp the logic he preferred.

"Elspeth." He flattened a hand on the door. Raw need, heart more than body, rolled through him. "I want to marry you. It simply must happen. You must see that."

"Must? That is a pretty statement of devotion."

James wished he had saved the matter for morning and a clearer head. "Perhaps we should discuss it tomorrow." *Must, should.* He ought to tell her that he was also obligated to meet the conditions of Lady Struan's will, and she was a perfect choice for a fairy bride. But he had a feeling she would not welcome that news.

"Do not feel obligated," she said, as if she had heard his thoughts. His twin, Fiona, had the same knack with him. He frowned.

"I do," he said. "I regret it. I apologize. I intend to compensate for it."

"Let it be our secret. Good night."

*Our secret.* The words sent a sudden plunge of desire straight through him, unexpected, enticing. His feelings were jumbled, and the passion he felt for her went against his code of behavior, keeping himself to himself and others safely distant.

"The situation demands an honorable solution," he said.

"What good union could come of such a beginning? It is best forgotten. I am content with a wee bit of ruination. Marriage for the sake of obligation does not suit me."

"You would rather be ruined than marry the ogre your grandfather chose for you." The notion of her with another man made him close a fist. "I offer a far better solution."

"He is not an ogre. He is a reputable tailor with a good income and a fine house." Through the wood of the door, her voice had a soft intimacy. James leaned close to listen.

"Then what the devil is wrong with the fellow?" He felt annoyed. Jealous.

"He does not love me, nor I him. He lives in the city and I want to stay in the Highlands. And he is more interested in my grandfather's weaving business than in me."

"Then he is a fool." James closed his eyes.

"And he is not the one for me," she said.

"And who," he said softly, "would that be?"

"Well, no one now that I am ruined," she said crisply.

He knocked his brow against the door. "You are not ruined, not while I am here to make it otherwise. You would be the new Lady Struan," he added.

"You live in the city. You have work there. My work is here."

"I would live here part of the time." The more he tried to persuade her, the more he craved this marriage. Hope, that silly, storybook feeling, bloomed in him as never before. With her, his life would be better. With him, hers could be better too.

"Well," she said.

"It would benefit both of us. You need a secure situation. I… need a wife."

"I am sure several ladies of your acquaintance would be happy to hear that."

"I am not asking anyone else to marry me."

"Perhaps you should. They would be happy to live in the city."

"Is that part of your infernal stubbornness? I have to stay in the city. I am a professor at the university. We could spend the rest of our time here."

Silence. "I do not want to leave this glen. I would stay here."

"You came to Edinburgh. We met there."

"I was anxious to go home. But meeting you—was very nice."

"Listen to me, Elspeth MacArthur. I am a viscount. I own a fine estate," he said, and began to tick off on his fingers. "I have a respectable yearly income, or I will have if certain requirements are met. I have a house in Edinburgh and a respected position. I'm not unpleasant to look at, despite the bad leg. And I have written a volume on geology that weighs nearly as much as you do." He was surprised by his fervor. He was not one to tout himself or show desperation. Certainly he had never courted a girl with so much insistence. "Surely that counts for something."

"Impressive. You will have no difficulty finding a bride, sir."

Shoving a hand through his hair, he blew out a breath. "That is more difficult than you know. Marrying you would solve—some other issues."

"Legal…issues?"

She had an uncanny ability to ferret out his innermost thoughts. "Promise to marry me and I will tell you the whole of my…legal issues."

"No."

He leaned his forehead against the door. "I will not beg. Give me your answer tomorrow—before anyone arrives back at the house, aye?" He sighed. "I am not very good at this confounded courting business."

"Better than you think," she said. "I am honored that a titled gentleman who is very, very handsome, would ask me. I do not care if he is wealthy or not. I care where he wants to be, and if he loves me. And I do not mind the bad leg at all. I have a bad ankle myself. In fact, I must rest it now. So good night, sir."

"Blast it all," he muttered. *Love.* He had not mentioned that, and it was crucial. But he was still sorting that out. Oh, it was there. He needed to come to terms with it. Sentiment was not his strong point.

"You swear too much. It is a plague in your personality."

"Elspeth," he growled. "Please."

"Listen, James MacCarran. I want to stay in the Highlands, and you are a Lowland man. And I think you are eager to be away south again."

"Edinburgh is not that far south. You would have a comfortable life with me."

"I know," she said softly. "I know it. But let us be done with it for now, Lord Struan. It is late."

The more she denied him, the more he wanted her. "But tell me this." He leaned close to the door, speaking low. "Is there someone else? Is there a Highland man who has your heart?" Fool, he had never thought to ask.

"I wish he lived in this glen," she whispered. "He is a fine man. We loved sweetly with the fairy magic upon us, and he has my heart. But he thinks of obligations and legal issues and forgets to look into his own heart."

James went still, heart thumping. A lightning strike of hope went through him. "This fine man, is he the one for you?"

"So he likes to think. Away with you, James MacCarran," she

said crisply.

He sighed, head bowed. He felt touched deep, changed somehow. Stepping back, he went along the dark corridor.

He was not quite the same man who had knocked on that door a quarter-hour earlier. He was a man in love who finally knew it, and needed to set other matters aside and say so.

ELSPETH SMOOTHED THE skirts of her green woolen gown that had dried beside the hearthside overnight. She had brushed away the dried mud; some stains might be beyond saving but could be hidden with some new trim here and there, perhaps plaid bands and ribbons. Best hurry now, she told herself, for the morning was growing late. She had slept longer than she wanted, and ought to leave for home soon, or for Margaret Lamont's house—that had been her plan before she had slid down a muddy hill in Struan's garden.

Outside, rain still pattered against the window glass. Truly, she wanted to stay. Struan's marriage proposal echoed in her mind. The memory of his honest words and intimate voice sent a thrill through her. Refusing his offer had been harder than James could ever know.

Glancing into the mirror over the chest of drawers, she combed her fingers through her tousled hair and did her best to plait it in a single braid, tied with a ribbon slipped from her bonnet. Her favorite hat, like her dress, would never be the same again. She would never be same again, she thought. The time here had changed her.

She tossed her plaid shawl over her shoulders. More than her gown and bonnet had been ruined here. Gloriously, sweetly ruined.

Marrying him was what she wanted, if she was truthful with herself. But she was adamant about staying in the Highlands—and more adamant that James must not feel obligated to marry her, as he seemed to do.

She glanced out the window at the dreary, sodden landscape.

Walking home would be unwise, considering her twisted ankle. James had offered to drive her home, and she would accept it. Last night, listening to him through the door, she had felt stubborn at first—but her heart took over, and she had been on the verge of relenting, even though she feared he felt only obligation.

She had always wanted to remain in the Highlands where her heart and her nature belonged. Her grandfather had told her that a fairy spell bound her to the Highlands, and that same fairy spell would eventually send her back to the fairy realm. For years, she had felt the pull of the Highlands, believing simply that she loved her home and Highland life, that her grandfather's fairy stories were pretty tales, and that she was in no danger.

But those beliefs were shifting. Now she had seen the Fey and felt their influence and power. And now she realized that she was falling in love.

Grandda wanted her to fall in love—he had once said it might break the spell surrounding her, the spell she had not wanted to credit. She could love and marry James. That choice was open to her. But she could not bear to leave her home and the life she loved. Perhaps that, in itself, was due to the fairy spell Grandda had mentioned.

Donal MacArthur's solution for her was to remove her from danger by marrying her off to a Lowlander; any Lowlander would do, she thought wryly, for he was in a hurry to see it done before she turned twenty-one, the day the spell would change.

But now she saw that the Fey would threaten James as well, pull him into their realm with her. Donal MacArthur had succumbed to their thrall, and her father as well, so Grandda had said. She could not let that happen to James—and so she should not wed him.

LATER, THE HOUSE seemed empty as she wandered through. James was nowhere to be seen—she had meant to ask if he could drive her back to Kilcrennan as the rain continued and her ankle was not strong enough for the long walk. In the kitchen, she encountered the dogs resting by the hearth. The generous span of windows overlooking the garden showed steady rain, mist, and the sodden green lawn where she and Struan had tumbled to the grass with wild and tender kisses, while the fairy court rode past.

A tray sat on the long pine table, holding a silver pot, a china cup, a plate holding oatcakes and jam, and a folded paper. Steam twirled from the spout, fragrant with cocoa.

*Elspeth.* She touched the letters. His handwriting was strong, with a hint of roundness, like a secret tenderness, here and there. Nothing more, just her name. But he had taken time to prepare the tray. Then apparently he had left the house, perhaps to see to the horses as he had done last night.

Pouring a cup of chocolate, she sipped, nibbled an oatcake, and offered bits to the dogs as they came forward. Osgar nudged at her hand and urged her toward the door. Moments later, she wrapped a dry plaidie over her, pulled it over her head, and opened the door to let the three dogs out, walking out after them.

Limping slightly, she lifted her skirt out of the mud. Osgar came back and leaned against her as if to offer support. She patted his shoulder.

"Good dog," she said. "My loyal friend."

Looking up, she saw James approaching the house from the direction of the stables and outbuildings. He wore a greatcoat and hat, cane in one hand, the other shoved in a pocket, the coat flaring in the breeze.

"Good morning, Miss MacArthur," he said simply. She was not sure how to interpret his cool tone and faint smile. "Chilly and wet today."

"Lord Struan," she said with equal coolness. "The rain is still with us, but it is time I returned home, I think."

"I will drive you as soon as the roads allow. I walked out a little ways to look at their condition. The road beyond the house is quite muddy, but may improve as the day goes on. Stay as long as you like." His brief smile was suddenly heart-wrenching.

"I should go." She glanced away. "Is all well with the horses?"

"They are perfectly fine. So are the chickens and the cow in the byre past the stables. I may be a city lad, but I know a bit about country life. Most of our livestock are kept on the home farm a few miles along the glen, but some are here. The cow gave no milk this morning, though I did my best. Perhaps she was frightened by the storm."

"Or the Fey."

He tipped a brow to allow it. "Mrs. MacKimmie keeps some chickens penned here. I found four eggs." He pulled his hand from a side pocket to display one brown egg and repocketed it. "We can share breakfast."

"I would like that. And thank you for the hot chocolate and cakes. That was thoughtful." She turned to walk toward the house alongside him.

"Quite welcome. I am not a bad hand in the kitchen, as a bachelor with very few household staff. How is the ankle this morning?" He glanced down as they walked, her hindered gait as rhythmic as his. "I'll take you back soon. You seem anxious to escape."

"Not escape, I promise. But I cannot stay here alone with you."

"Unless we change our status."

She did not reply. Pale morning light mingled with soft rain and the ground was beset with runnels and puddles. Elspeth went carefully, and once or twice Struan set a hand under her arm, all in silence.

"Halloo! Lord Struan, halloo!"

"Who is that?" he asked. Elspeth had noticed two men walking along the mucky road toward the house. One wore a kilt, jacket, and dark bonnet with a plaid over his shoulder. The other was dressed in black with a tall black hat and a plaid over his shoulders for protection.

Elspeth felt her stomach sink. "Mr. Buchanan and his son," she explained. "He is the blacksmith, and his son is the kirk minister down the glen. They will draw a quick conclusion seeing us together, and news will travel fast. The Buchanans do not guard their tongues well, and neither do their wives."

"Then we may as well meet our fate." James took her arm to escort her toward the stile in the low stone wall that separated Struan lands from the road.

"Och, the new laird, and Miss MacArthur too!" the older man said.

Elspeth smiled. "Good day, Mr. Buchanan. Lord Struan, this is Mr. Willie Buchanan, our local blacksmith, and his son, Mr. John Buchanan. He is the reverend in the glen kirk."

"Good to meet you," Struan told both, shaking their hands. Looking like old and younger twins, the Buchanans tipped their hats to Elspeth and then to the viscount.

"It is a fine soft day," the blacksmith said.

"Aye," Struan said. "Hopefully it will clear soon."

"The clouds are thick yet, and dark over the mountains to the west there. More rain to come," Willie Buchanan predicted.

"I would have come sooner to welcome you, sir," said the younger man, "but for the poor weather and my parish duties. What a surprise to find you here, Miss MacArthur," he continued. "I thought you would be at Kilcrennan, snug by the fireside. We stopped there this morning to see if all was well after the storm, and Mrs. Graham said you were away to Margaret Lamont's house. She thought you might be safely there."

"I—set out for Margaret's house but had some difficulty in the storm. Lord Struan, ah, came to my assistance."

"Did he now?" The elder narrowed his eyes. "What sort of assistance?"

"A dry roof and an offer to drive the young lady home," Struan said.

"I see," the old smith said. Elspeth wondered what he meant.

"We should be on our way, just walking about to see if all is well after the big storm. And off to see that my auld mum is well too. We cannae take the pony cart, see, the roads are that bad. The river and stream are floody, too. And the stone bridge down the way is washed out. Some part of it collapsed, and it is not safe for the time being."

"Oh! But I would need to go home that way."

"You will have to take the long way over the hills," the young reverend said. "No cart or gig can take the road or the bridge until things dry up again and some repair can be made. Perhaps Mr. Lamont can do that, he has a good hand with such things."

"Is MacKimmie here, then, and Mrs. MacKimmie?" Willie Buchanan asked. "I have greetings for Mrs. MacKimmie from my wife."

"Not at present, Mr. Buchanan, but I will tell her you called," Struan replied.

"Not home? Perhaps MacKimmie then."

"Not here at the moment," Struan said.

"Ah." Mr. Buchanan glanced at his son. "Not here."

Elspeth shivered at the implication and drew her plaid closer, for the drizzle increased while they stood there. The gentlemen adjusted hat brims and jacket collars against the wet and the wind, and she hoped the Highlanders would hurry onward, but they did not seem to be in a hurry. Shifting her weight to her uninjured foot, she glanced up at James, and saw the quick look exchanged between the Buchanans.

"Yer Southron housemaids ran off, I heard," Mr. Buchanan said. "We saw yer groom taking the lasses down the road just yesterday."

"Apparently they dislike ghosts and fairies," Struan said. "I am not much troubled by them myself."

"Och, Lowlanders," the blacksmith said. "Well, it is custom in this glen to avoid Struan lands when it is time for the fairy riding. You are a brave man to stay here at this time. Did no one warn you?"

"I am aware of the tradition, but decided to stay."

The elder Buchanan nodded. "Elspeth MacArthur, are you sure himself understands the whole of it?"

"He does," she answered, lifting her chin.

"You will find Highlanders a superstitious lot, Lord Struan," the reverend said. "The people of this glen have their legends and traditions. We are all familiar with them. But some put real faith in them." He looked at Elspeth. "It is not a matter of religious faith, nor paganism or godlessness, as some suggest. It is part of the unique Celtic character. As pastor, I let it be and find no harm in it."

"That is wise, sir," Struan said. "The legends are certainly fanciful."

"The stories are more than amusement," Elspeth said. "They are part of the cultural legacy of the Highlands. Many put store in them with good reason."

"Of course," the elder Buchanan agreed. "I recall that Lady Struan was quite interested in the fairy legends in this glen. She would drive about in her ponycart to talk to people and learn about the local customs."

"My grandmother did love her work," Struan said affably. "The skies look rather dreadful, gentlemen. Will you come in for tea, or something stronger?"

"No thank you." The reverend smiled. "We will be on our way. Miss MacArthur, may we see you home? We would be glad to walk you back to Kilcrennan."

"Thank you, it will not be necessary," she said with a smile.

"No need to impose on the good laird," the elder Buchanan said. "Yer grandfather would want ye home. He's expected home soon from the city if the roads permit."

"I will see Miss MacArthur home very soon," Struan said.

"Sir, you must be very busy. We can do it," the elder man insisted.

"Da, perhaps they are courting," the reverend murmured, but it was audible to all.

"Lord Struan is a friend," Elspeth said, feeling indignant. "We met in Edinburgh months ago."

"Just so," Struan agreed. Though he did not touch her, she felt his strength and support infuse her. She lifted her chin and stared defiantly at the smith and his son.

"Ah." Buchanan glanced at his son, then back again. "Well, my lord, we will move on, and good day."

"Good day, Miss MacArthur," the reverend said.

The smith tipped his hat to Elspeth and spoke in Gaelic. *"Mìle deagh dhùrachd dhut nad àm ri teachd, Eilidh, nighean Dhòmhnaill."*

A thousand good wishes to you in your future, Elspeth, daughter of Donal."

She thanked him in that language, and the men moved on. Then she picked up her skirt and hurried toward the house, limping unevenly. Catching up to her, Struan reached to open the door first to allow her to enter.

"What is it?" he asked.

She whirled. "Did you hear that?"

"I do not speak Gaelic."

"He spoke a Gaelic blessing that is used for an engaged couple!"

"Engaged?" He frowned.

"Either he assumed that, or he was implying that I had best marry or be disgraced. He will spread a rumor about it, sure as we stand here."

"Indeed," he said thoughtfully. "If we announce our engagement, that would disprove any rumors."

"You are trying hard to convince me," she said.

"You are trying hard to refuse. But this is the best solution to avoid scandal and harm to your reputation." He bent to pet the two terriers nosing at his boots and jumping up for attention as he spoke.

"Highlanders do not fret over scandal the way Southrons do. There will be some whispering, and Buchanan never minds his own business, but I would not be judged unfairly as I might be in the city. Even lasses who might have babies out of wedlock are not severely judged or sent away. It is understood that such things happen."

"Aye," Struan said wryly. "They do."

She felt a hot blush move into her throat and face. "My cousin was caught out like that at sixteen. Her family treated her kindly and raised the child as their own. A few years later, my cousin married another man who was glad to have her. He is a good husband to her. As for my wee transgression," she said, "I would not have to marry the tailor, and I could stay at Kilcrennan in peace to do my work."

"Weaving?" he asked. "I understand your grandfather makes fine tartan."

"I am a weaver too. This is my work." She lifted a corner of the plaid draped around her shoulders. "But weaving is no occupation for a viscountess, if I were to marry you."

"I would never discourage you from doing what you want. My grandmother did as she pleased, chasing fairy legends and writing stories. If she had set her mind on weaving, I assure you the walls of this place would be draped in plaid. She never let convention deter her, even after she died," he added.

"She also spent a good part of the year in Edinburgh. I will not abandon this place to go south for tea parties and such. A husband is not expected to give up his work, but a wife takes on other duties. Marriage, a household, children."

"Marry me, decide your duties, and spend as much time here as you like."

Elspeth busied herself ruffling Osgar's silky ears. "Away from my husband? You would not want that."

"We can easily keep two homes, Elspeth," he said quietly.

"Why are you so determined? Most men caught in a compromise would be glad to be free of it."

He picked up Nellie the terrier and scrubbed his fingers under her jaw. "You require a husband for honor. And I require a wife."

"Require?" That felt like a blow. "I cannot marry a man who

values obligation above valuing his wife."

"I did not mean that, my dear lass," he murmured.

"I do not know what to do," she burst out. She swept past him and went through the kitchen toward the stairs, heart beating hard. Some raw need urged her to turn back and ask what this was truly all about for him. But she ran on.

Her stubbornness was wavering. She wanted to marry him. Even if he did not feel the same, his offer was consistent. Perhaps he was wavering too.

But if she did waver, if she did marry, it would have to be for love.

Every part of her knew she had begun to love him, and she hoped he cared for her. The fervor that had burned between them last night seemed to prove it, and yet—something else stood between them, she thought.

Then she remembered Charlotte Sinclair, who had seemed so possessive of his attentions in Edinburgh. What if he had planned to marry Miss Sinclair, but now felt obliged to a Highland girl in this awkward situation?

"Damnation," he said behind her.

Elspeth whirled, so lost in thought that she had not heard him in the hallway. "What is it?"

"I forgot the eggs." He took his hand from his pocket, eggshells in his palm, clear and golden slime coating his fingers.

She laughed, part giggle and part sob in relief and surprise. James laughed sheepishly, egg dripping on his coat, his boots, and the floor. The terriers began to lick at the floor and his shoes.

"I still have these." He produced two eggs from the other pocket. "Miss MacArthur, would you care to share a very small breakfast?"

With a sigh, she felt herself surrender. "That would be lovely."

Seeing his crooked half-grin, his damp brown hair and sky-blue eyes, the wide shoulders and lean build, she remembered how good those arms, those lips felt. She melted, yearning to run to him. Yet she stayed where she stood.

Truth be told, she did not want to leave Struan House and its laird now, if ever. The pull she felt was strong, and each moment added more to it.

He tapped his walking stick in the hallway as if it was an accessory, not a necessity, and held out a hand to usher her toward the kitchen stairs. He was pragmatic and yet passionate, skeptical yet willing to understand. He was neat in his appearance, yet his study was in disarray.

And here he stood with rain dripping from his fine coat, egg smeared on his hands, one terrier licking his boot and another pawing at him in adoration. He laughed and her heart turned in delight.

"Can you cook eggs, Lord Struan?"

"Actually, no. I was rather hoping you knew. Though I will try if you need to rest your foot."

He would do that for her, cook eggs while she rested. It felt like a peace offering of sorts. Hope bloomed in her heart again.

But she feared that he might regret his proposal if he knew that she might be the daughter of a fairy, with a grandfather bound in bargain to the Fey.

For now, she just wanted more of his company before she had to leave. And she wanted a little food too. She followed him, dogs trotting beside them.

# Chapter Eleven

SURVEYING THE DAUNTING pile of papers and books on his untidy desk, James sighed, then resumed reading his grandmother's manuscript. Having Elspeth here, a happy yet bewildering distraction, had brought respite from the task, but it must be tended and finished. And he was still required to find a bride with fairy blood, or one claiming to be so.

Elspeth could meet or exceed any standard in a wife, fanciful bloodline or none, if he could only convince her to marry him. Her stubbornness was resolute and puzzling. Once he took her home and met her grandfather, he would do his best to court her.

If this fairy-like girl continued to refuse him, he and his siblings could lose everything. He could hardly explain to her his reason to marry her. More to the point, he was quite fond—more, he loved the girl, felt sure of it now—but his grandmother's will left him blessed little choice in the matter.

Shaking his head, frustrated, he turned the page of the manuscript. He had nearly finished reading and had made inroads with research and notes. Fairy lore puzzled him, certainly, but the accounts that Lady Struan had recorded, mostly encounters with fairies and the supernatural, were quite entertaining.

He would rather study ancient rock formations than fairies. With each day, he was falling behind on his research. For now, science vied with fancy and was losing.

Despite Elspeth's claim about fairies in the garden, he had

noticed nothing but odd drifting fog and strong winds, all explained by poor weather. He was somewhat concerned about her insistence on fairies—but he was also realizing how deeply embedded the local traditions were in this glen. Elspeth had learned it in childhood.

Rain pattered against the windows and the chair creaked beneath him as he set the well-thumbed manuscript aside. The work was challenging, but nothing seemed as crucial as coaxing Elspeth MacArthur to marry him.

Time was an increasing factor. Before he had come to Struan house, he had thought to offer the estate for sale—a practical solution to the multitude of problems posed by his grandmother's will. The mad conditions of marriage and fairy whatnot tied up the funds, and a sale could solve that. Accordingly, he had written to Mr. Browne to ask him to search for a buyer.

A reply had come within a week. James took that letter from a desk drawer and read it again. *The Right Hon. The Viscount Struan*, it began. *My Lord, Rec'd your inquiry and yr request is understood and is within yr rights as heir. I can recommend two interested parties, a Scottish lord and an English gentleman. Both could generously satisfy the sale. Pls advise. Yrs, Geo. Browne, Esq.*

If the place sold, James planned to divide the funds among his siblings to rescue their financial straits too, saving all their dreams. His dream had been modest enough, just freedom to pursue geological research. Now he had another dream— marriage and a family someday.

That new possibility told him to rethink selling the place. Letting go of Struan House would be more difficult than he thought, for he loved its beauty, its atmosphere, its remoteness too. And his circumstances had shifted dramatically.

He returned to the work, and after a while heard the click of dog paws on the wooden floor and the swish of skirts. Glancing through the adjoining doorway, he saw Elspeth perusing the library shelves, while Osgar plopped down nearby. Rising, James went to the door.

She turned. "Do not let me disturb your work. I only came here to read." She held up a book. "Fairy stories. May I look at it?" She sounded formal. Careful.

"You are welcome to read or borrow anything here you like."

"Thank you. The rain is letting up," she added, glancing toward a window.

He noticed that she grasped a chair as she moved along. "You ought to be off your feet," he said.

"I can manage."

Had the looming departure put them on formal terms now? He wanted to help her, take her into his arms. The issue of compromise and marriage was not resolved in his mind, though she seemed set in her decision. As she crossed the library, the room seemed vast, the distance far, as if he had lost her already.

"It's a handsome room, this library," he said, trying for conversation, strolling into the room. He would not retreat against her cool silence. Not yet.

"It is," she agreed. "You must be very proud of it."

"Aye." He did not want to sell—that suddenly became very clear. "It is a place one would want to keep forever in a family."

"Indeed." She paused by a glass display cabinet. "Do you know much about these stones?"

He joined her, glad of the excuse to be near her, and peered over her shoulder at some stones displayed there. He had not paid much attention to them. "Looks like mostly quartz," he said. "That one is a very nice cairngorm, and the reddish one is a fine bit of jasper."

"Why are they displayed here? Did your grandmother collect stones?"

"My grandfather collected various objects he found on the grounds and had a case made to display them. I remember playing with the stones when I was a lad, the few times I was here, and my siblings and I would bring odd bits to our grandfather, hoping he would like them. My sister and I were curious about nature and science, and I grew very interested in geology.

Fiona as well, though she has focused on ancient fossils—the imprints left by shells and tiny creatures. Those are more difficult to find than rocks," he said with a smile.

"What of this one?" She pointed at a large blue stone.

"I have not seen that one before. My grandmother must have put it in the case later, perhaps when the grotto was created. I am sure they found some good stones in the process. This one is a very nice specimen of agate, a form of quartz."

"Very pretty," she said, leaning close, as he did.

"They call these Scotch pebbles." The round stone was large enough to fill a man's palm; sliced in cross-section with an outer shell of crusted rock, its core was a crystalline structure formed of wavy rings in shades of blue. "Agate occurs in volcanic rock, but the blue sort is rather rare. I have not seen it often in the Highlands."

"It almost glows," she said.

"It has extraordinary luminosity. I wonder if it is local or was found elsewhere."

"Could I see it more closely?"

James rattled the little door. "I do not know where Mrs. MacKimmie put the key. When she returns, we can open it."

"I will not be here then," she said. He saw sudden tension in her shoulders, in the nape of her neck. He wanted to touch her, ease it away.

"Then you must come back. And bring your grandfather." He recalled something she had said about the stone. "You were looking for a valuable stone that your grandfather lost in our garden, were you not? Is this the stone?"

"It might be." She leaned toward the glass again, her arm brushing his. He watched her, savoring her elegant profile, the blush filling her cheeks. She glanced up.

"What else do you know about agate?" she asked.

"They are often found in Scotland. It is a type of quartz called chalcedony," he went on. "They occur in beds of sedimentary rock, granite or sandstone, and were likely exposed to enormous heat eons ago, heat such as a volcano produces. Good agate like this one is not generally found in this area, as far as I know."

"If it is my grandfather's stone, he found it here years ago, at the top of your garden before the grotto was added."

"Here! Are you certain?"

"I remember that it was blue and striated. This might be the one. He called it a fairy stone. These hills once belonged to the fairies, they say. Supposedly there is a gateway to the fairy realm on the Struan estate."

"Is that why the fairies ride through?"

She smiled. "I thought you did not believe that."

"Many such legends are based on natural phenomena. I would like to add some geological notes to my grandmother's fairy book, as I am reviewing it in hopes of completing it. A fairy stone found on Struan lands would be a charming addition."

"Charming," she said. "But not authentic proof."

"Does such proof even exist? Nonetheless, I would like to add elements such as this. Perhaps," he said, as the thought struck him, "you would be kind enough to assist me with some of the local legends."

"I could, but Grandda knows a great deal more than I do."

"I would like to hear what he has to say on the subject."

She tilted her head. "So you want to know the truth about fairies?"

"I prefer truth to fancy, but aye."

"The truth might surprise you. At least, Grandda might say so."

He laughed. "I do want to hear how he found a fairy stone, though he lost it."

"He found it where the grotto is now. But he left it there. It is poor manners to take what belongs to the fairies, so they say."

"Construction in the grotto must have unearthed it, and my grandmother took it for her collection. Did removing it go against what these fairies want?" He chuckled.

"It is disrespectful to alter a fairy site. That would include the grotto."

"So they trample our grounds every October. Mystery solved," he said wryly.

"Surely you come across such legends in your geological work."

"I have heard that fairies are associated with hills, groves, wells, springs, caves, and so on. Though in Scotland, one must wonder what is *not* a fairy site."

"If the hill behind your house did belong to them and was changed, they might be displeased. Folk in this glen have been fleeing the fairy riding for generations."

"We need not worry too much. It is all imagination."

She slid him an odd, assessing look and strolled away. When she paused by the fireplace to hold her hands out to its warmth, she looked up at the landscape painting that hung above the mantel. "That is beautiful. I had forgotten it was here."

"It is marvelous," he said, joining her to study the painting in its ornate gilt frame. "My grandmother loved it. A local artist, she said once." The scene showed a meadow and a grove of trees whipping in the wind. The sky was purple, pink, and deep blue, a gorgeous twilight scatted with stars. Tucked in the landscape, tiny people danced about while others rode past. It seemed quaint to him and he had never given it much attention.

"I loved it too," Elspeth said. "Grandda and I sometimes visited here for tea with Lady Struan, and I would study the wee dancers and white horses and the magical twilight sky." She smiled up at him. "The local artist was my father."

He peered close at the signature in a bottom corner. "Niall Mac—MacArthur. Your father, indeed!"

"He had a gift for such, though he was a weaver too. He painted this the year before I was born, Grandda told me, and Lady Struan bought it from him. It is a fairy painting. Do you see?"

"I thought it was just trees and such." The twilight sky and billowing trees were rendered with a deft hand, he saw now. Looking closer, he saw the dancers wore gossamer veils with a glow of light around them, while cloaked figures rode on horseback between the trees.

"A skilled and imaginative artist. I am impressed. So my grandparents knew your family before you were born?"

"Aye, they would have. Long ago, the Struan estate was owned by my great-great-grandfather, who sold it to your kin. That was before the Jacobites rebelled, but many Highlanders were failing due to English laws and invasions of property."

"I knew it was acquired a century ago, but did not know it originally belonged to the MacArthurs. Is Niall MacArthur living at Kilcrennan too? You never mentioned."

"He—is gone. I never knew him or my mother. Grandda raised me from infancy."

"Oh, I see. I am sorry." He felt touched deeply by that. "I know what that is like. My parents died when I was eight," he said. "My siblings and I were separated into the care of relatives. My aunt, Lady Rankin—you met her last August—raised Fiona and I in Edinburgh. We are twins, and stayed together. Patrick and William went to other kin."

Her gaze was warm with understanding. She rested a hand on his arm briefly. "So we are both orphans."

"I would hope we have happier things in common."

"A love of fairy lore?" She laughed. He loved the silvery sound of it. "So you are a twin! I liked your sister very much. I am glad you had each other during those years."

"She liked you as well." The day they had met Elspeth at the ladies' assembly, Fiona had agreed with Sir Walter Scott that James must see her again.

Fate had apparently arranged it. He frowned, bemused by the notion.

"Thank you for telling me that. I think you do not share much about yourself."

"There is safety in secrets," he agreed.

"Sharing something so personal takes trust. So thank you." Her clear, steady gaze met his. The sense that she understood him, perhaps as kindly and sympathetically as his twin, washed over him.

"Trust is important, aye." Though he did not come easily to that, he realized he trusted Elspeth, though he did not know her entirely and suspected she had secrets too.

"Do you remember your parents?" she asked.

"I have good memories of them." He still felt a sharp sense of loss there, and did not willingly open that door. "My father was a scholar, a good man, calm and fair. My mother—kind. Lovely," he added, unable to say more. Each time he thought of her, he remembered her beautiful voice and imagined roses and lavender, her favorite flowers.

"Lavender," Elspeth said. She inhaled, eyes closed. "I can smell it somewhere." Startled, he shook his head. "There are no flowers in here."

"You are fortunate to have siblings," she went on. "I have none, and I know very little about my parents. Grandfather does not talk about them much, but he says—well, you would laugh. He says they are with the fairies." She looked away.

"I would not laugh at that. Your Grandda is an interesting character."

"Very. Sometimes I dream about my parents and hope they were like the beautiful couple in my dreams. Grandda says aye, but he likes me to be happy."

"Of course." He studied the painting again, and a new detail caught his eye. "Did your mother model for your father? One of the girls looks like you."

"Truly?" She rose on tiptoe, wobbling on her injured foot. James steadied her arm. "Oh, I see! That one—and another here, and there too. They look alike."

"They resemble you. And there is something about the shape of her face." As she glanced up at him, he touched her cheek, her chin. "Aye, much the same."

Touching her felt like heaven. He lifted her chin with a finger. She smelled wonderful, cool rain and warm woman. Lavender too, somehow. It was comforting—and exhilarating.

She smiled. "I wonder if my father painted her. Grandda never said. I do not know what she looked like, nor do I know her kin. Their marriage was brief. She died with my birth. And he left. Died. I do not know much about it."

"If that is her, she was a beauty, and you favor her."

"This is like a gift, something of my parents to keep. Thank you!" She rose and kissed his cheek.

He sucked in a breath and set both hands at her waist, then pulled her toward him for a new kiss that she returned willingly. Heat pulsed through him, a desire for more, for this comfort and ease and excitement.

She sighed and slid her hand along his collar, touched his jaw—and leaned away. "I must go," she whispered, looking up. He could lose himself in those eyes, silvery and magical somehow.

"You need not rush." He brushed back her hair, kissed her brow.

"But I must," she murmured. Caught in his arms, she did not break his hold, resting her head for moment on his chest. "If the roads allow, I should go home. Grandda and our housekeeper will be worried if I do not return soon. I apologize for being so much trouble. Please do not feel obligated. You know—about marriage."

"I would feel better about this if we did marry. To be honest, it might be convenient for both of us, and much to our liking."

"Liking?" She sounded disappointed.

He should have phrased it differently, should have said what his mind had begun to whisper. *Love.* It was a revelation, but still forming.

She moved away from the fireplace and her father's painting. "You have work to do and must have other plans. I am in the way here."

"You are not." He suddenly remembered. "I am expecting guests in a few days. My aunt is coming up with some others to tour the Highlands. They will stop here."

"Will your sister come up as well?"

"She is, and our younger brother too. Miss Sinclair also. You may remember her."

"Oh. The one who set her cap for you." She glanced at him.

"I give her no encouragement."

"But she is lovely, and a wealthy heiress, I heard it said, and so a part of Edinburgh society. She would be an ideal wife for a viscount."

"So would you." He tipped his head. "It seems we are both eager to avoid other engagements. What if I asked you again to marry me?"

She tilted her head, eyes twinkling. "You are persistent."

"I am," he said firmly. "I do not regret having an obligation to ask."

She stepped back. "But I am keeping you from your work. Is there a gig or cart that will do on the roads?"

Rebuffed again, though not sure why, he was unwilling to give up. "Very well. We will leave it for now. There is an old gig in the stable. I will fit it up with one of the horses."

He had felt they were on the edge of real agreement, felt his life about to change for the better. But things had whirled again without warning. She was a fickle thing—or else there was something that frightened her.

"Tell me. Is there some reason you are so reluctant to marry?"

"Why would you think that? It is just not—necessary." She moved along, fingers tracing over the spines of books. "Are you doing some research for your grandmother's book about fairy lore? Is it something you must do here, or in Edinburgh?"

Deflected again. "It is a condition of her will that I finish the book. Some research and annotations are needed. I have found books here that will be helpful."

She pulled a book, opened it, slid it back. "But you do not believe in fairies."

"Not particularly, but it makes no difference to the work. Her book is a thorough compilation of stories and personal accounts. I will add more, and then if it is published, readers can decide for themselves what they believe."

"The author as well. One must believe wholeheartedly in what one does."

That simple truth gave him pause. "But many write about a subject they are knowledgeable about, even if they do not necessarily agree."

"Just as one may make a marriage without love, if there is an obligation?" She examined another book.

He inclined his head. "Is that the trouble, Miss MacArthur?"

"Marriage needs love."

"Not everyone would agree with that, though it is a pretty notion."

"A pretty notion." She flipped the pages of a book. "Are you sure you want my assistance with your book? We might have to mutually agree on the subject."

"What?" He was distracted by the lovely curve of the back of her neck, small and vulnerable just where her glossy dark hair was rolled in a braid; he was distracted by the delicate shell of her ear. And he was preoccupied by her response and her questions. She wanted to know how he felt. That was fair, though he was not entirely certain. This was moving fast, and overt sentiment went strongly against his nature.

"Miss MacArthur," he said. "I care. I do."

She kept her back to him, studying open pages. "Do you?"

He touched her shoulder, then traced a finger along the back of her neck. She turned quickly, sweetly, into his arms.

The kiss happened naturally, familiar now, tenderness without ruse or agreement. He knew the risks, knew he was losing his heart, his very soul here and now. He wanted to lose those to her. Brushing his lips over her cheek, her earlobe, he remembered the fierce passion of the night before that had so overtaken him. Drawing back, he set her a little apart, reluctant again to let the depth of his feelings show. He was not used to this.

"What if we were engaged briefly? You could break it off when you want. If you want," he added.

"It is a wicked bargain." She tapped a finger on his chest. "Never make a bargain with the fairy ilk."

He went still, reminded of his grandmother's demand. "Are you of the fairy ilk?"

"Who knows?" She looped her arms around his neck. He could not resist her, felt a spinning within so compelling that he pulled her close, kissed her. He felt like a man drowning, and she his capricious, beautiful rope.

He drew back. "Any more of that, my lass, and we should forego an engagement and marry quick."

"If we both agreed."

"You drive a tough bargain," he murmured, and took her face in his hands to kiss her, feeling her arch against him, feeling her sigh on his lips.

The door to the study pushed open then, and at the creak of the door, James looked up to see Osgar enter with the terriers trotting after. He had forgotten the hounds had been there and had wandered off. He scratched the wolfhound's great gray head as the dog pushed between them.

"Enter the fairy hound to rescue his mistress."

"He wants to remind me to leave before anything else happens here." Then she closed her eyes. "But we will not be alone for long."

"The MacKimmies will not be here until later today. Perhaps tomorrow with the bad roads."

She shook her head, her back to the window, silhouetted in the light. "Someone is coming to the house. A girl. There is a coach not far behind. And I feel that my grandfather is already returning. He will be home tonight, sooner than I thought."

"The lass with the Sight knows all," James said, bewildered.

"She does, sometimes."

He glanced through the window at a view that spanned eastward, and saw gray drizzle and mist floating in long clusters over hills purple with heather.

Then, far off, he saw a small figure, a woman walking along the ridge of a hill. Moments later, a coach rounded the base of a hill, coming slowly along the muddy track.

"Someone is coming," she said. "I told you."

Puzzled, James shook his head. "Even if you had the eyes of a hawk, you could not have seen them coming. Your back was turned to the window."

"Now will you believe me, James MacCarran?" she asked quietly. "I know things. I am not what you think I am, nor am I much suited to life in the city."

He struggled to piece all this together, yet desire warmed him, and a sense of hope rose in him, rusty and yet there. He did not understand her, but he wanted her quite desperately now. But he would not make a fool of himself by falling for fairy nonsense. Everything had an explanation. Everything.

"Then we should go, sooner than—I wanted." As she walked past him, a feeling overwhelmed him, physical desire mingling with deep longing. "Elspeth."

She spun and reached out just as he took her into his arms and kissed her again, long and thoroughly, and she returned a fervent kiss that erased doubt, frustration, time itself.

Then he drew back, brushed her hair back, kissed her brow. "You cannot deny that there is something strong between us. Shall we agree on an engagement? I will speak to your grandfather."

She shook her head. "I think not."

"Fickle lass. I thought you were ready to agree."

"I am. And then it changes. Perhaps it is my fairy blood," she said lightly. "They do say it is in my kin, far back. Or more recently," she added.

"You have no idea," he said, "how much I want to believe that."

"Perhaps you will come around to it someday." She smiled, whimsical, amused, and walked ahead of him.

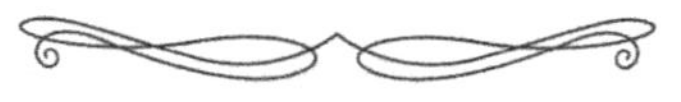

# Chapter Twelve

SOON ENOUGH AND too soon, for she was that conflicted about leaving Struan House, Elspeth sat in the creaky old gig beside James. He slowed as a carriage came along the road toward them and slowed.

"Good afternoon, Angus MacKimmie," James called. "And Mrs. MacKimmie. Good to see you back so soon."

The housekeeper, sitting in the coach with a maidservant, leaned forward. "My lord, good to see you as well. My daughter has enough help, and with your guests arriving soon, next week, I thought I would be needed here. Good day, Miss MacArthur," she added, looking a bit surprised.

"Mrs. MacKimmie," Elspeth said, blushing. "Lord Struan kindly offered to give me a ride to Kilcrennan."

James nodded without explanation. Sensing the housekeeper bursting to know, Elspeth only smiled.

"How are the roads, MacKimmie?" James asked.

"Well enough, depending where you go. Over to Kilcrennan, watch out for the bridge." He peered toward Elspeth. "Good afternoon, Miss MacArthur," he said, tipping his hat.

"We heard the bridge had some damage," James said.

"There's mud gushing down the hills to swamp the road in places," MacKimmie went on, "and some trees are down. The stone bridge is nearly washed over. I wouldna go that way, sir."

Elspeth hung back in silence as James thanked him, and she

felt pure relief when the vehicles rattled in opposite directions. "Thank you for not saying anything about yesterday."

"No need to explain," he replied, eyes intent on the road.

"Mrs. MacKimmie is a good-hearted soul and would say naught about it. But Willie Buchanan and his son may let everyone know our business."

"With luck, they will soon hear of an engagement, and no harm done. I imagine secrets do not keep long in a small glen."

"The fairies keep their secrets. Humans have more trouble with it."

"I think you have a few secrets yourself," he murmured.

"As do you."

"You are sniffing them out with your Highland powers," he said.

She lifted her chin, feeling a bit hurt. "Most people take me at my word."

"I am a cautious sort. But I trust you tell the truth where you see it. Now, I have a question for you."

"I will not marry you."

"Fair enough. We will leave it at that. I only want to know when you might be free to assist me with my grandmother's book."

She looked at him from under her bonnet rim. "When do you need me?"

His keen glance told her all his thoughts. "Anytime, lass. At your will."

"I could come to Struan any day you like."

"I will fetch you Monday, would that suit?"

She nodded, heart pounding. "What about your guests?"

"They will not be here yet. I want to work on Grandmother's papers as much as possible until then."

"Do you plan to go back to Edinburgh after that?"

"I have lectures to give, and other work, aye."

She nodded, bouncing on the seat as the gig hit a rut. James murmured about the poor roads as he guided the horse and vehicle around curves that took the road upward. Reaching the ridge, the descent was steep and the road was marred by runnels and mud. Drizzle dampened Elspeth's bonnet, shawl, the lap robe tucked around her, and James's hat and coat. The road seemed slippery under the wheels, the fog thick.

"This weather is miserable," she said.

"The fairies are not happy with us," he remarked. He slapped the reins and pulled on the brake a bit as he guided the horse downward in silence. He was focused and capable, and Elspeth was quiet, gripping the side for support.

"Devilish weather," he muttered then. "I have yet to see this glen in the sunshine. There has been mist, rain, and the deluge of the Apocalypse ever since I arrived. Your wee fairies might have intended to bring us together by sending you down a mudslide into my arms. But they could give us some sun now."

"That would be nice," she agreed. Grandda had taught her to see meaning in everything around her. Nothing, he said, was as simple as it appeared.

Ahead, she glimpsed the old bridge. As they rounded a challenging curve, James concentrated on his task and Elspeth watched the water of the wide and rocky burn that rushed under the bridge.

"James!" she said then. "The water is very high today."

He drew on the reins. "Wait here. I want to look at the bridge." He leaped down to the road.

Not content to wait, she climbed down too, lifting her hems out of the mud to follow him toward the bridge, which spanned a small gorge. Her boot heels sank in the mud, her walking impeded by her stiff ankle. Her skirt snagged on gorse and she tugged it free, then joined James at the edge of the wide stream.

The wooden bridge spanned a gap of twenty feet or so, the stone pylons embedded in earth and rock. The stream gushed through and lapped at the sides of the arched bridge, water splashing over the planks. The stream was the color of milky tea.

"Careful," James murmured, taking her elbow.

"The burn is rarely this high." Along the sides of the gorge, tree roots and bracken thrust out of the water, and fallen branches swept by in the fast current.

"Is there another place to cross?"

"There's a level place two miles or so that way, at the head of the gorge. But the burn is very wide there and one must step from rock to rock to cross. There is no bridge. It's opposite the way to Kilcrennan, and would make the journey even longer."

"We do not have much choice unless we return to Struan and wait for the water to subside. Is there no other access?"

"Not close by. Some people jump the gap," she said. "Downstream there's a leap, where one side of the gorge is higher than the other." She pointed in the other direction.

He laughed. "I will not chance that, nor should you, though I would not be surprised if you have given it a go in the past."

"Is that intuition, sir?" she asked, amused.

"Only logic, Miss MacArthur, knowing you."

She smiled. Learning more about him each moment, she knew he had true warmth and heart beneath his cool exterior. Despite his staunch skepticism, he did not dismiss her intuition. "True, once I did try the Leap with friends when I was young. They made it, but I fell and broke an arm. I could make it, I think, now that I am taller."

"Out of the question."

She remembered his leg then. "Of course," she murmured.

"You have a turned ankle, and what of our horse and gig? I wonder if we could walk the horse over the bridge without the gig." James went forward to step tentatively on the bridge, jumping up and down to test its soundness, then walking toward the middle.

Elspeth heard the low groan of wood and iron. "No, stop!"

He moved back to the grass. "It might hold, but the water could wash over at any moment. We must go upstream to cross, or return to Struan."

"The bridge will hold me. I can cross here. You return to

Struan with the horse and gig. You need not escort me all the way home." She did not want to say farewell but did not want him to take the risk for her.

"So the viscount traps you at Struan overnight, then tosses you out of his gig to walk home on a poor ankle, in a storm, over an unsafe bridge? My lass, they write ballads about such cruel lovers as that. And your grandfather would call for a hanging."

*Lover,* she thought, thrilled at the casual way he said it, with such acceptance. "He would bring a reverend, not a rope."

"Which is worse, to Miss MacArthur's thinking?" he asked wryly.

She only laughed, walking back to the gig beside him. He lifted her inside, his hands firm at her waist, then leaped up and took the reins to turn the placid mare. Then he guided the horse along the earthen track beside the gorge in the direction of the other crossing. Below, the water rushed and brimmed nearly to its sodden banks.

Nearing the fording place, where the sides of the gorge disappeared to flatter moorland, Elspeth saw that the run-off had flooded the moorland to either side. "The crossing on foot is over there," she said. "The rocks are flat and it is usually easy to walk across. But the water is too high now."

"Aye." He stopped the horse. "That is no easy crossing there. Our wheels could bog down."

She nodded. The burn had overflowed its banks, creating a swampy area to either side. The rocks used for crossing on foot were mostly submerged.

"How deep is it over there? Are there good-sized rocks we could use to step across?" He pointed downstream.

"It is not too rocky there, and usually is just inches deep. But more today."

"I think the gig can make it across. If the horse will not falter, we'll do all right. Hold on." He set the horse forward before Elspeth could protest.

Under his skilled and certain hands, the gig rattled steadily across the boggy ground. Elspeth clung to the seat, grabbing James's sleeve with her other hand, his arm tensing as he guided reins and horse.

Then they were fording the burn, the horse moving through the flow, the gig following. Elspeth squealed in alarm at the swirl and rush of the current.

"We'll be fine," James said. Within moments, the water swirled to the hubs, then nearly the tops, of the wheels, splashing over James's boots and soaking Elspeth's hem.

"Turn back," she said, clutching the seat.

"We will be fine, my girl." The horse stepped through the surge. As water sluiced over the floorboards, Elspeth shrieked faintly.

Halfway across, the horse stopped, and the wheels seemed stuck, the gig shuddering in the current. Water slopped over the floorboards, wetting Elspeth's shoes and skirts. The horse pulled again, whinnied, stopped.

"Stay here," James told Elspeth, and stepped down into water that surged around his legs. The tail of his frock coat floated behind him as he surged ahead and took the horse's bridle. He spoke quietly, patting the mare's nose, then moved forward, the horse following. Within moments, the gig lurched free.

Elspeth drew her legs up to the seat, water washing over the floorboards. The horse gave a hesitant whicker but plowed steadily through the water in response to the man whose calm and caution made the girl and horse feel safe.

Holding the bridle, James led the horse ahead carefully, slipping a bit in the swirling water, his hat tipping off as he caught himself. Elspeth bent to snatch up the hat as it swirled past.

The gig surged dripping from the water, horse and man guiding. As it lurched up to the opposite bank, James climbed inside.

"Well done!" Elspeth handed him his hat. "Kilcrennan is north, that way."

"There's something to be said for funding new roads," James said, as the gig rolled along the rutted, muddy track.

"As laird of Struan, you could pay for repairs rather than wait for the Crown to fix the roads. They are in no hurry to fix up the Highlands after they laid straight new roads through the hills to quell the Scots a hundred years back."

"And much good it did. Highlanders are a stubborn lot," he said.

"We are." She laughed, and he did too, and they rode quietly toward Kilcrennan and her grandfather.

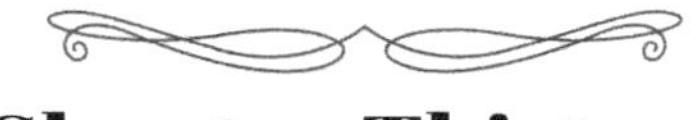

# Chapter Thirteen

JAMES SHRUGGED INTO a borrowed tartan waistcoat of dark green with black and yellow accents, then wrapped a clean neckcloth around the high collar of a fresh linen shirt. The borrowed things, including tan trousers and a coat of gray superfine, all made for a tall man, fit well enough. Mrs. Graham, the housekeeper, had provided some of Mr. MacArthur's things, showing James to a guest room to change.

"MacArthur is glad to lend them to you. My lord, we are grateful to you for taking care of Miss Elspeth and seeing her safe home."

*Safe home*, James thought, savoring the phrase. Mrs. Graham might have guessed he and Elspeth had been alone, yet the woman seemed unbothered.

Knotting the neckcloth, about to go downstairs for the hearty tea Mrs. Graham had promised, he stopped at the window to gaze over the courtyard of the quaint and modest estate of house, old stone tower, and outbuildings. MacArthur had nearly two thousand acres, Elspeth had explained as they rode to Kilcrennan. The place was old, tilted, shabby, cramped, showing charm as well as age. Most of the outbuildings, Elspeth had said, were weaving cottages. Beyond, misty blue mountains marched into the distance beneath a wide sky that promised to clear soon.

Then he saw Elspeth crossing the yard, dry and dressed in a pale gray gown with a plaid of soft colors wrapped over her shoulders. Just the sight of her tugged at his heart, bringing an inexpressible yearning. He knew now, clearly and certainly, that he loved her, felt his feelings expand far beyond obligation and the absurd demands of his grandmother's will. Life would never be the same for him without that fey and fascinating girl by his side.

Now a gig and horse rolled into the yard, and the driver, an older gentleman, stepped out. Perhaps this was Donal MacArthur, James wondered. The man looked strong and fit in a dark brown coat over a red plaid kilt and stockings in the Highland way. Seeing Elspeth in the yard, he flung his arms wide and she ran to be enveloped in a hug. James heard her laugh, heard her grandfather's booming reply.

"Home, wee girl! I worried you had vanished in the fairy riding!"

"The fairies did not take me, Grandda. I was safe at Struan House."

"Struan! What is this?"

Mrs. Graham hurried to greet MacArthur too, and James was surprised to see the housekeeper give and receive kisses from both. As they walked toward the house, Donal and Mrs. Graham both wrapped arms about Elspeth, the three of them snug, supportive, and loving.

James sucked in a breath as the yearning grew powerful, unsatisfied, almost a physical hurt. Years ago he had known such warmth, the joy and laughter of parents, siblings, servants who were kin and helpers. There was always ease of affection in that home. But his parents had died and the children were sent away, and he and Fiona had lived with well-meaning but stern Lady Rankin. They'd had only each other for years.

That stale old loneliness still pulled, for he felt the outsider again. Then Donal MacArthur looked up, saw him at the window, grinned widely and lifted a hand to welcome him. Elspeth looked up and waved.

Feeling some relief, he headed for the stairs.

THE HEARTY TEA was supper, James discovered. The generous spread was served in the dining room, where he sat with Elspeth and Mrs. Graham, with MacArthur himself coming soon after seeing to some tasks in the cottages. James glanced around the cozy room with its lovely blue walls, planked floor, and a table set with crisp linens, delicate china, and a silver service that even fussy Aunt Rankin would be proud to have.

The fare was excellent, too, hot rolls and butter, cold sliced lamb, rowan jelly, small cakes and biscuits, and steaming black tea. Elspeth poured, and James felt comfortable enough to help himself liberally and laugh at the light conversation.

Lady Rankin, James thought, would have her nose out of joint to discover this Highland family not crude and backward, but warm and civilized. She had maintained that opinion even though her sister, Lady Struan, had gone north—and so Aunt Rankin had rarely sent James and Fiona, as her wards, to visit their grandparents.

"You will catch your death of colds in the north and come home undisciplined and have to be educated all over again," she would claim.

But he and Fiona had been happy there, exploring and free. By the time he had gone to university in Glasgow and was offered a teaching position in Edinburgh, he did his best to visit his widowed grandmother, wanting to spend more time in the Highlands, though it was not always practical. His twin Fiona found more opportunity than he, for she studied the Gaelic language, gained some proficiency, and joined a ladies' society that sent her north to teach and help in Highland glens.

But here, James felt immediately and utterly at home, and savored it as quietly as he savored the tea, the cakes, and the company. He watched Elspeth, admiring her simple loveliness again. The pale gray wool and the creamy tartan in lavender and rose flattered her complexion. When she smiled at him, the dimples at the corners of her mouth made him smile, too.

"That is a handsome shawl, Miss MacArthur," he said.

"It is one of my weaving pieces. Could I could give you a length for your twin sister? I would be honored."

"Thank you," he murmured. "I would love to see the looms where you work."

"Of course." A blush seeped into her cheeks, and her eyes sparkled. He felt she remembered, as he did, lovely secrets between them.

"Please stay the night, Lord Struan," Mrs. Graham said. "It is going dark, and the roads will not be improved yet."

He had no desire to make that trip alone in the dark. And he had no desire to leave Elspeth yet. "I will gratefully accept, if it is agreeable."

"Of course," Elspeth said. "Grandda will come in soon. He will be pleased."

"Mrs. Graham," James said. "Miss MacArthur told me that you are a cousin on her mother's side. I know some of the Grahams in Edinburgh. The younger Sir John Graham is a friend—a road engineer with a keen interest in geology, so we have worked together. I saw them at the king's reception in Edinburgh, where, ah, Miss MacArthur and I first met." He glanced at Elspeth and way.

"Oh, aye, sir, those Grahams are cousins, and Sir Hector Graham too, who is now Deputy Lord Provost. He has three lovely daughters—Ellison, Deirdre, and Juliet. But they keep to Edinburgh for the most part."

"Sometimes they visit Strathniven here in Perthshire," Elspeth said, "but we do not see them often." As she spoke, the drawing room door opened and Donal MacArthur entered.

"Lord Struan!" he boomed. "So good to meet you, sir!" James stood to clasp his hand. "Welcome to Kilcrennan!"

"Lord Struan will be our guest for the night, Mr. MacArthur," Mrs. Graham said, sounding more like a wife than a housekeeper.

"Excellent," MacArthur said, sitting beside Elspeth to accept a cup of steaming tea, heavily sweetened, from Mrs. Graham, and then a plate of cold meat and rolls.

"I appreciate the loan of the clothing, sir," James said. "My things got quite wet as we crossed some high water."

"Down by the Durchan Water, Grandda," Elspeth supplied. "It was very floody but Lord Struan got us safely across."

"We are even further in your debt, sir," Donal MacArthur said. "Souls have been swept away in lesser floods than we've seen this week. I had the de'il of a time coming back from Edinburgh. Would have arrived sooner if not for the high waters and poor roads. I saw the Buchanans along the way and heard that Elspeth had been caught stranded at Struan House. That worried me. But I see all is well."

James caught Elspeth's glance and looked away. "All is well, sir."

The man leaned forward. "I understand you are a professor at the university."

"I teach natural philosophy, specifically geological sciences, and do some exploration and research as well."

"Rocks and such, hey! A good subject of study. You are new to Struan House, I think? You were named viscount when your grandfather passed a few years back, yet Lady Struan, who I considered a friend, said that her grandson kept to the city."

"Struan House was my grandmother's home, and she kept the estate. I would not usurp that, and my lecturing duties and research keeps me very busy."

MacArthur nodded, spearing another roll with a two-pronged fork. He glanced at Elspeth. "The Laird of Struan stays much in the city," he said, popping a chunk of buttered roll into his mouth.

"I know," she said tersely.

"Where's the yarns from Margaret, then?" Donal MacArthur asked. "Is your cousin well? How did Lord Struan come to take you home?"

"I never made it over to Margaret's." Elspeth set down her tea, cheeks high pink. James saw bravado spark in her eyes. "I was at Struan House, stranded there by the weather."

"Ah. The Buchanans thought so." Donal looked from her to James and back again. James felt like a boy caught out at school. "And the MacKimmies away and all."

"What do you mean?" Elspeth asked warily.

"Reverend Buchanan and his father told me you were caught out in the rains, and that they suspected you and Lord Struan were together in interesting circumstances, were his words. Is there something I should know?"

James sat straighter. "Sir, if may I be frank. Miss MacArthur stayed at Struan House, aye. She had a mishap and was injured, and with the rains, could not travel."

"She twisted her ankle, Donal MacArthur," Mrs. Graham said. "I looked at it myself today and made her soak it in a salt bath. She must rest and cannot walk about the hills for a while. Did you not see her limping in the yard?"

"I did see," Donal said. "Injured. Go on, sir." He fixed James with a stern stare.

"Given the storm and her injury, I offered her hospitality at Struan House. My housekeeper and servants were detained elsewhere, unable to return yet."

"The storm and the fairy riding," Donal MacArthur said. "And then?"

"Grandda, it could not be helped," Elspeth said.

"Alone together," her grandfather murmured.

"Lord Struan was a cordial host." Elspeth lifted her chin. "The Buchanans have no right to suggest otherwise."

James saw temper flaring in the older man's leonine eye, but MacArthur held his composure. So Elspeth got her temper, her spark, and her dignity too from this man.

"She turned her ankle, Donal," Mrs. Graham reminded him.

"I fell in the mud," Elspeth said. "I could hardly walk. It was unfortunate."

"Unfortunate," MacArthur repeated. "For two days!" he thundered then.

"Oh dearie!" Mrs. Graham fanned herself. "MacArthur, compose yourself!"

Elspeth's cheeks burned as bright as her eyes. "Fortunately, Lord Struan was there to help me," she said. "Imagine if I had been truly alone out there."

MacArthur tapped his fingers on the table. "I commend you for considering my granddaughter's well-being, sir, but what of her reputation?"

"We were in extraordinary circumstances," James said.

"Extraordinary," Elspeth repeated. "Grandfather, I saw the fairies riding!"

"What!" MacArthur stared.

"Over Struan lands," she said. "We heard the horses. Or I did. And I saw—" She stopped. "I will tell you later. It was an exceptional night."

"How exceptional was it," her grandfather growled.

"Lord Struan was an utter gentleman," she said, lifting her chin.

James blew out a breath, not sure that was entirely true. "I understand the situation appears dire, Mr. MacArthur. I know such things can jeopardize the reputation of an entire family. I am prepared to make it right."

"Make it right?" Donal MacArthur regarded him, then Elspeth. James felt his heart beat fast, anticipating. "You would offer to marry her?"

"I have done so already. I would ask your blessing." He could not look at Elspeth just then, but felt her hot gaze on him. He knew this was not how she wanted to reveal it.

"Huh." MacArthur leaned toward Elspeth. "And will you have the man, then?"

"No," she said, and set down her teacup.

"He's a fine gentleman with a title and property, and seems to have good morals. I believe he has a good heart as well. I believe you found a good one."

"He is, he does, and I have. But my answer is no."

"He has a fine estate," MacArthur went on as if she had not

blatantly refused. "Sir, may I assume that your income is excellent?"

"I am, ah, comfortable," James said, feeling distinctly uncomfortable.

"There," MacArthur blustered, waving a hand. "And he has a teaching position and a house in Edinburgh as well. He can take you to the Lowlands."

"I do and I can," James told Elspeth. "If you want."

"I do not care to go to the Lowlands again," Elspeth said firmly, quietly.

"Highland or Lowland, the decision was made when you stayed the night at Struan House," MacArthur said. "The two of you make a fine match."

"We do," James ventured.

"We do, but I do not want to marry," Elspeth said.

"Peggy Graham thinks you must marry, do you not, madam?" MacArthur boomed.

"Lord Struan is a fine gentleman and Elspeth is fortunate," Mrs. Graham said. "But if the lass refuses, she has her reasons and you should listen."

Despite that, Donal MacArthur raised his china cup in salute. "To Struan!"

"Grandda, you must listen. But I see you will not." Elspeth stood and went to the door. "I have weaving to do. This matter is not decided, so do not celebrate." She left.

"There, that's done," MacArthur said in a satisfied tone. "She will be married."

"Let her make up her own mind, Donal MacArthur," Mrs. Graham said.

"Stubborn as yon lass is, we must interfere. Eh, Struan?"

"I like her stubbornness, sir. And she has her reasons to refuse." James stood. "I will do my best, I promise. But she cannot be forced. I think you know that. Mrs. Graham, thank you for tea." He nodded and went to the door.

"Hoo hoo!" Donal crowed as James left. "A wedding for sure, Peggy dear!"

THE LOOM CLICKED and the heddle bars shifted as Elspeth pressed the foot pedals. She threw the small threaded shuttle from right to left, then another left to right, through the gap between the threads. All the while she swayed her body side to side, back and forth with the steady rhythm of loom and shuttle. Her hands moved quickly, the repetition soothing, erasing all but the moment. That respite was what she needed.

She pressed the treadle again to shift the wooden heddle bar that brought one set of warp threads down, creating a tunnel between the layered yarns. Tossing another threaded shuttle through the gap, she caught it with her left hand as it sailed through. The next push of the treadle dropped the warp threads to snug the weft thread in another color into the weave. Tossing the shuttle through again, she dropped it and picked up another color.

Quick and nimble she went, warp threads clicking, yellow and black, the weft threads sailing through, red and black. The woolen cloth grew in length by inches, the span only as wide as the reach of her arms as the cloth turned on the wooden roller that pressed against her taut belly as she leaned to the work.

The rhythms spoke to her. *Go to him; stay here; go to him; stay here. Go to Struan, leave Kilcrennan,* said the loom. She tossed another shuttle, pressed the treadle. *Love him, keep him, love him, keep him,* said the loom.

She took up the shuttle and flung it, right to left. Catch the shuttle, press the treadle; catch the shuttle; press the treadle. She did not want to think, she only wanted to lose herself in the warp and the weft and the rolling of the cloth.

A decision must be made. Yet someone waited for this fine tartan and would treasure it. That would do for now.

But it was not enough to fill a lifetime.

*Catch the shuttle, press the treadle. Yellow goes over, black comes back; red flies through, black follows. Love him, keep him, go to him.*


JAMES PAUSED IN the open doorway of the weaving cottage, shoulder leaned against the doorjamb as he watched the weaver so absorbed in her work that she did not look up.

He had never seen tartan cloth produced on a loom. He had always taken the woolen fabric for granted, not thinking how it came into existence, only what it cost, or how it looked, or how it kept a man dry and warm, free and comfortable.

After a few moments watching the loom and the weaver, he saw how the parts worked together, how the colored yarns flew and interwove into the plaid pattern as the cloth formed, spooling taut and handsome over the roller.

But the weaver held his greater attention.

He was fascinated by the girl and her skill, how she sat on a chair leaning into the loom, back straight, arms out, hands swift, as if she held a harp sideways in her lap to play a rhythm of clicks and shushes and swoops, every motion deft and efficient. The loom shuddered gently, the roller turned, the cloth grew under her steady hands.

She was focused, calm and entranced, a soft light on her face. She did not see him watching her. He appreciated her swan-like grace, her supple curves, her beauty. What she did was dance-like and almost seductive, so that his body stirred, and he wanted her fiercely, deeply, body and sweet soul. And he saw more than a beautiful weaver at work.

He saw her gift, and her love, for the weaving, and he understood why she did not want to leave Kilcrennan or go to the Lowlands. She was part of this place, this devotion. In Edinburgh, she would feel smaller, lesser, her weaving not respected for an ancient and honorable craft, but merely an industry and an activity unsuitable to a viscountess. This was more than a pastime for her. This was her art, and she was devoted to it.

He would never ask her to leave this behind. In silence, he turned away.

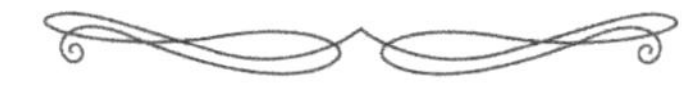

# Chapter Fourteen

"THE RAIN WILL clear overnight," Donal MacArthur remarked. "Whisky, sir?"

James turned as the older man entered the parlor and went to a shelf containing a round ceramic bottle and glasses.

"Thank you," he agreed. "And thank you for your hospitality, Mr. MacArthur."

"We are glad of your company and your help for my granddaughter. She mentioned you intend to complete Lady Struan's unfinished book."

"I am working on her pages for now, though I must return to Edinburgh and the university in a few weeks." He wondered if he would go alone, as it seemed he might never convince Elspeth to marry him.

"I see." MacArthur poured the drams and handed one to James.

James sipped. "Excellent stuff," he said, as the warmth spread through him. "Is it from a local distiller? Mellow, yet with subtle power. Extraordinarily pleasant." He sipped again. "I've never tasted the like for quality."

"'Gie us the drink, to make us wink,'" MacArthur recited Robert Burns, and James chuckled. "A MacGregor cousin makes this in his small distillery up in the hills. So long as he makes enough family and friends, 'tis legal." He grinned.

"Ah, good." James was aware that the manufacture of illicit

whisky and its export via smugglers was rampant in the Highlands despite legal strictures. "I wish your cousin well in his enterprise. This is fine stuff."

"He always sends some to Kilcrennan. He calls this fairy brew."

James sipped again. "Because it is delicate as well as powerful?"

"And because it is made from dew according to a recipe from the Fey."

"The Fey, is it." The whisky warmed like fire yet soothed his throat and his spirit too, relaxing him. "Your cousin would be a wealthy man if he could sell this outright."

"*Tcha!* The taxes would be too high to bother. There would be no profit left. My cousin does well enough exporting his other whiskies, and we shall say little of that to protect him, hey. For this brew, he respects his responsibility to the *Daoine Sìth*, and will not profit from their recipe. Fairy dew makes his fairy brew." He winked.

"*Dow-in shee.*" James attempted the Gaelic. "My sister has a knack for the Gaelic, learned from our nanny. I did not pick up much of it myself."

"You had a Highland nanny in Edinburgh?"

"I was born in the Perthshire hills and spent years in the Highlands before I came south to live with relatives."

"Then you are a Highland man at heart, for all that."

"I suppose I am. Mr. MacArthur, do you believe in this fairy business?"

"Oh, I do," was the firm answer. Then the man took a long swallow.

"My grandmother mentions you in her manuscript. She was impressed with your knowledge of fairy lore. She devoted pages to your stories."

"Did she?" Donal MacArthur carried the bottle and sat in a threadbare brocade chair, indicating the other for James. "I am flattered. We were good acquaintances, and I am pleased to be in her wee book." He raised his glass. "To Lady Struan, a friend to the Kilcrennan weaver and a friend to the fairies too."

"She also mentioned Niall MacArthur."

"My son. Elspeth's father."

"So I understand. His painting hangs in the library at Struan House."

"The fairy grove, aye. He painted that just before he disappeared."

"Disappeared?" James raised his brows.

MacArthur refilled his glass and poured another dram for James. "He was lured by the charms of a fairy lass."

"Some lasses have a way of enchanting a fellow."

"Some, aye. And some are of the fairy ilk." MacArthur sighed. "Niall roamed the hills to make his drawings—he was gifted, that lad—and he worked at the weaving too. One day he went out with his drawing box, and never came back. He met a fairy lass and went over to the fairies with her."

Unsure how to respond to that, James sipped. Perhaps the man embellished the account to hide the shame of a young man running off and leaving a small daughter and presumably a wife. "What a tragedy to lose him. I am sorry," he said carefully.

"Sad for us, but he enjoys life where he is. One loses all sense of time and responsibility in the fairy realm. A day there is like a year here. A week is seven years. I know this myself."

"Oh?" James tipped his head, skeptical, trying to remember something his grandmother had written, but he thought best to move the subject along. "So Miss MacArthur did not know her father?"

"Never saw him except in her dreams. She has a gift, you know. The Highland Sight." He tapped his forehead.

"So I have seen." That was undeniable and inexplicable.

"It can be a gift from the fairies." The old man sighed. "Mrs. Graham and I have raised her to be a proper lass, even took her to Edinburgh for her debut with her Graham cousins. But she prefers to be here, and she is a brilliant weaver, I will say. But I must be honest, sir." MacArthur leaned forward. "I want to see her married, and happy—and far away from here."

"She seems determined to stay."

"Do not give up your suit, sir," Donal said.

"I cannot force her to agree. She is very stubborn."

"Soon she will turn twenty-one, and then—well." MacArthur stopped. "They have won, what's done is done."

Surely the weaver had imbibed too much drink and spoke in riddles and delusions. "Does her age matter? She is far from a spinster."

"She would not mind that. But she must wed." Donal sipped more whisky, and leaned toward James again. "I went to Edinburgh to talk to a flourishing tailor there about taking Elspeth's hand. But I found I did not like him so well as before. Now you are here, and I am thinking, this is the lad for my wee Elspeth!'"

Silent, unsure how to answer, James returned MacArthur's gaze.

"Good then," the man said half to himself. "What do you teach, though you are a wealthy lord?"

"Geology," James said, knowing he should divest the man of his opinion about his wealth. Later for that. "Rocks. Earth."

"Ah! You can help us find the gold!" He raised his glass. "You are the one."

"I would be happy to look for gold if it is in these hills. Some parts of the Highlands contain veins of gold running through the rock." Now his head was buzzing too, from the strong fairy whisky. "My grandmother wrote about a legend of some fairy gold."

"A legend in this very glen," MacArthur said. "I must tell you—ah, Elspeth!"

Looking up to see Elspeth in the doorway, James stood. "Miss MacArthur."

"Lord Struan." She approached, limping only slightly, her gait improved some. He offered her his chair, and she sat, settling her gray skirts around her. He slid a footstool toward her so that she could rest her foot, showing a narrow black slipper and a hint of white stocking.

"What a fine man to give you a wee stool for the wee foot," MacArthur said.

"Aye," Elspeth said. "Is it the fairy brew you are drinking?"

"It is, and fine stuff. Struan likes it."

Hiding a smile, James leaned against the mantelpiece. The whisky made him mellow, warm, content. He could almost believe in fairies just then, and could imagine Elspeth as their queen with her delicate beauty, dark lashes sweeping above pink cheeks, her hair soft as black silk.

When she glanced at him, he saw she was neither amused nor content.

"Elspeth, have some of Dougal MacGregor's fairy brew. 'Twill take the pain from your foot. Oh. I should not say his whole name," he mumbled.

"It is safe with me, sir," James reassured him.

"I like your lairdie," MacArthur told Elspeth. "Will you have some, lass?"

"A bit, thank you. A swallow—enough!" Elspeth said as her grandfather poured. "I hope you warned Struan about this brew. It is rather strong."

"Och, he's done well with two drams and no weakness. 'We are na fou,'" he quoted, raising his glass. "'Well, na that fou—'"

"'But just a drappie in our ee,'" James said, completing the Burns line.

MacArthur boomed a laugh. "Elspeth, lass, marry this laddie, do!"

"Aye, do," James echoed softly, feeling more comfortable by the moment. He loved this place, he loved this family, he loved this fairy brew, which was loosening his usual restraint. And he very much loved the daughter of this place. He raised his glass in a small salute to her.

"Away wi' you," she said. Her gaze melted his heart just then.

"Never," he said. Surely it was the whisky. And yet he meant it. He would never leave her, fairy or not. He would convince her. He had to.

"Beware the fairy brew, my lord," she murmured.

"And beware the wee fairy lass," he replied. She laughed.

"It's late, Grandfather," she said. "Our guest wants an early start."

"Women always have practical notions when there is good whisky to be had," MacArthur complained. "First let me tell Struan about the fairy gold. He must hear the truth of it."

"Grandda," she said.

"Go on, sir," James replied, intrigued.


*DEAR GOD, NOT all the truth*, Elspeth thought in a panic. "Grandda—"

"Long ago, they do say," Donal began, "the *Daoine Síth* of this glen had a treasure so fine, it shone like the sun inside their hillside palaces. They had gold and silver and precious stones from deep in the earth, from mines tended only by the Fey, and treasure more precious than we can imagine. Every glen has its fairies, and every fairy clan has its treasure. And this was marvelous to behold."

Elspeth watched James as he listened intently, one shoulder leaned against the mantelpiece, letting her have his chair. He was relaxed and so handsome, looking as if he belonged here. Her heart quickened.

"Long ago, my MacArthur ancestor found their hidden cache," Donal continued. "MacArthurs are the oldest clan in the Highlands, and it must be true or we would not claim it, aye?"

James laughed, and Elspeth smiled. Just being near him made her feel so good, warm and happy, with a precious excitement sparkling within her.

She could marry him, she thought, and feel this way for a lifetime. It would be like a dream come true. All she had to do was accept.

But the power of the Fey made that almost impossible.

She wished her gift of Sight would show her the reason he was so determined, but she could not penetrate his inscrutable thoughts. Why did he insist on a bride? She felt he cared for her now, yet he had not acknowledged it. She knew how she felt. But if it was true that she was fairy-born—as her grandfather insisted—she could not draw James into her life.

"This MacArthur found the fairy treasure," Donal was saying, "and he hid it away to ransom his kinsman, a piper who had been stolen away by the fairies. They would not give the piper back, for they liked his music. They demanded the return of their treasure. He refused. So they played havoc in the glen, stealing away humans, playing tricks. The thief himself took a fairy bolt in his leg and died, and so the secret hiding place was never found.

"Ever since," he continued, "they have stolen glen folk and made wicked bargains. And they will do mischief until their gold is returned."

"The fairy riding," James said. "Is that why some are frightened of it?"

"They fear the fairies will take them away in revenge, aye."

"How long ago was this treasure taken, if it really happened?"

"Three hundred years, and aye, it happened."

"Can it be found? Are there any clues, or maps?"

"I have looked. Many have searched. If it is located, two keys are needed to open it. One key is a certain stone. The other—" He looked toward Elspeth.

She shook her head to silence her grandfather from saying she herself was the other key—or so Donal claimed.

"Miss MacArthur was looking for a stone in the garden at Struan House," James said. "The blue agate in the library case, is that the one in this legend?"

"You found the bonny blue stone?" MacArthur demanded.

"There is one like that at Struan House," she admitted. "But we do not know if it is the key in the tale about the treasure."

"Likely it is. I want to see it."

"Gold, silver, some gemstones are found now and again in the Highlands, either naturally formed in the earth, or buried by ancient people," James said. "It could be called fairy gold. It is easy to see how such legends come about."

"But this is real," Donal said.

"How would you know it was fairy gold? How could you ever return it?"

"I know how," Donal replied.

Elspeth hoped her grandfather would move on. He clearly had more than enough whisky in him. "Grandda," she began.

"Are there clues in family lore, since this fellow was an ancestor? Maps, anything in writing?" James asked.

"He was a farmer, not a scholar. This is all we know. The treasure is somewhere in this glen, and needs two keys, a blue stone, and…well, we know what the second key is. The Fey need human help to find the missing treasure. My ancestor outwitted them, see," Donal said. "They will not be happy until it is found. Without it, they are not at ease."

"A fairy's aim is to be happy, in harmony with nature and the earth," Elspeth added. "Living is an art to them, pleasure and delight and enchantment. They cannot fulfill that if they are uneasy over something stolen from them."

"They are a temperamental lot," Donal said.

"We call them the Good Neighbors," Elspeth said. "But they would be better neighbors if they had their gold."

"Certainly people have searched for this treasure," James said.

"Many, without success," Donal MacArthur said.

"Such an interesting tale. I want to be sure it is in Grandmother's book."

"Oh no, you must not put that in the book," Elspeth said.

"Local legends are important to her book," he answered.

"Elspeth is right, you cannot include all the details. Some part of it must be left unsaid. The fairies will be very angry if their secrets are told."

"Grandda, enough," Elspeth said. "Struan does not believe in the Fey."

"But it is fascinating," James countered.

"You do not *believe* it," she said. "That is the difference."

"I believe what can be proven."

"He'll believe soon enough," Donal said. "He's writing a fairy book, he's drinking fairy brew. And he's in the thrall of our wee fairy lass. He's fallen to the glamourie."

"The glamourie?" James asked. "My grandmother wrote of it. A fairy enchantment that changes our perception of the world, makes us see reality differently, something like that."

"The glamourie is all over you, sir. The lass has the knack of it."

"That she does," James said, meeting her gaze.

# Chapter Fifteen

STIRRING DEEP IN the night, a bit groggy from the whisky, James wondered what had woken him. He heard voices, felt as if shadows moved around him. Sitting up, he craved fresh air to clear his head. The fairy brew, as MacArthur had called it, had been stronger and more lasting than he thought.

Dressing in trousers and boots, shrugging the borrowed frock coat over his shirt, he left the house to walk through the courtyard and follow the earthen lane that led toward the weaving cottages. The night was cool and overcast, and a ringed moon flowed its beams through the clouds. Fog curled low on the ground, and meadows and orchards stretched into the dark distance.

His footfalls echoed quietly, and soon he heard the fast, clacking rhythm of a loom. Faint light glowed in one of the weaving cottages. Was Elspeth awake too? The cadence of the loom was furious and passionate.

He went close and peered through the square window beside the door.

Not Elspeth, but Donal seated at the large loom. A lantern lit the space, the rest in shadow. The man worked very quickly, shifting and moving, lacking Elspeth's grace but working with power, speed, and certainty.

Watching, James frowned, then gaped. MacArthur worked so fast that James could hardly follow the movements. His hands, the shuttle, the yarns, the loom were all a blur. A red tartan pattern gathered rapidly on the roller, faster than seemed possible.

James rubbed a hand over his eyes and looked again. The loom whirred, clicked, shuddered, and the weaver sped through his work like a demon. The incredible pace seemed beyond what a man could do.

Had the whisky been that strong? Was he dreaming?

"Come away!" A hand touched his arm, and James turned to see Elspeth. "James, please," she whispered.

He drew her close. "Look! What is he doing?"

"Working. Hush," she said, touching her fingers to his lips. He circled an arm around her, drew her close. She wore a dark plaid over a pale nightgown, her hair loose and long and silky dark.

"Why are you out here?" he asked. "Did the noise of the loom wake you?"

"I woke, and I knew you were out here, so I came. I can feel you when you are about," she whispered. "As if you are…part of me."

He understood. He felt it too. Only he and his twin sister had ever had such a tie, but now—was it possible to love someone so quickly, trust them so completely?

"Come away," she whispered, drawing him into shadows away from the window. "We should not be here. We must not watch him."

"He works the loom like the devil himself. What is it?"

She sighed. "It is the secret of his weaving. He guards it. We must leave." She tugged at his arm.

"That pace is inhuman." He glanced through the window again, from a hidden angle. As if in a whirlwind, Donal snatched the new roll of tartan from the loom, set the frame, and began anew, all at a steady and astonishing speed.

"It is how he does it. It is how he produces excellent cloth very quickly."

"I watched you today at the loom. You were all skill and grace." He set his arms around her. "But this is unearthly."

"That is true."

A chill slid down his spine. "Please explain."

"It is the fairy gift upon him," she murmured. "Years ago, he was given the fairy gift, the ability to weave a month's work in an evening."

"Go on," he said skeptically. "A fairy gift?"

"A kind of spell."

"Away wi' you," he said gently. "I did not have that much whisky, lass."

Her eyes were wide and sincere. "It is due to the whisky you drank that you can see this tonight."

"I am not fou," he jested. "No' that fou." But she was utterly serious.

"Listen! The fairy brew lets some of us see fairy magic. Without that, you might simply see the man at his usual weaving."

He frowned. "Your grandfather said your gift of Sight came from the fairies. I thought it was just another term for what some Highland folk can do."

"Some are gifted by the fairies at birth. Grandda insists I was."

Everything in him wanted to deny what he heard. Yet he felt a strange and almost dreadful sense—what if it was true and real? The small hairs lifted on his arms, on his neck. "What do you mean?"

"I am a good weaver, and can make a length of tartan in a few days. When the magic comes over him like this, Grandda can make a dozen plaids in a night," she said. "I wonder if he wanted you to see this. He gave you the fairy brew that he shares with no one but me. And then he set to the weaving where anyone might see him."

"That was deliberate?"

"Aye, he would do that. He wants to pull you to us, you see."

"I see," he said slowly.

"But we will not let him know you were here, aye? Only I

know, and Peggy Graham too, but she prefers to ignore it."

"I would prefer that too. Any moment now I shall wake in my bed with a thick head from whisky." He paused. "Would you want to be there and wake together?" He drew her closer. "We could arrange that with a vicar."

"Hush you," she murmured, smiled, and set a finger to his lips. Then she took his face between her hands, lifted on her toes, and kissed him.

Slow, tender, surprise and delight, the kiss sank through him, crown to sole. His body surged, craved. He caught her by the waist, dipped his head, kissed her hard and sure until she arched against him. Then she pulled back.

"That was very real," she whispered.

"So is this." He traced his thumb along the delicious weight of her breast.

"Jamie," she breathed, pressing against him.

He closed his eyes. Only his sister ever called him that boyhood name. On Elspeth's lips, it felt intimate, fitting, with the ring of love to it. *Love.* He needed to tell her so.

"Come away," she said. "Go back to sleep."

"This is a dream, aye? Not even your fairy whisky can prove to me that I've seen fairy magic." His heart thumped like a drum. Leaning down, he nuzzled his lips over her cheek, traced to her lips, and kissed her again.

Her lips opened for him and she sighed against his mouth. "This is real, and so is that in the cottage," she whispered. "Let yourself trust what you see."

Kissing her again, he drew back and pulled her into his embrace. Trusting did not come easily to him, yet Elspeth MacArthur challenged him, drew him, challenged him again. She had a kind of magic about her, a captivating charm he had never encountered before. She pushed him to think beyond what he had had always known.

"I trust that I saw a man weaving like a lunatic. And I trust I have a lovely lass in my arms. And I trust that I am falling in love with her."

His heart pounded to say it.

She drew back. "Is it so?"

"I think so. Does it change your mind?"

"I might be falling too. But it only makes things—more complicated."

"I think it could simplify things." He brushed his hand over her soft hair, down her cheek, touched her lower lip. Then he kissed her again, touching the merest tip of his tongue to hers. She opened her mouth a little, inviting him.

This was real. This was reassuring, breath and flesh and passion certain in his body. He needed her that way, and he wanted to spend his life with her.

Yet she was the most alluring and stubborn creature he had ever met.

She pressed against him now, lips urgent, lush, and soft under his. She pulled back and looked up. "What is real now," she whispered, "are your feelings for me, and mine for you."

Again she echoed his thoughts. "You are a conundrum."

"Come away," she said, and drew him through shadows and fog.

As they approached her weaving cottage, its windows dark, she pulled him toward the shadows along the side wall. There she set her back against the stone and lifted her arms to his shoulders. He tugged her to him at the small of her back, taut and slim and sweet against him. Swathed in darkness and quiet, he kissed her again, deep and fervent, slow and tender.

A sort of wildness entered him, heart thudding, body craving. He cautioned himself to slow, consider, and he did—until she pulled him hard against her, kissing him with opened lips and moist, curious tongue. He was full, hard, aching for her, and her fervor equaled his now. He followed the craving as far as she would allow, standing in the lee of the stone wall, lost in needful kisses and touches.

She tossed the plaid she wore around them, a warm, soft

shield, and he bunched her night rail under his palms, her body slender and heated beneath the fabric. His body quickened all through like fire as she ran eager hands along his shoulders, then under his coat, fingers tugging at his shirt, then warm over his skin. Her touch teased, tantalized as he pressed her against the wall, his hunger driving him now. He was changing in the moment, opening to her, trusting her with his desire, his vulnerability. Unsettling to lose that accustomed reserve, but he had to be truthful and honest with her, with what he felt.

His reliable, dull, carefully constructed life had been shifting ever since he met her months ago, culminating in the here and now. What had seemed fanciful and impossible to his logical mind was shifting too, and the feelings he had strictly guarded were opening too. Why did he feel such love for her, so quickly? Impulse was unlike him. But the certainty that he loved her felt true.

He surrendered to the moment, her permission clear, her fervor rising in pace with his. She felt solid and real in his arms, willing and ready. Questions of magic and fairies faded. This was all that mattered just now, this need, this love.

Yet he was a thinker, a scientist, a questioner, not used to surrendering to the body or the heart. He hesitated.

She did too, her breath ragged as his. "What?"

"What are we doing, my lass?"

"Whatever it is, I like it. Come with me," she whispered. Taking his hand, she led him around the corner to the cottage door, and pulled at the latch. He lifted her in his arms, pushed the door open, stepped inside, and kicked the door shut behind them.

The small dark room smelled of wood and wool, smelled of peace and order. He set her down, and she drew him to a dark corner with shelves and baskets of plaid cloth. She drew out a blanket and tossed it to the floor, tugging him down to his knees with her.

"What do you want, love," he murmured.

"What we will," she said.

"There are consequences," he murmured.

"Could be," she whispered. "We will think of it later. Come to me."

SHE DID NOT care about consequences or compromise, Elspeth realized as she drew James down with her to the soft plaid rumpled on the floor. She only cared about the moment, the pulse of longing, her need to be with him. They would not be disturbed here, and she wanted this as much as he did. She would think about what to do later—should there be a child. Oh aye, then marriage. But she did not want to think about that either.

Deep inside, she knew what she would do now. Somehow she would marry him, find a way to stay safely with him. Later for all that. The new certainty of it compelled her forward. He loved her, and she knew it for truth. Just knew it.

She knelt, circled her arms around his neck, let her body cleave to his. He streamed his fingers through her hair, cupped her head, kissed her, achingly tender. His lips traced along her cheek, her ear.

"What is this between us?" His lips traced, touched. She closed her eyes.

"Love," she said. "Not magic. Just us. Just love." She touched his beard, like fine sand under her fingertips. "And we may do what we will here."

His sigh became a groan as he soothed his hands over her shoulders, over her night braid, loosening the strands to spill down her back. Shivers cascaded through her. She returned his kiss, felt his heat and hard body through the fabric of her nightgown. She pressed close, felt his heartbeat thudding against hers, and she pulled at his sleeves to strip off his coat. He tossed it aside, its thick warmth adding to the nest that cushioned them as she dropped lower with him.

Now his kisses plummeted deeply through her, made her breathless. She fit her body to his, delicious quivers running through her as his fingers smoothed over throat, breasts. She tightened, tingled as his fingers grazed over nipples, and she arched for more. She felt as if she would do anything he asked.

But would she marry him, truly? The thought made her pause her breath. She ducked her head away, felt sad as he kissed her hair, her cheek, her throat. What if this was the last time she would ever be in his arms? What if he never asked her to marry him again, accepting her denials? What if he went away?

She felt a fool, caught between choices, thinking one way, thinking the other, body and heart wanting this, head and fear for the future wanting something else. Surrendering all that, she kissed him again, hungry for touch, for what was offered in the instant. *Take joy from this now*, she told herself.

Sliding her fingers through his thick, wavy hair, she leaned back to let him kiss downward, throat and breast, until she cried out softly and slid her hands under his shirt, smoothing over his warm, firm skin, his thundering heartbeat.

He groaned, fingers finding, teasing, lips caressing, and she gasped as he tugged aside her gown to touch his lips, warm and pliant, to her breasts, one, the other, his hand at both. Lightning shot through her and she moved, pleading, melting with urgency, feeling buttery and willing as his lips traced and his hands grazed and raw need pulsed through her.

*I love you, I will marry you*—she wanted desperately to say it. Yet she held the words back, letting her body say what she held back.

If the vows became real, she would fear for him and what they had.

He lay her back in the thick bed of plaids, matching breast and chest, hip and hip as he slipped his fingers under her gown, finding her deepest parts. She tugged, arched, could not get enough, fast enough, heart pounding, body rocking, begging and seeking more. She felt the hardness of him through his breeches, and ached to give herself to him without thought of what might happen later.

So she let passion replace thought, wildness displace logic, need overwhelm reason. She tugged as buttons and cloth fell away, her hands hot over his skin, his hands rousing over her, slipping into her. She found the length of him, like velvet over hot iron, and she moved boldly to shape him with her hand, skin on skin, heat to heat. He groaned fiercely, lifted to kiss her mouth.

"Love me," she said, without thought.

"I do," his voice gruff, breaths mingling, hands skimming.

"I do too," she murmured, and shifted, breathed out, let her body ask. And soon he found her, slipped inside her just there, and she surged and gasped as she took him into her. His lips covered her cry as she felt a spark catch like flame, and she rocked, rocked like the mindless rhythm of the loom, shimmering and aching as she felt him go deeper, raising that exquisite fire higher, as he rocked with her in release. And she sobbed out, feeling something precious and something missing all at once.

"I wanted—that with you—" she began breathlessly.

"My love," he whispered, ragged, brushing back her hair, "now there will be a wedding quick, whether you want it or not. What do you say?"

Sighing, heart thumping, she pulled the generous plaid over both of them, curled with him, still aching, yearning, not sure what to say.

He kissed her lightly. "I mean to marry you, Elspeth MacArthur."

"If I marry," she said, "it would be to you."

"If. Well then," he said, sitting up. "There is progress."

"You are a patient man," she said.

"In love with an infernally stubborn lass, woe be it to him."

# Chapter Sixteen

GOOD GRANITE WAS abundant in Glen Struan, James realized, standing atop a high hill overlooking his grandmother's house—his house, now. The morning air was fresh, the sunlight invigorating. He took up hammer and chisel and went back to his work.

He tapped away at the stone until another chunk broke away from the stone ledge that ran under the hillside behind the house. The rock broke easily, crusted sedimentary rock and limestone and red sandstone. James felt sure the layers stretched deep inside the string of hills near the house. More tapping revealed veins of granite just below the surface, a much harder composite studded with glittering quartz and smoky cairngorm.

Angus MacKimmie had told him of a quarry in the glen that produced sandstone and limestone, with some granite and trap rock so hard it was not easily quarried. James was pleased to see the variety of deposits as he worked. The granite and basalt in this glen could reinforce his research and theory about the geological makeup of the central Highlands.

Next he broke off bits of limestone that showed fossil traces. Fiona would want to examine them, as she was particularly fascinated by fossils. Dropping the bits into a leather bag, he set aside the tall, gnarled walking stick that Angus had given him to help with strenuous hill-climbing. Then he pulled a small leather notebook and wood-wrapped pencil lead from a pocket, sat down, and made notes.

> *Granite and whinstone formations 100 ft. plus above level of house,* he wrote. *Deposits indicate internal heat that fused masses together to create beds of sedimentary rock...molten material extruded from terrestrial core, cooled as crust, becoming volcanic rock. Evidence strong. Basalt, dolerite, gray granite. Traces of red sandstone too.*

Excellent material for lectures, he thought, and he could use this for the scientific volume he was writing for the university. His project relied on theories that included a catastrophic development thousands of years ago, stupendous heaving shifts of ancient land and sea masses. Other scientists theorized that early land masses and rocky formations had evolved slowly as a result of gradual erosion. James leaned toward the Catastrophists, as they called themselves, though he agreed in some details with the Uniformitarianists. Both were right in parts, but he was convinced that catastrophe had been the larger factor, judging by the evidence.

Granite required tremendous heat to form, which could indicate volcanic activity. He was pleased to find rich sources of granite this far into the Highlands, a considerable distance away from volcanoes such as the old remainder near Edinburgh. He was also pleased to find the beds on Struan property, giving him access and dominion.

What he had discovered was worthy of more exploration and could be an enormous contribution to piecing together a geological picture of Earth's creation. The discoveries about eons long ago also helped indicate future terrestrial evolution. He intended to explore that further in his scholarly work.

Seated in the brisk wind, he searched the leather bag he had brought that held chisels, hammers, and a loupe—two small hinged magnifying lenses banded in brass. The bag also contained chunks of unfired clay to test the streaking properties of minerals, along with bits of metals and shards of wood to test hardness and density. In addition, he also had a small vial of hydrochloric acid, well-capped, to dissolve sedimentary deposits so that he could clean and identify rock. He had brought all of that with him to Struan in hopes of making progress here.

Hearing the dogs bark, he looked down the slope to see Angus climbing toward him, Osgar and Nellie running alongside. The terrier reached him first and James rubbed her head.

"Your guests are arriving, sir," Angus said, pointing southeast.

"Sooner than expected! I had a letter from my aunt saying they would be here Thursday. It's but Wednesday."

"Mrs. MacKimmie has the house more than ready," her husband said.

"Of course." Struan House sparkled, from polished furniture to silver and glass, and clean counterpanes and fresh linens were in all the guest rooms.

Now in the distance, he saw a black coach and matched four following the road. "Two or three miles away, are they?"

"Aye, and that's a fine private coach," Angus MacKimmie said. "I sent a groom ahead to lead them to the house. The roads are still muddy and rutted, and will stay so until they can be fixed," he added bluntly. "Yon coachman best go slow."

"I wish we had the means to fix the roads and the bridge." James understood Angus's broad hint. He sighed. Watching the road, he knew he must stop his work and go greet his guests. Dropping his things into the satchel, he shouldered it and took up the walking stick to descend the hill with Angus and the dogs.

The young groom came along the road on foot, one of Angus's nephews, a kilted boy with red hair and an elfin grin. MacKimmie went to meet him while James went more slowly, using the stick to balance his uneven gait.

The pockets of his tweed jacket sagged, for he had dropped rock specimens into those too. The loose, comfortable coat had been a gift from Donal MacArthur, a package that had arrived at Struan House two days after his visit to Kilcrennan House. Its sturdy woolen weave was handsome, warm, and impervious to damp. He wondered how long it had taken for Donal to weave the cloth, and who had made such a fine coat.

Yet he had received no message from Elspeth, and that puzzled and troubled him. He had sent a note of thanks for the coat, extending a dinner invitation and inquiring politely after Miss MacArthur, adding his hope that she would like to help with his research as she had mentioned.

He still waited for an answer. He had considered riding to Kilcrennan, but pride and uncertainty delayed him, as well as the need to work on the fairy book as well as his scientific research. He had quickly reverted to the familiar shell closing over him again. What he had felt with Elspeth was freeing, but he could wait. He would wait forever so long as he had hope.

But he would not ask her to marry him again. She had refused enough, and he was not keen on feeling the fool. Let her decide. He knew he would be happiest with her, but he also knew he was capable of moving on if need be. Daydreaming was not in his character, but he had found solace in imagining her in his house, in his life, doing what she willed. Lately he wondered if that avenue of dreams had closed.

Yet if he could not find an appropriate Highland bride to fulfill his grandmother's will, he would jeopardize everything for himself and his siblings. And if he did not marry soon, Lady Rankin was sure to push Charlotte Sinclair at him. But she could not fulfill any requirement he had. Only one lass could do that.

Well, he was accustomed to a solitary, modest life, and he could go on. He could sell Struan House and generate funds that way. But it would break his heart.

Angus returned, pointing toward the carriage coming closer. "Davie says there are three gentlemen in the coach, and others following in a second coach."

"Ah. We shall see who they are soon."

"Very soon. That driver is flyin' fast on a poor road."

Smiling at another broad hint, James stood waiting on the sloping foot of the hillside as the first vehicle rolled along. It was a handsome black barouche drawn by four powerful bays with whipping black manes. Angus lifted his arm and the coach slowed and stopped. For a moment, James was reminded of the devil's coach said to haunt some Highland roads. He huffed at the thought, wondering who had accompanied his aunt.

The coach door opened and his brother Patrick leaped down. Pleased, James moved to greet him with a handshake and a thump on the shoulder.

"James, you look well! Country laird and all agrees with you," Patrick said, grinning. "The others are following—Fiona, Aunt Rankin, Philip, and Miss Sinclair. They should be here soon."

"Very good. Who is with you?" The carriage door opened and a second man emerged. "Sir John! Excellent to see you," James said, stepping forward to extend his hand as John Graham approached.

"Struan! Good to see you." John tipped his hat, blond hair bright in the sun. "I hope you do not mind the intrusion. I know you did not expect all of us, but we had a business endeavor north of here, so Patrick invited us. Lord Eldin was generous enough to offer the use of his carriage for the trip."

"Eldin?" James tensed, hearing his cousin's name. He glanced toward the barouche as a third man, still inside, looked out the open door. He was dressed all in black, from his hat and dark hair to his polished boots. He leaned forward.

"Greetings, Struan. I see no reason to get out now, with the driver about to take us to the house." Nicholas MacCarran, Lord Eldin, waved a hand briefly.

"Eldin. Welcome," James said.

"No doubt you're surprised to see us," Cousin Nicholas said. "Sir John and I had business near here—I have a building project near Loch Katrine—so we thought it efficient to travel with Patrick."

"Of course," James said. "Will you stay the night?"

"Just for luncheon," Eldin answered, as if Struan House was an inn. "Our business is in the north, and we must reach our hotel by evening."

"I see. Go ahead and ride up to the house. I'll walk and meet you there."

"I'll walk with you," Patrick offered as John Graham climbed back into the coach. Angus and the groom joined the driver above, and they set off.

"Sorry, couldn't be helped," Patrick said. "Nick is persistent."

"True. He talked our uncle into selling the clan seat to him years back."

Patrick huffed. "He and John are heading north to look at renovations for an old castle near Loch Katrine. Nick intends to open a new hotel there. With more tourists coming to the Highlands, more accommodations are needed. Eldin hired John Graham as an engineer to build private roads and so on."

"The locals might deem it too much improvement to suit them," James murmured. "Well, we shall see. I understand Aunt Rankin plans to tour the Highlands."

"She's quite enthused about it. She will stay at Struan for a night or two, as she is in a hurry to get going. You know how she can be. She'll breeze through the Highlands and barely appreciate it, but once home, she will be an expert to impress her friends."

"Indeed. I am surprised you are with her. You have scant patience for her entourage. Fiona is with her?"

"I could not have borne the company for long without her! Aunt Rankin is dragging along her insufferable nephew, Philip, and Miss Sinclair. The latter for your benefit, I am sure."

"No doubt," James muttered.

"I would have begged off entirely, but I wanted to see you. And I have been appointed to a position in the Highlands. Excise Officer in a northern area. I am to work with a local sheriff up here, starting in a few weeks."

"Splendid! A far better use of your talents than clerking documents in the Signet Courts. And you have a taste for adventure."

"Smugglers abound in those hills, so it should prove interesting."

"Just be careful. Smuggling is useful for some, and dangerous to others." James thought of the elusive MacGregor who made fairy brew and other illicit whiskies.

"I am to assist Mr. Dougal MacGregor, a sheriff there," Patrick said.

That was Elspeth's cousin's name. James masked his surprise. "I am glad Fiona decided to come along."

"She's arranging to teach at a Gaelic school, and wanted to see you before she leaves. She has requirements to fulfill as we all do, thanks to Grandmother." Patrick glanced at James. "Any luck with yours?"

"I am making my way through the fairy book. But I have not married a fairy yet."

"They are not thick upon the ground, I imagine."

"More than you'd think," James drawled. They reached the stone gates leading to the house. "If I cannot meet that requirement—I may have to sell Struan House. We can divide the profit and no longer pursue Grandmother's fairy nonsense."

"We must not lose this property, James. Our family loved this place. The house and estate are the true legacy, more than the funds."

"Fairy brides are—elusive," James said curtly. And unwilling, he thought. "A sale would help all of our finances."

"Aye, but we might lose the inheritance to Eldin. Do not forget that."

"I am aware," James said.

Ahead, the barouche had reached the house's formal entrance. Lord Eldin stepped down, drenched in black, turning his haughty, handsome head to assess the place.

"Perhaps Mr. Browne can more liberally interpret the will," James said.

"We can ask," Patrick said. "I spent several hours in a coach with Lord Raven over there. He is cold as ice, as if someone plucked the heart out of him. I recall him being pleasant enough when were lads. I wonder what happened."

"He was. I wonder too." James had nearly forgotten that Cousin Nick had been a good companion in boyhood. But he had heard rumors of betrayal and scandal since, though he knew little about it. He strode forward, ready to act as host and laird to uphold the Highland hospitality that dictated courtesy no matter the guest.

As they entered the house together, James thought of what Patrick had said. *It's as if someone plucked the heart out of him.* That came from hurt, he thought, and wondered again why the Earl of Eldin would have turned so unfeeling, if indeed that was the case. Perhaps it was a protective ruse.

A shout from Angus MacKimmie caught his attention, and James turned to see a landau entering the earthen drive. He walked forward to meet it. As the driver opened the door, Sir Philip stepped out first with a mumbled greeting. Then James and Patrick assisted the ladies to the ground.

"James! Lord Struan, rather!" Lady Rankin exclaimed. "How good to see you. What absolutely dreadful roads you have up here. Look who I brought with me."

Fiona stepped out, her smile quick and bright, her kiss for James light on his cheek. Smoothing the creases from her gray skirt and short jacket, she moved aside as Charlotte Sinclair stepped out.

She twitched the ivory skirts spilling gracefully beneath a red velvet spencer, and patted her blond hair under a straw hat looped with crimson ribbons. She stretched out her hand. "Dear James, how I've missed you!"

"Miss Sinclair," he said, his voice cool. He overlooked her move to offer her gloved hand for a kiss. As Charlotte tucked her arm in his, he could only think of Elspeth.

"It is good to see everyone," he said to all. "Welcome to Struan House."


LATER, WHILE THEY enjoyed Mrs. MacKimmie's excellent luncheon of cold mutton, mashed turnips, and more, James listened as his aunt talked of her touring plans in great detail. The woman scarcely took a breath despite attempts by others to talk as well.

"Miss Sinclair has the headache and has gone to her room," Lady Rankin told Mrs. MacKimmie for the third time. "Send a tray up to her, please."

"Aye, madam, we've seen to it," Mrs. MacKimmie answered.

"James, you must find us a local guide," Lady Rankin said next. He nodded, pushing around a piece of lamb and a spoonful of rowan jelly. "Sir Walter planned to join us on our trip, but he was unable at the last moment. I am so disappointed. He would have been a superb guide on our journey through the Trossachs. His poem is set there, you know, *The Lady of the Lake*."

"I know it well, Aunt," James said.

"Although he gave us a most excellent travelogue for the area, written out in his very own hand. Fiona has it. Did you remember to bring it?"

"I did, Aunt." Fiona reached into a pocket to produce a folded letter, opening it to show James, seated beside her, a page densely covered with handwritten suggestions.

"We are excited to see Loch Katrine, so beautifully described in his poem," Lady Rankin went on. "Lady Murray told me last week at tea that the views are breathtaking there. Fiona, do bring your sketchbook so that later we may enjoy pictures of our trip."

"I will, Aunt."

"The area is popular with tourists," Eldin commented. "In fact, I plan to open an establishment near there. Recently I purchased an old castle to refurbish into a hotel."

"How nice that will be!" Lady Rankin said.

Silent, James noticed that Patrick and Fiona applied themselves to the meal, as did John Graham, while Philip and Lady Rankin expressed interest in Eldin's project.

"You should all visit when the place is ready for guests," Eldin said. "We would extend a reasonable price to family." Patrick looked at Fiona and rolled his eyes.

"Thank you, dear Nicholas," Lady Rankin said. "Fiona, do consider his new hotel for your accommodations if your teaching assignment is near there."

"Cousin Fiona would be more than welcome," Eldin said.

"I will be teaching in a glen there long before the place is done," Fiona said flatly.

After Lady Rankin and Fiona retired to their rooms to rest, James stayed with the gentlemen to have coffee at the table, a more casual choice than retiring to the parlor. When Graham asked about local Highland whisky, James fetched a bottle from a stock that Lady Struan had acquired. Eldin held up a hand in curt refusal—the man had Spartan tastes—while the others accepted drams. James drank only coffee, spooning a little sugar in the hot, bitter liquid. He was reminded of Elspeth and her sweet tooth for sugar in her tea. She was never far from his mind.

They discussed engineering efforts throughout Scotland, which James found quite interesting. John Graham had much to say, while Eldin brusquely commented, though he seemed keen to learn about plans near Loch Katrine.

"However, the roads in your little glen here are in very poor condition," Eldin told James. "I hope you have plans to repair them, as viscount here."

"Recent storms did some damage. I will ask Mr. MacKimmie to hire a few men to repair the bridge near here. And repairs are needed elsewhere, I know."

"The roads the Highland Commission planned several years ago are nearly complete," John Graham said. "The work of Telford and others is making a difference throughout the Highlands. Between the new roads and older highways created under General Wade for the British campaign a century ago, the Highlands are more accessible than ever. It is good for tourism, which could prove good for Scotland."

"I wonder if this glen was included in those plans," James said. "Otherwise the cost of repairs could be considerable."

"Submit an inquiry and a report on conditions here to the

Commissioners for Roads and Bridges in the Highlands," Graham said. "I know the fellow in charge. They would send an engineer to assess the problem. It might take time but could solve things."

"May as well pay for it yourself, Struan," Philip said, "if the roads and bridges are on your estate. Get the thing designed and hire the laborers and workmen."

"Unless you lack funds for repairs," Eldin said.

"If it must be done, I will take care of it," James said curtly.

"Allow me to offer a donation for the work," Eldin responded.

"Why would you do that?" James responded, wary.

His cousin shrugged. "It is a pretty glen. And I hear it is a place of fairy legends, too. I'm partial to such things," he murmured.

Was the man mocking them, or trying to lay claim to Lady Struan's book? James narrowed his eyes. "The legends here are similar to many in the Highlands. As for the work needed in the glen, I appreciate the offer, but it is solely my concern, sir."

"I do not offer out of the goodness of my heart," Eldin said. "This glen could provide a thoroughfare toward Loch Katrine and therefore my hotel. So I would prefer that your roads and bridges be in good repair."

"I will keep that in mind," James said, tight-lipped. After all, his cousin stood to gain if the MacCarran siblings did not meet the will requirements.

"How is your geology research going, Struan?" Philip Rankin asked. "And something about folklore too, as I understand it."

"It is progressing nicely."

"A while ago," Eldin began, "I heard a tale of lost fairy gold in this glen. Have you encountered such a story?"

"Only in passing," James answered. "There is nothing much to it. My grandmother did not even mention it in her notes."

"She was a thorough scholar of folklore," Eldin said. "I am sure she entrusted her work to you in good faith."

"I am doing my best."

"Gold?" Patrick looked intrigued. "A bit of gold would solve a lot of problems."

"Certainly people must have looked for it," Eldin said. "Temptation is strong where legends of treasure exist."

"True. Have you encountered my MacArthur cousins while you have been here, Struan?" John Graham asked. James turned, grateful for a new subject. "I wish I had time for a visit, but alas we are set to meet with architects in the morning."

"I have met Mrs. Peggy Graham and the MacArthurs," James said carefully. "They are quite well."

"Excellent! Please give them my best regards."

"You must invite them to dinner while we are here," Patrick said. "I remember meeting John's cousin Miss MacArthur in Edinburgh. Lovely girl."

Sipping his coffee, James nodded. "She is."

"She was quite taken with you in Edinburgh." Philip grinned. "The kisses flowed that afternoon, as I recall! You and Miss MacArthur seemed in agreement."

"Met a Highland lass, did you?" Eldin asked. "Very good."

Sensing the edge in the tone, James smiled flatly. He would be glad to see Eldin's fancy barouche depart along the same rough and rutted glen road the man had complained about. And may the very de'il bounce him back to hell, he thought uncharitably. For some reason he was glad that Eldin would not meet Elspeth MacArthur.

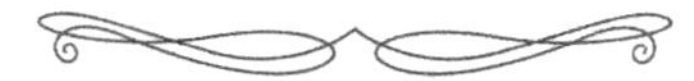

# Chapter Seventeen

MOVING A HEAVY roll of tartan, Elspeth set down the bolt, tugged the roller free, and set it again on the loom. Removing the last yarn sett from the loom took a little time as she wound the spare yarns into bundles and thought about the next design. After completing a length of commissioned tartan, she now planned to weave a gift length to give to James at Struan. It would be a reason to see him again.

No matter what happened, she wanted to give him something she had woven. Then some part of her would always be with him.

A fortnight had passed since he had visited, and she had thrown herself into her work. She did not have her grandfather's otherworldly work habits, but she kept a pace fast enough to be creative and productive.

She had managed to be too busy to talk much with her grandfather about Struan and marriage and her future, though he tried. She tried not to think about it, but the matter burdened her heart and soul.

Now, she left the weaving cottage and went into the storage house where yarns and supplies were kept. Inside its dimness, sunbeams poured through cracks in the shutters. Motes and woolen fibers floated on the light. From a shelf, she took a copy of Wilson's *Key Pattern Book* and sat at the worktable turning the pages.

Published by an Edinburgh tailor years earlier, the book contained hundreds of tartan designs assigned to particular clans. Some were based on old clan traditions, while many had been invented more recently. Tartan patterns and clan associations were part of the craze for Highland culture that accompanied the king's visit to Scotland. And that had benefitted the Kilcrennan weavers and other weavers too.

Immersed in studying the meticulous hand-colored tartans on the pages, she was surprised to hear a knock. The door opened to admit a young woman.

"Margaret!" Elspeth jumped up to embrace her cousin. "How nice to see you!"

Margaret Lamont smiled, round face beaming, brown eyes sparkling. Her red hair was tucked in a thick braid wrapped over the crown of her head, making her seem even taller, her full figure party due to another babe on the way. She was a brawny lass, as Donal MacArthur sometimes described her, with wide shoulders, strong arms, and hands pink from working with raw wool and dye baths.

"Reverend Buchanan brought me here on his way through," Margaret explained.

"Dear Margaret! You look good," Elspeth said. "I hope you are working less with this babe coming. The dye baths are not good for your back, and the smell could make you ill."

"My husband found others do the dyeing for now, so I am spinning and combing. Today I had some free time and my mother is watching the children, so I thought to visit you. I love seeing what you and Uncle Donal are weaving with my yarns."

"Your yarns are wonderful! I've finished several tartans this week. I came here to search out a new pattern."

Margaret peered at the book open on the table. "What a great book it is," she said, and began speaking softly in Gaelic, as she and Elspeth sometimes did. It was Margaret's native tongue. "Tartan is in such demand now. The demand will keep us all busy."

"I'm glad. Grandda is very content when he's busy at the weaving."

"What sett will you choose?" Margaret turned a page or two.

"I was looking for, ah, MacCarran."

"Lord Struan's plaid?" Margaret asked. "I heard you were seen at Struan House with him. Reverend Buchanan told me. Uncle Donal said so too, just now in the yard when I saw him. He and Peggy Graham hinted at—something going on with you two."

Elspeth blushed. "Grandda cannot keep a secret."

"He has your best interest at heart."

Elspeth sighed and turned another page. "I want to weave a plaid so Lord Struan can have a kilt made up in Edinburgh when he returns."

"Would this be your wedding gift to him?"

"*Och*, Grandda has indeed been chatty!"

"It is customary for a bride to make her husband a tartan of his clan if she has the skill for it. And you do."

"It may be more of a parting gift," Elspeth admitted.

"Is it? Peggy Graham and your grandfather think otherwise," Margaret said quietly. "They love you so much, and hope the best for you. And those Buchanans are gossipy sorts. Do not whatever they say. Your grandfather and Peggy seem to like Struan very much." Margaret touched Elspeth's shoulder. "They said he offered marriage."

"He did."

Margaret nodded. "I see. Do you love him?"

Turning another page, Elspeth sighed again. "This kerfuffle is all my doing. I asked him to ruin me, Margaret," she confessed.

"Asked him to what?" Margaret blinked. "Did he?"

"Only a little, and I wanted it. And I thought it would help me escape the marriage Grandda tried to arrange with a tailor. But I did not think that—well, it is no matter now."

"Your grandfather wants you to marry well and leave Kilcrennan, I know that."

"He does. And now his mind is set on Lord Struan."

"What is wrong with that, if you like what happened with him?" Margaret smiled.

Elspeth felt heat fill her cheeks. "Grandda wants my happiness, but I need to stay here at Kilcrennan, not go south with a husband. I thought no one would ever marry me if I were compromised. But Struan offered, and offered again, and is waiting, unless he has given up by now."

"I have not seen him, but Peggy says he is a lovely braw man. A good man."

"Oh, he is," she said quickly. "And he was a gentleman with me, truly. I never expected that—" Her voice caught. "Oh, dear."

"So you fell in love? And what is the trouble with that, then?"

"It is so confusing." Elspeth flipped pages. "I cannot find the pattern I want."

"The MacCarrans are a small clan. They may not be in this book."

She was relieved that Margaret left the other topic. "We have other books, older ones that Grandda uses. Perhaps it is there." Elspeth a black leather notebook from the shelf, very worn, with slips of paper stuck among its tattered pages. She paged through and finally stopped. "MacCarran! Here it is."

They leaned together to study a page of sketches and charts showing weaving patterns. "'The MacCarrans are a sept of the MacDonalds of the Isles,' it says. My great-great-grandfather wrote these notes. Interesting!" Elspeth said.

"It says here that the Kilcrennan weavers made a tartan for a MacCarran laird in the years of peace," Margaret said. "That would have been before the Jacobites. What a blessing to have these old notes. The ancient plaids were not always specific to a clan, but varied depending on local weavers and the plant dyes they had available."

"The MacCarran is very authentic, then." Elspeth studied the design and color notes. "Twenty warp threads of deep blue, twenty warp of forest green, ten weft threads of red, five of white," she read. "That repeat would be very handsome."

"I heard something about the MacCarrans long ago," Margaret said. "A small clan with an interesting history. Do you know their clan motto?"

Elspeth shook her head. "Lord Struan mentioned a tale of a fairy ancestor, but he does not believe in such things himself. It is all fancy, he says."

"Then he needs to spend more here with you and Uncle Donal," Margaret laughed. "Ask your viscount about the MacCarran motto."

"He is not my viscount." Elspeth took a scrap of paper and a bit of charcoal from a box on the table and copied the sett pattern. "I do not know when I will see him again. But I can weave this for him and send it to him if he leaves for Edinburgh."

"Perhaps he will take it to Uncle Donal's tailor friend," Margaret said.

"I do not care what he does with it." Elspeth copied carefully, not looking up.

"It will be a fine gift and you should deliver it yourself."

She glanced at her cousin in surprise. "Me, go to Edinburgh?"

Margaret smiled. "Weave fast, and go to Struan House."

Her heartbeat went fast. "I suppose I could."

"This is what I remember. The MacCarrans had a golden cup in their castle seat that was very ancient, a gift from a fairy ancestor. Around its base was a motto."

"What was that?"

"Love makes its own magic," she said.

"Oh! That is beautiful. He never said." Elspeth felt tears sting her eyes.

"I thought you might like it."

"Oh, Margaret, what have I done?"

"Only you can say, and only you can make it right. Ask your heart what it wants, and follow that."

"I thought he proposed to me out of responsibility. But the situation was my own doing. And Grandda needs me here, even if he says he does not."

"Such things can be sorted out, especially if you love him."

She shrugged. "I do. And I think he cares for me too."

"What more do you need?" Margaret asked gently.

"It is more complicated than that. I feel I must stay here always."

"Sometimes love seems so complicated, yet it is a simple, beautiful thing." Margaret smiled. "If you love him, tell him. Give the man a chance."

Elspeth gave her a hug. Suddenly she wanted to weep. "I am so glad you came by today. Help me pick the yarns."

"Gladly." While they worked together finding skeins in the colors of the MacCarran plaid, her thoughts tumbled.

She would turn twenty-one in just a few days, when her grandfather had said she would belong by fairy bargain to that realm. She still did not know whether to believe it, and Margaret knew nothing of it.

Later, after Margaret had shared tea with them, and the stable groom agreed to drive her home so she would not have to walk the distance, Elspeth set out to find her grandfather in his weaving cottage. He was there, the light of candles glowing in the window. She knocked, and Donal glanced up as she brought some yarns for his work as an excuse. Things needed to be said.

"Grandfather," she began.

"Aye then, what is it?" He paused his work, his pace normal that evening.

"Kilcrennan is flourishing. And that depends on your ability to weave so quickly."

He nodded. "Aye. Go on."

"We can meet orders for tartan faster than many others, though only we know why. Otherwise, to do all this work, we would need eight or ten weavers to fill our orders. There are not that many weavers in this glen. Margaret's Robbie is a weaver too and could merge his business with ours to help."

"I have been meaning to speak to Margaret's Robbie about

that very thing. I will not be here forever at Kilcrennan."

"Oh you will," Elspeth insisted. "And I will help. You and I and Robbie could train new weavers. Margaret is a fine weaver too, but she has children that keep her busy for now. And with the tartan madness upon the city folk, Kilcrennan weavers will keep growing."

"We do not need to fill all those requests, you know."

"You have put your heart and soul into it. And we have relied on your magic."

"I suppose we have," he agreed. "I think Kilcrennan tartan cloth casts its own spell. Wearing our plaids brings happiness to people here and in the south."

"It does. Grandda, please listen. You said yourself that if I fell in love, the magic would end. It would break the fairy spells over us. So I cannot fall in love. All this magic in the weaving would end. Kilcrennan would end."

"Perhaps that is not so bad. You would be happy. That would be worth it. But I want to see you safely away from here. I have not changed my mind about that."

"What makes you think I am unhappy? I love Kilcrennan. I love my work."

"It is enough for now. But not for all your life."

She sighed. "Do you remember the day you took me to the place where the fairy portal is hidden, and you told me about the fairies and all? I was fourteen. You said if I ever found true love, all binding agreements would be broken."

"Is that the problem?" he asked quietly. "You are in love and it scares you."

She nodded wordlessly.

"Love is the greatest magic humans possess," he said. "It is more powerful than fairy magic. It can remake any spell, solve any problem, satisfy any bargain, defeat any ill of body or soul."

*Love makes its own magic.* She remembered the motto of the MacCarrans. "But I cannot knowingly let Kilcrennan—and you— come to an end."

"Your happiness is all I have ever wanted, lass. Your happiness and safety. I do not want to lose you to the fairies. But I will happily lose you to a man who loves you."

"What about your happiness and your incredible gift? Truly, I still do not know if I believe all of this or not. What if I stay and they never come for me? What if we find another way to make peace with all this? I will not destroy it for you."

"Is that why you refused Struan? For me?"

She nodded, knowing it for the truth, fighting tears. "Also because of the threat to Struan if he should marry me—who knows what would happen to him, or to you, if I fall in love and leave this place? There is the lost fairy treasure to find too."

"Ah," he said. "You are so like the fairies. Capricious. Charming. Beautiful."

"Please listen," she pleaded. "I want to stay at Kilcrennan, and never fall in love."

"Too late," Donal said. "You are far gone in love now. That is the real treasure, lass. Do not give it up for any reason."


SCRATCHING HIS INKED pen over paper, James sat at his desk recording his most recent findings and thoughts. Earlier that day, while afternoon sun slanted golden through the windows, he had labeled the rocks and bits he had collected up in the hills, arranging them neatly on a small table. Now he was eager to develop his thoughts about the finds.

> *Lava, volcanoes, floods, tidal waves, earthquakes, and other catastrophes caused massive shifts of land and sea,* he wrote. *The physical record formed then and remains now in rock and stone: ripples and layers seen in rock, cracks formed in mud that dried in the heat of the sun and turned to stone, and the fossil remains of marine shells, plants, mammals, and reptiles—*

Osgar sat up from his nap by the desk and whined. James glanced down. "Did you know," he said to the dog, "that even before the Greeks, man has noted evidence of a long-ago sea that surged as high as the mountains? Did you know whole continents once lay underwater? Or so we think. Rock preserves a record of the truth and the secrets of the earth and astute observers can interpret them. The past is key to our present and our future. Ah!" He scribbled the words.

The dog tipped his head as if trying to understand. James sighed and thought of Elspeth, who would surely have listened and asked something that would stir his thinking. He felt a sharp longing, missing her. She was never far from his thoughts.

Sanding the ink, blowing gently, he set the paper aside and reached for his grandmother's manuscript. He needed to finish this wretched fairy business and move on with his research—though he dreaded breaking ties with Elspeth when the fairy nonsense was done.

A knock at the door had Osgar leaping to his feet with a deep *woof*. James stood and opened to door to admit Eldin, who looked his usual grim and unreadable.

"Come in, Nick. May I send for coffee or tea?"

"Thank you, no. John and I will depart shortly for Loch Katrine. What a handsome animal," his cousin said, petting Osgar. "A proud and ancient breed."

"Aye." James wished Osgar would growl at him, but the wolfhound merely nudged his head under Eldin's hand for more. Greedy beast.

"I only need a moment of your time. Mr. Browne mentioned to me that you may sell this house. I am prepared to offer generously for it."

James frowned. "I have not decided."

"James," his cousin said. "You should know that the addendum in Aunt Struan's will regarding my role in the inheritance was entirely her doing. I did not influence her."

"You corresponded with her often over business dealings, so you could easily have discussed it with her."

"I only assisted her in some investments. She placed some

capital in enterprises such as jute, herrings, and salt to support Scottish industry. She made more than a little profit in illicit trading as well to support the whisky industry in particular. My aunt believed that Highlanders had suffered enough in the Jacobite rebellion and the Clearances that tossed them from their rightful homes and lands. Her intention was to help Scotland, but she earned extra funds that way." He shrugged. "She seems to have added me to the will as a contingency if her wishes are not met."

"Then you know the conditions of the will."

"I do, and I wish all of you luck with it. Very unusual." His eyes were an intense dark blue, cool and hawkish.

"Some of us are convinced that you exerted influence over her."

"I did not. Nor was I responsible for other unfortunate events in the family," he responded in a cold tone. "I am unfairly accused of causing Archie MacCarran's death."

"You watched our cousin, Fiona's betrothed, fight and die on a bloody battlefield and stood by when he needed help," James growled. "You choose to save yourself."

He glanced down at James's leg. "You did not save him either. But you were seriously injured and must not recall the day correctly."

"I do," James said, on the verge of throwing the man out. Beside him, Osgar barked loudly and trotted to the window that overlooked the lane that led to the house, then stood to his impressive height, paws on the glass, barking again.

"What is it?" Eldin asked.

"Visitors," James said, seeing a gig pass beneath the trees to approach the house. The dog woofed again. "Down, lad," James told Osgar. But he knew why the wolfhound was excited. A person dear to him was on her way. Dear to James as well.

Elspeth rode beside Donal MacArthur. She wore a plaid shawl, and her bonnet partly covered her dark-as-night hair.

"Ah," Eldin said. "Would this be the Highland bride, by chance?"

James frowned at that, wondering how his cousin had heard about that. The Earl of Eldin was an odd one, though. Perhaps, like Elspeth, he had the Sight.

"I do not know what you mean." James patted Osgar's great gray head.

"I think you do. But as I said, I will not take up your time. I only wished to extend an offer to purchase the place. I have fond memories of visiting my aunt and uncle here."

James wanted to ask if the man had any fondness in him. "Thank you. Good day."

After a moment, calling Osgar to follow, he left the room. As soon as he stepped into the corridor, a shriek echoed overhead. He glanced around just as Mrs. MacKimmie came around the corner.

"*Och,* the banshee is awake again! But our laird is already here, and it is only the weaver and his granddaughter arriving. Oh!" She looked at him. "Oh, aye!"

"What is it, Mrs. MacKimmie?"

"What if the laird's bride is here?" she asked with a mischievous smile.

He huffed a wry laugh. "Please prepare tea for the MacArthurs."


"GRANDDA, THIS IS not the way back to Kilcrennan!" Elspeth said as her grandfather turned down the earthen lane that led to Struan House. The manor, visible through the trees, was a pale stone elegance backed by autumn-bright hills under a blue sky.

"The glen road is in poor condition after the flooding. We'll go this way."

"This only goes to Struan House."

"I forgot to answer the laird's dinner invitation."

"Send our refusal by post or messenger. Stop, please. I am not ready to see Lord Struan today," she added miserably, reaching up to tuck loose tendrils of hair under her shabby brown bonnet, then smooth her equally shabby brown skirts and the old red plaid over her shoulders. She was dressed for weaving and errands, not for company, certainly not to see Struan. Pinching her cheeks, she realized they were likely already pink from the chilled air and sudden embarrassment.

"The laird also asked you to work with him on his writings. And to marry him. If you want to refuse him, do it yourself, for I will not."

"What a devious thing to do, Grandda!"

"I am not proud of it, but here we are," he said as the gig rumbled along the forested lane. "Remember when I told you how I met the fairy queen and fell under her glamourie? I am reminded of that today."

"And the fairies gave you the gift of weaving. I know the tale. Very pretty. And I still wonder—but why tell me now? Just turn around and go home."

"I did not tell you all of it."

"We have no time for a new fairy tale here. Turn, please!" She pointed back.

He drove on. "I made a wicked bargain with the queen," he said. "I did it to protect my family and further my trade. I bartered for the weaving gift and promised her my time and companionship because she lured me with her charm. But I was wrong to agree, and I pay for it every seven years."

She looked over at him. "What are you saying?"

"I became the queen's lover," he said, "and she calls me back to her."

Elspeth shook her head. "I do not want to hear this."

"You should, because you must understand the danger they bring to anyone who dismisses their power. I cannot break the spell that binds me. It is a wicked trap. I betrayed my dear wife in that bargain. She knew I was caught by a fairy lover and yet she loved me still." He glanced at Elspeth. "I would give anything to be forgiven for that."

"If you could break the spell, you would lose your weaving gift."

He stopped the vehicle under the trees. "I would give it all up," he said, "never visit the Fey again, never see Niall again. I would give it all up for your happiness, and for the privilege of telling Peggy Graham I love her," he added.

"Peggy! I thought so!" Elspeth set a hand to her heart. "Does she know?"

"Not all of it. Peggy is a fine woman who does not question my past or my secrets. I think she loves me. Ah, well." He lifted the reins again. "I do not want you to make the same mistakes I made."

"What do you mean?"

"Do not sacrifice your love and happiness just so I can weave in my strange manner and visit the Fey on my appointed day. Do not risk your own safety with the Fey. They cannot be trusted. I want to be quit of all that madness now."

She nodded, thoughtful. "Are you sure love would break the spells over us?"

"Niall himself told me so. But we cannot live in fear of what the Fey might do. I want you to accept Lord Struan's proposal."

"But he has a house in Edinburgh and I want to stay with you at Kilcrennan."

"Marry him and you will see it differently. Go in there and tell your laird you love him. Just do that."

She had told him and he had said the same, and yet she had retreated. Now hope bubbled up inside her. She wanted to leap out of the gig and run to the house to find him. "If I did that, and things changed for you, what about your work?"

"A weaver is what I am. I would just be slower." He gave a sad chuckle.

"What about the fairy treasure? Is that real?" Was any of this real?

"It has never been found. I will bargain with them again. They do love to bargain," he said wryly. "And this time, I will take you out of it somehow. You deserve to be happy."

"If all of this is true," she said, "you will risk too much."

"You believe some, but not all—what will it take to convince you? I weave with a madness over me, which you have seen with your own eyes. Then believe the rest, lass."

"It could be the whisky upon you."

"Why do you think they call it fairy brew? Stubborn lass," he grumbled. He flexed the reins to urge the horse along the drive toward the house. "There is another reason for you to marry Struan. Did he see me at the weaving? I thought he did."

She glanced away, remembering that passionate, private night with James. "He did see something," she admitted.

"That secret must stay with us, so he must become part of the family. So there."

"Grandda, did you give him the fairy brew deliberately to allow that to happen?"

"Perhaps I did." He chuckled again.

Moments later, the gig rolled to a stop before the wide entrance steps. Elspeth hastily smoothed her skirt and tugged at her bonnet.

"What was that noise?" Donal asked.

"They have a banshee," she said, looking up at the house.

"Ah, I nearly forgot! Then that is your sign, lass. Go tell your laird what you feel. It is time to be true and good to yourself."

She stepped down just as Angus MacKimmie walked toward them, calling a greeting. Though conflicted, she felt hope rising. But she wondered how much of the extraordinary truth about her family she could reasonably explain.

Hearing footsteps, she looked up to see James coming toward the gig. She drew a shaky breath. "Good afternoon, Lord Struan."

"Miss MacArthur," he said, his eyes so blue, so serious. He inclined his head. "What a nice surprise."

She began to answer, but sensed suddenly that he was tense. He glanced back at the house, and she saw others coming out as well. Some faces were familiar—Sir John Graham, Miss Fiona MacCarran, and others.

"I beg pardon, sir," she said to James. "We forgot you might have guests."

"That does not matter in the least," he murmured. "I am glad to see you."

"Miss MacArthur!" Fiona MacCarran came forward to take her hand. Then John Graham reached to kiss her cheek.

"Cousin Elspeth, how good to see you," John said. "Cousin Donal, greetings, man!" He walked around the gig to talk with her grandfather.

James touched her elbow. "Miss MacArthur, you may remember my youngest brother, Patrick." She smiled up him as a woman and a tall man dressed in black came outside as well.

"You remember Miss Sinclair," James said then.

"I do," Elspeth said politely as Charlotte Sinclair gave her a tight little smile. The young woman stood so close to James that her shoulder pressed his arm.

Feeling a jolt to see that, thinking she might be too late after all, Elspeth kept her smile in place. "How do you do, Miss Sinclair. How good to see that you all found the chance to visit the Highlands together."

"We came with Lady Rankin to visit James, er, Lord Struan and we look forward to touring the countryside." Charlotte turned up her smile like a lamp as she looked at James. "Tomorrow I will lure him away from his books to take us around."

"And this is my cousin, Lord Eldin," James said, almost cutting her off. "Miss MacArthur of Kilcrennan." Elspeth turned almost gratefully toward the stranger.

"A true Highland girl. I am charmed." Eldin inclined his head. At first glance, he looked like a dark, avenging angel, his face flawlessly handsome but stern, his physique neat in his black clothing. But Elspeth sensed something unsettling about him. She frowned as he extended his hand for her gloved fingers.

The world went dizzy for a moment, shadowy with a smoky haze. She saw James and his cousin in a different place, a brown meadow with a chaos of smoke surrounding men in bright red jackets and dark tartan kilts—the uniform of the Highland Black

Watch. James and Eldin held bayoneted guns, James seated with a bloody gash above his knee, Eldin standing over him, A Highlander lay dead at their feet. The image disappeared, and instead she saw both men staring at her now.

"Miss MacArthur, are you ill?" Eldin asked.

Only a few seconds had passed, she was sure. She pulled her fingers from Eldin's cordial grip. "You—" she whispered, "you were there. James was hurt—the other died."

"Elspeth. Miss MacArthur," James murmured, taking her arm. "Come inside."

"What is this?" Lord Eldin asked sharply. "Do you have the Sight?"

"Come inside. We will have tea," James said firmly, leading her up the steps. As the others turned to follow more slowly, Elspeth leaned into his sure strength, grateful for his calm, for she was trembling. He guided her to the library where Mrs. MacKimmie had laid an elaborate tea on the large round table and brought her to a wing chair by the fireplace.

"Sit here. What happened?" he asked quietly. "One of your visions?"

"Odd," she said, putting a shaking hand to her brow. "I saw you and Lord Eldin in regimental dress on a battlefield, I think." She told him quietly, quickly, while the others wandered into the room. "You had a gash above the knee. There was a dead Highlander."

"Dear God," he said. "I never told you about all that. I was wounded," he whispered. "Another cousin was killed. Eldin was with us."

"Oh my," she breathed.

"Would you like some whisky? You are shaking."

"Just tea," she said with a rueful laugh. "I am fine now."

"Drat, here they come," he said, and turned as the others entered, talking, finding seats, exploring the room and perusing the teapots, cakes, and small sandwiches laid out.

Eldin came to her. "Miss MacArthur. You seemed overcome."

"I am perfectly fine, sir." She rose to her feet.

"So you have the Sight," he murmured, and closed his eyes. "Ah. Fairy-held. A gift. Interesting." He leaned toward her. "I have a touch of it myself, so I understand."

She had sensed something odd about Eldin. Perhaps that was it. James returned, and she felt a sharp tension between him and Eldin, as if the cousin posed a threat.

"You and John will be leaving soon, but I hope you will stay for tea," he said.

"Of course," Eldin said, and went to the table.

She rose from the chair and followed James. Charlotte, taking the role of hostess that properly belonged to James's twin, Fiona, was pouring tea; she handed James a plate of sugar biscuits, calling those his favorite.

Feeling small and invisible, Elspeth brightened to see her grandfather. "Lass?" he asked, sounding concerned.

"I am fine, Grandda. What would you like?" she asked, gesturing to the table.

"Whatever makes you happy, that is all I want."

"Ah, that would be one of Mrs. MacKimmie's cinnamon seed cakes, then," she said, reaching for a plate.

# Chapter Eighteen

"WHAT A SUBSTANTIAL tea," Charlotte remarked, after the group had sated themselves on the generous spread of cold meat, sausage rolls, sweet biscuits, cakes, a fruit compôte and more.

"A Highland tea is much like a supper, Miss Sinclair," Mrs. MacKimmie said, having come in with a made to clear some dishes away.

Charlotte Sinclair looked startled that a housekeeper had spoken to her.

"The laird often takes his tea this way, with a small supper late in the evening," Mrs. MacKimmie continued. "I will serve soup later. Better to have an informal meal, as you must be tired from the long journey up here."

"Thank you for the excellent tea, Mrs. MacKimmie," Fiona said sweetly, while beside her Charlotte looked offended. "We should have an early evening before we go out tomorrow."

Elspeth glanced at James. He stood beside her chair, cup and saucer cradled in his hand. "I should go," she said, setting her cup on a table. "I only came by today hoping to, ah, help with your work as we discussed."

"Did you? Good." He leaned an elbow on the back of her chair, and she looked up into his eyes, sincere blue, the safest, most wonderful eyes in the room to her just now. She wanted to stay here with him, but felt distinctly uncomfortable with others who were part of his life when she was not yet sure of her role in it.

"My lord," Charlotte said. "Tell us about this beautiful house. For instance, I want to know more about the pretty curiosities in the display cases. Come over here and look." She beckoned to him.

"Fiona can tell you about the rocks there," he said, smiling. Charlotte only frowned as Fiona went to the display case with her to look at the stones there.

"I had forgotten that your guests might be here," Elspeth said to James. "You are too busy today. We can discuss the fairy book another time. Grandda has errands and so we should leave. Thank you for the hospitality."

"Stay," he said quickly.

Donal MacArthur, standing by the fireplace studying the painting above the mantel, glanced over at Elspeth. He held a teacup in one hand and nibbled a bit of lemon cake tucked in a napkin. "Thank you, Struan," he said. "I do have errands, but perhaps my granddaughter could stay until I return for her."

"She may stay as long as she likes." James smiled.

*What if I want to stay forever?* she thought. But with Charlotte Sinclair here now, perhaps James would feel differently about marrying a Highland girl. There was no chance for a private discussion with him, but perhaps fate had interfered. Charlotte was possessive of James and was making a show of staying near him. His impulsive offer of marriage might have already faded in his mind.

That hurt too much to dwell on. She stood. "Grandda, I will come with you. Lord Struan has guests to entertain."

"If he does not mind, we do not," Donal said. "I will be back. See if you can assist with his papers, as promised."

"I could, I suppose," she said hesitantly, glancing at James.

"Good." He gestured for her to follow him into his study. Seeing that, Charlotte hurried over to take his arm.

"James, are your friends leaving? How nice to see you again," she told Elspeth. "Dear Struan, you must tell me about this pretty blue stone in the case. I quite like it."

"Mr. MacArthur is leaving for a little while, and Miss MacArthur is staying for the afternoon. She has promised to help me with something I am writing."

"Oh," Charlotte said with a pout, and walked away.

"That one has an angel's face and the manners of a magpie," Donal said.

James chuckled, then turned as his sister called and excused himself.

Elspeth looked at her grandfather. "Now I need to stay to make sure the magpie does not claim your fairy stone for her own."

"Best do that, lass. I looked at it during tea. That is the stone the fairy queen gave me, and we must have it back. Besides, it is your right to be here. You love the man," he added low. "Stay and tell him."

"I will not squabble with the other lass over him," she whispered. "He wants me or he does not. It remains to be seen."

"I see it but you do not. Before I go, come look at Niall's painting with me."

She crossed the little distance to the fireplace with him. "Struan noticed that one of the women looks like me. I hoped she might be a likeness of my mother."

He craned his neck to peer closely. "She does look like you—and your mother too. She was a beautiful fairy woman with black hair and silvery eyes. So aye, it could be. Now look over here." He pointed. "I wonder if you will see what I saw. And you should show your laird if we are correct."

For a moment, she glanced back to see James standing beside Charlotte Sinclair, who nudged close to him. The woman's blond hair shone in the sunlight from the window, and his hair gleamed too, chestnut touched with gold. They were a handsome couple, she thought, and sighed.

Gazing up at her father's landscape painting, she studied the moorland rinsed in purple twilight, and the delicate details of forest, mist, and the play of color in the sky. Then she noticed a detail she had not seen before.

A dark rock wall was depicted to one side of the painting, and as she moved her head, the color and shape came together to form a narrow cave mouth, tall niche. Inside the dark crevice, she saw the painterly glimmer of tiny dabs and dots of color.

"Grandda, is that—could it be—gold inside a cave?'

"I thought so too. Ah, it is getting late. I must go. I will be back." He patted her shoulder. "And here comes your laird. Tell him."

"Not my laird," she whispered.

He smiled and left, taking his leave of James, who then came toward her.

"Your grandfather said you had something to show me," James said.

She nodded, tilting her head for a better perspective as she looked up at the artwork. Then she touched his sleeve. "Look! There, at the right. Do you see a cave? What else do you see?"

He studied it in silence, then nodded. "Look at that. It could be a pile of gold and jewels, maybe pearls. It looks like a pirate's treasure in the shadows there. I never noticed it before."

"Nor did I. My father included so much detail with the fairy riders, the woman who looks like me, or my mother—Grandda just said so too. And now a cave with a hidden pile of treasure. What if he left clues for others to find?"

"But the legends are well known here. He just added them to his painting."

"It is more than that. I feel it." She tilted her head again. "That rocky cliff looks familiar. I have seen it somewhere."

He leaned sideways, his shoulder touching hers, his head angled as he spoke softly to her. "Then we should look for that, and see if we can find a cave and your fairy treasure. And then," he whispered, "perhaps your fairies will dance at our wedding."

She stared at him. "Wedding?" Her heartbeat leaped.

"If you like." His voice was low, compelling, so dear to her. She leaned close. But they could not talk about this here. It needed time and privacy.

"I thought you did not believe in fairy nonsense," she whispered.

"I had the impression you are not convinced either. Certainly not like your grandfather, who regards fairies to be as real as the people in this room."

She sighed. "But—what if this is proof?"

"Of fairy legends and stolen treasure, aye."

"Please, can we talk somewhere?" She set a hand on his sleeve.

"Fairies and treasure! How exciting! Tell us more," Charlotte said, coming near.

THERE WAS JUST no blasted privacy in this place, James thought, as Charlotte joined them. He felt hounded by the girl, who seemed blithe and pleased. Just now, he desperately wanted—needed—time alone with Elspeth. And somehow, even with Charlotte tracking his every move, he wanted to speak privately with Fiona and Patrick too. His siblings deserved to know that he had asked Elspeth to marry him, and that he was diligently working toward—and hoping for—her agreement.

Despite her refusals and his impatience with her at times, he would not give up on her, or the future he wanted to share with her.

"Treasure?" Patrick asked, coming closer, Fiona by his side. "We overheard! Fairies are endlessly fascinating. Fiona loves them too."

"Have you discovered much about fairies here at Struan House?" Fiona asked.

"Just in Grandmother's manuscript," he said.

"Lost treasure and fairies!" Charlotte said. "Perhaps we could look for them!"

"Unlikely. There are some entertaining Highland tales locally.

That is all," James said. "Isn't that so, Miss MacArthur?" She nodded, eyes wide.

"Look. This painting has fairies riding through it." Fiona stepped closer.

Charlotte shoved between Elspeth and James to gaze at the picture. "Very pretty, though it might be nicer in a bedroom or a parlor than in here. Perhaps you could move it if I chose a good spot for it upstairs, Struan."

"I like it here," he answered. "Our grandmother was fond of it. And Miss MacArthur's father was the artist."

"Truly father?" Charlotte looked at Elspeth with surprise. "Then your family will want to have it back when Struan House is sold."

"You are selling Struan?" Wide-eyed, she met his gaze, silvery eyes distressed.

"Not yet," he said, frowning.

"He wants to be rid of the place, and one can hardly blame him, a drafty old house so far from the city." Charlotte tucked her hand in his elbow. "He has many responsibilities in Edinburgh, and this house needs attention, unless we—er, he—wants to spend a good part of the year in the Highlands."

"I may do that." With a stiff smile, he moved away from Charlotte, who seemed oblivious so often to what he said and did when it did not meet her expectation.

"Lord Struan, would you truly sell this grand old place?" Sir Philip asked in a jovial tone as he came toward them with Lady Rankin on his arm. "Then I might want to buy it myself."

"I am sorry I missed tea, but I needed to rest," James's aunt said, grasping his hand for a moment. "Miss MacArthur, how nice to see you again. Do you live nearby?"

"I do, my lady. My grandfather and I live down in the glen at Kilcrennan."

"Is your grandfather the weaver?" Sir Philip asked. "I have kilts made from Kilcrennan cloth. Fine stuff!"

"Weaving! Do you employ small children in your factory?"

Charlotte asked.

"Good heavens, Miss Sinclair," James muttered.

"Just myself when I was younger," Elspeth said, mischief glinting in her eyes. "I am a weaver too," she added. James noticed Charlotte and Lady Rankin raise their eyebrows at that. "We weave the cloth on handlooms, like my great-grandfather and his father before him, and my grandmothers too."

"Mr. MacArthur is an old-school artisan, and Miss MacArthur is very gifted in the craft also." James spoke with pride, hoping they heard it.

"Highland weaving is an ancient craft, a true art form in the Highlands," Fiona added. "Tartan cloth is quite popular now, so they must be very busy. We can thank Sir Walter Scott for reviving a sense of Scottish character and heritage. People are keen for anything Scotch these days," she added.

"It seems that way." James silently blessed his sister for her praise.

"You genuinely appreciate the Highlands, Miss MacCarran," Elspeth said.

"I do. I love being in Highlands. James and I spent some wonderful holidays here at Struan House."

"Fiona now works with a Highland society, teaching English to native Gaelic speakers," James explained to Elspeth.

"Wonderful! Since you were both here as children, I am surprised we did not meet sooner," Elspeth said.

*I wish we had,* James thought. His childhood might have been happier. "We were here for a fortnight once or twice a year. We wandered the hills with our grandfather, Lord Struan. But we did not meet many local children that I recall."

Elspeth nodded, about to speak, when Mrs. MacKimmie returned to clear the tea table. The servants had not yet returned from fleeing for the fairy riding, so the woman had more work than usual. James handed her his empty cup with quiet thanks.

"Mr. MacKimmie told Philip and I that there are fairies out in your garden," Lady Rankin said. "I would love to see them. Little garden figurines, I suppose he meant."

"*Och,* MacKimmie likely meant our real fairies," Mrs. MacKimmie said, looking up. Lady Rankin gasped to hear from her, while James smiled, glancing at Elspeth.

"Oh aye, fairies are abundant here," Elspeth said with a little smile.

He enjoyed the stunned silence that followed, and smiled to see Charlotte's gaping expression.

"Part of the charming folderol of the Highlands," he told them. "I did not believe it myself when I came here, but the Highlands are making a believer even out of me."

"Fascinating," Fiona said. "Has anyone truly seen fairies here?"

"There are many stories in the glen," Elspeth said. "Tradition says the fairies ride across Struan lands at this time every year for one or more nights. Lord Struan and I saw them the other evening," she added. "Or we thought we did."

Blast, James thought. That was a bit too honest. He wondered if Elspeth meant to shock Charlotte in particular, though he knew his siblings would be more than interested, given their grandmother's odd will.

"You...and Lord Struan did what?" Charlotte asked.

"Saw the fairies," Elspeth said. "Or at least we thought so."

"You and Lord Struan were together at night?" Charlotte squeaked out.

"We were outside and saw something quite eerie."

"Alone?" Charlotte asked. The rest of them were silent.

James blew out a breath. "Alone for a bit," he said, taking the chance. "Miss MacArthur was in a bit of a kerfuffle and I came to her assistance. But I cannot vouch for seeing fairies. It was probably mist."

"Lord Struan kindly helped me when I was caught in a storm," Elspeth said. "And perhaps I was the only one who saw fairies riding through."

"Good God," Philip said. "I was just out there but saw nothing so good as that!"

"Alone," Charlotte repeated. "Here. At night."

"What did the fairies look like?" Fiona asked, head tilted in curiosity.

"Just a thick mist," James reassured her.

"Beautiful young people on pretty horses," Elspeth said.

"Shapes in the mist," James clarified.

"*Och,* and what a storm that was," Mrs. MacKimmie said, holding the tea tray, in no hurry to depart. "A fierce storm, rain for days. The roads flooded and the bridge broke. It was kind of Struan to rescue Miss MacArthur."

"Are you finished clearing, Mrs. MacKimmie?" Lady Rankin asked.

"So you were here, too, Mrs. MacKimmie," Fiona said.

"Struan House is my home, Miss MacCarran," the housekeeper replied.

With a sigh of relief, James nodded his gratitude to the housekeeper, who smiled, tray clattering as she went to the door.

"James, do enlighten us," Lady Rankin said. "I am confused."

"Miss MacArthur was stranded here in a devilish Highland gale. Just for a bit until the weather cleared."

"I see," Charlotte said coldly.

"I suppose it could not be helped," Lady Rankin decided, "and you had a capable chaperone in Mrs. MacKimmie, even if her manners are quite forward."

"She is an excellent housekeeper. A treasure," James replied.

"An excellent woman," Elspeth said.

"And the fairies?" Patrick asked. "They were beautiful, you say?"

"So lovely," Elspeth said. "Lord Struan insists it was imagination, but I saw them as clear as I see you now."

Fiona touched Elspeth's shoulder. "How wonderful!"

"How frightening," Charlotte said sourly.

"You might see them yourself the next time they ride," Elspeth said.

James nearly groaned aloud. Elspeth was putting them on now, especially Charlotte; he knew by her tone and the twinkle in her eyes.

"This is silly," Charlotte murmured with an angry glower for Elspeth, which she then turned on him. He felt sorry for her, for he could never give her what she wanted. Her idea of loving someone was to be haughty and possessive, not kind or encouraging.

Just then he noticed how Philip Rankin looked at Charlotte, how he stood close to her and focused on her with a lot of admiration. Philip was haughty in his way, but also clever and jolly, and had a good income. And he seemed smitten with Charlotte. She needed a man who adored her and was thick enough to overlook her flaws. If she took notice of Philip, she would find a good match under her very nose.

"Not silly, Miss Sinclair," James said then. "Fairy lore is part of the Highland culture. And there are things in heaven and earth that we cannot understand, as the great Bard once said. Is it not so, Sir Philip?"

"Huh, indeed," Philip said. "I would like to hear your thoughts, Miss Sinclair."

"I would love to see fairies in the wild," Fiona murmured. "I would love to make sketches of them." James remembered that was part of Fiona's assignment in the will.

"If you look for them, remember to ask their permission before you draw what you see," Elspeth told his sister. "Or they may try to steal you away."

"Who, Highland savages?" Lady Rankin put a hand to her bosom.

"Fairies, Aunt," Patrick said. "It is said they steal people away to their world."

Lady Rankin gasped. "How can that be?"

"If the Fey are angered, they may do anything out of revenge," Elspeth said.

"So they say. But—these are all just stories," James said.

Whether genuine or lunatic, he wanted to end this before someone mocked what Elspeth said or believed, because he loved her.

He did. But he had no time for that revelation. "Miss MacArthur is quite the expert in fairy lore," he said. "And I am reminded that she kindly offered to advise me on local folklore today, a subject that interests me very much. If you will excuse us, I would like to show her what I have been working on."

He ushered her into the study, then drew her around behind the door into the shadows. "Elspeth," he growled.

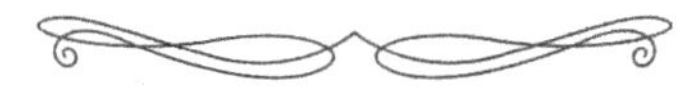

# Chapter Nineteen

"DO LEAVE THE door open," Elspeth said. "Else Charlotte might knock it down."

"Let her," James said, but yanked it open, standing behind it with her. "Now tell me what you were going on about back there."

"Fairies. Your sister was quite interested. Miss Sinclair is not pleased. And your lady aunt looked as if she would faint when you dragged me in here."

"She likely fears fairies are everywhere now and will come after her. I thought it best to get you away before you revealed all your fairy secrets, or invited the blasted fairies into the blasted room!" he said too loudly.

"Which fairy secrets? And keep your voice down."

"Your grandfather's peculiar weaving habits, for one. Your father's fate, painting fairies and then disappearing, or whatever he did. And I will shout if I must. Let them come after us."

"So you do believe!" She smiled.

"I would not go that far, my lass. But I admit what seems unusual for most is normal for you. Is that enough acceptance?"

She tilted her head. "It will do."

Her eyes, just then, were clear aquamarine lit with silver. But he would not tell her how beautiful they were. Not then, or he would be lost and want to pull her into his arms and tell her even more. "That is the best I can offer."

"James, listen," she said, as if she hardly heard. "I realized something, looking at the painting. Something about my father."

"Tell me, then."

"I think he went out to paint and sketch, and saw the *Sith* out there and drew them, then he would have gone home to paint them. That would fix their images for posterity. They would not like that. So they took him in forfeit. I wonder if Grandda knows that. It makes sense," she added.

"It sounds preposterous to me," he said. He was tired of fairy nonsense, even if he was wavering on the topic now, surrounded by it and seeing things he would never have believed if he had not met her. But he was not ready to admit it. "Blasted nonsense," he added for good measure.

"Your language deteriorates when you are upset."

"A casualty of the war, my vocabulary. Go on."

"I know, because I saw it here"—she tapped her brow—"and I just knew that my father painted the fairies and fell in love with one of them. And so they stole him away."

He shook his head, huffed in surrender. If he was to trust her, he would have to believe her. It shook the foundations of reason, but he had to give credence to some of what she and her grandfather said and did. Because he loved her, and owed her that trust.

He was more lost than he thought possible. Reaching out, he traced his fingers over her soft hair, cupped her chin, tilted it. His body throbbed at that simple touch. "Beg pardon. So you just knew, in your way. Go on. I am listening."

"And I saw, in my mind, your sister walking in the hills carrying a sketchbook. Does she have a habit of that?"

"She does. What else?"

"She could be watched by fairies. She must take care to avoid a bad fate."

"Fiona is like me and too pragmatic to see them. If she ever did, they would have a devil of a time getting her to go with them. My sister may seem calm and composed, but she would give the fairies such a fuss they would be glad to escape with their lives. If they exist," he added hastily.

"What promise did you and Fiona make to your grandmother?" she asked.

"And just when," he said, resigned, "did that revelation come to you?"

"When I was talking to Fiona. *Did* you make a promise to Lady Struan?"

"The book."

"Something more, I think."

He exhaled hard, thoughtful. Sooner or later, he had to tell her. "My grandmother set conditions on the inheritance. I must finish her fairy book—and find myself a Highland bride. To be specific, a fairy bride."

"A fairy bride," she repeated. She crossed her arms. Tapped her fingers.

"Otherwise there will be precious little inheritance, and most will go to Eldin."

"Eldin. I see." She watched him. "And so you met me."

"Elspeth, it was not that way," he said.

She pushed at his chest. "You knew this all along, yet said nothing!"

"We both have secrets," he said.


"SECRETS!" ELSPETH'S TEMPER fumed as she realized he had kept this from her. She glared up at him. "I may not have told you everything, but I never deceived you."

"Nor I you." When she pushed at him again, he gripped her wrist, drew her close.

She allowed it, though she felt furious, confused, even betrayed. But when he touched her, she relented, and when he cupped her cheek, her thoughts and feelings collided. Her need to be in his arms won out.

"You wanted a fairy bride, and so you let me go on the Fey. And then you asked me to marry you."

"I did, and I would again," he said low. "I owed it to you by the end of that evening, if you recall."

"I thought that was only out of obligation. But you had another reason," she hissed. "Your inheritance! How convenient for you that I came by!"

"I wanted to marry you." She began to walk away, but he took her shoulders and set her behind the door again. "I still do."

"Because of my unbelievable but very convenient tie to the fairies."

"That was part of it. But not all!"

"Why did you not tell me?" And why, she suddenly thought, had her intuition not told her? Love had befuddled her. That was why.

"I would not know a fairy from a fishwife. And you repeatedly refused my offer. So no explanation seemed necessary."

"I had my reasons for refusing," she said, looking away.

"And I had mine for asking," he whispered, standing so close that Elspeth tilted back her head, feeling he might kiss her, wanting it. When he touched his nose to hers, questing, she sighed and accepted his kiss, her hand curling in his, her knees gone weak. Then she toughened and pushed him away.

"There are people in the next room," she said.

"Let them come in. They will witness me proposing to you—again." His face was so close, his breath soft on her cheek. She sighed, closed her eyes.

Then opened them in a renewed glare. "I trusted you."

"And you can. Know this, Elspeth. I would trust you with my life," he said, then sighed. "I love you, do you not see it? This has happened so quickly, but I feel sure of it now. And it is not in my nature to say such things. But I love you, all of you, fairy or not fairy. It is as if a kind of magic has come over me."

Her breath caught. She wanted to throw herself into his arms. She nodded. "It has been very quick, aye. I feel the same. But there is something I must tell you."

"What is that?"

She drew a breath. "My mother was a fairy. Or so my grandfather insists."

"Good God," he said.

A knock sounded on the other side of the open door. Elspeth leaped, startled. James scowled. "Who is it?" he asked in a gruff tone.

"Fiona and Patrick. The rest of them went out to the garden. May we come in?"

Sighing, he pulled the door open and stepped out. Elspeth came out too, smoothing her gown, tucking strands of hair into place. James waved his siblings inside and shut the door.

"Now," Patrick said, "what's the kerfuffle here? Aunt Rankin went up to her room, afraid vindictive fairy sorts are lying in wait for her outside. Charlotte dragged Philip with her, fuming over you leaving with Miss MacArthur. And the two of you have been in here whispering rather loudly."

Elspeth stood by, silent, hands folded, cheeks blazing.

"We have much to discuss, Miss MacArthur and I," James said.

Fiona turned. "Miss MacArthur, this may sound absurd, and I apologize, but I must ask. Are there any rumors of fairy blood in your family?"

Elspeth lifted her chin. "I believe so."

"Quite possibly," James said, and ran a hand through his hair as if flustered.

"Excellent! James, you found her!"

"Found me," Elspeth repeated stiffly. "Good for you, sir."

He leaned against his desk. "You may as well know that Miss MacArthur is just finding out about this…fairy requirement. And she is not happy with me over it."

"When fairies are angered, they are not cooperative," Elspeth snapped. "What is the requirement? Is there more?"

"Our grandmother's will requires each of us to find and marry someone of fairy blood," Fiona said. "Grandmother wanted to restore the fairy legacy to our family line."

"Otherwise, none of us can inherit," Patrick said, "And Lord Eldin gets it all."

"Oh dear," Elspeth said.

"Exactly," James said. "Now you know."

Stunned, she stared at the three of them. "Perhaps Lady Struan wanted to change your minds about the *Daoine Sith,* knowing you might not believe without evidence."

"The dowin shee?" Patrick asked.

"The fairies," Fiona translated. "The peaceful ones, it means."

"Not so peaceful when crossed," James drawled.

"Lady Struan may have thought that if your brother were to live here," Elspeth said, "he would need to understand the importance of fairy tradition in this glen."

Patrick nodded. "That could be. She knew more about the subject than most, and probably thought all of us far too practical and in need of more imagination."

"She might think Elspeth the perfect bit of proof," James mused.

"I wonder if Grandmother lured you here, James," Fiona said. "Perhaps she intended all along to bring you two together. She may have wanted this for you."

Elspeth caught her breath as they all turned to look at her. She met James's gaze for a moment, that blue tidepool drawing her in. "If you believe it, it may simply be so."

"Is that all it takes?" he asked gently. "When she came here to the house in that storm," he explained, "circumstances were such that it was prudent for me to offer marriage. Given all the fairy nonsense—er, the lore in Elspeth's family, Grandmother may have hoped we would meet."

"But I refused him," Elspeth said.

"Oh dear!" Fiona said. "I hope you will reconsider."

"Miss MacArthur, if I may say so," Patrick said, "if you do have a trace of fairy blood, it would be a great service to all of us if you would marry our brother."

"You will not convince the stubborn lass," James murmured.

A movement beyond the window caught her attention, and Elspeth looked out to see her grandfather's gig advancing along the road toward Struan. He was returning already. She could risk telling them the whole truth now or keep her secrets to herself, and lose her chance at happiness.

In a few days she would turn twenty-one and her life might change irrevocably. She had not wanted to drag James into that, even if she was not entirely sure what might happen. It sounded preposterous even to her, and she had grown up with it.

But Donal MacArthur was right. She had fallen in love. It was too late to stop that. True love could break the hold the fairies had over her family. But until the treasure was found and returned, Donal would remain in their thrall, so he said.

She drew a breath. "True, I have fairy blood through my mother," she said. "And I believe I have seen the *Daoine Síth*. Some things I know, and other things I struggle to accept, just like you. I know it is difficult to believe. But for me and mine, these tales have always been so. I do not know if others can accept that. If you can accept that," she told James.

"I can." He took her hands in his. "Marry me and find out."

Behind her, Elspeth heard Fiona catch back a sob, and Patrick beamed.

Elspeth nodded slowly. Finally, all of a sudden and certain, she knew. "Well then, I will marry you—on one condition."

"What is that?" He rubbed his thumb over her fingers, warm and compelling.

She straightened her shoulders, aware of the risk, feeling as if she stood on a high cliff edge—and only their clasped hands, their love, could save them both.

"I will marry you, but we must find the lost fairy treasure first. And all this must happen before my birthday."

"Your birthday? When is that?" he asked.

"Next week. The twentieth of October. I will turn twenty-one."

"Goodness. Why before then?"

"On that birthday, the Fey have vowed to take me away. So my grandfather says."

"Gracious," Fiona said. "This is—like nothing I have ever heard."

"We can only try," he said simply.

"And I have an idea where we can look. Tomorrow, then, if you please."

"Tomorrow," he said.

"It is not for the riches of the thing, and I do not care if you are a wealthy man or not," she said. "Please trust me. The treasure must be found for all our sakes."

"What if we married and took time to search these hills for treasure?"

"Because I do not know how long we will have together," she blurted. "A lifetime or a few days. If the treasure is not found soon, the bargain Grandda made years ago with the Fey could cause terrible grief. You are part of that now."

He drew her into his arms, regardless of his siblings standing near. "Even if we have only days, I would marry you. If we have a lifetime, I will marry you. Trust that."

"I do," she whispered. "And I believe we will find it now. I think my father left the clues in his painting."

"Then we will try." He kissed her brow lightly. Elspeth heard Fiona catch her breath again. A warmth like sunlight went through her—happiness, passion, hope. She tilted her head to kiss him, and stood in his embrace for a moment. She wanted to be with him forever, felt so grateful to have found him.

Yet she could not lose the sense of danger gathering all around.

Then Fiona hugged her and Patrick kissed her cheek, both welcoming her into their family. Smiling, she tried to ignore the feeling that she had just thrown down a gauntlet to fate and the Fey.

Yet this was the only choice where she could be true to herself. Quick as this had all come about, James already seemed part of her soul. Any differences between them only enriched their match, one changeable and airy, one solid and earthlike, each helping the other to grow. It felt right, despite the risks.

"James, please," she murmured. "Help me find it tomorrow. We must."

"We will try. When my aunt and the others go off to tour the Highlands, we will stay here, you and I, and search in the glen. Do you know where to look?"

"My grandfather has searched throughout the glen for years. But my father's picture shows something that may help, though we have to puzzle it out."

"The little cave in the landscape?" he asked.

"Grandmother called the painting a pretty picture of Ben Venue," Fiona said. "She told me that once. Might that be a clue?"

"*A' Bheinn Mheanbh!*" Elspeth gasped, nodded. "That is the Gaelic. It is a small mountain near Loch Katrine. Your aunt's party may go past it tomorrow on their tour."

"Then we must all go with them, and you too, Miss MacArthur," Patrick said.

"Elspeth," she told him, smiling, as he and Fiona did too.

"Then we will scale Ben Venue if we must," James said. "Ask your grandfather to come as well, to help us search. We will all slip away and look for treasure, aye?"

"Charlotte will not like that very much," Elspeth said.

"Charlotte is not my concern," James said. "You are." He set an arm around her shoulders. She sighed, relaxing against him.

"I know this seems impossible," she said. "But I am grateful."

"If I can meet my grandmother's preposterous conditions, Miss MacArthur, and find myself a fairy bride, I think anything is possible."

Tears stung her eyes, though she smiled. If Grandda was right, it was dangerous indeed. If they failed, she might never see James again.

A rapping sounded on the door, and Patrick opened it. "Mrs. MacKimmie!"

"Begging pardon, sir. Mr. MacArthur is here and asking for Miss Elspeth."

Elspeth nodded, squeezed James's hand, and murmured farewell. She could not find adequate words, filled with gratitude, excitement, love—and a hint of dread.


LATE THAT NIGHT, James held the blue agate up to the glow of the lamplight. He had found the key to the case and removed the stone, wanting to give it to Elspeth. Her promise to marry him at last had given him hope, and the condition she had requested did not seem insurmountable. If stones like this existed nearby, then he might find crystals and even a bit of fool's gold—iron pyrite— to satisfy the quest for a horde of treasure.

Had Elspeth set a Herculean task to see how sincere he was about fairy legends? His sincerity toward her was without question, but he understood her need to challenge. He wanted her to know that his proposal was because he loved her, wanted her, and not because of the inheritance. That it could satisfy Lady Struan's will was simply a benefit now. He wanted to be her husband regardless.

He looked forward to the outing in the morning, as Elspeth and Donal would join the group for their Highland tour, acting as guides. While Donal might not be as well-versed in Sir Walter Scott's poetry as the others, who wanted to see sites they had read about, he knew Donal would make the day an entertaining adventure.

Then he wondered if Elspeth had told her grandfather about their engagement. For now, it was best kept a secret among just a few.

He turned the agate again in the light. At its heart was a cluster of tiny clear crystals in a toothy formation that reminded him whimsically of a miniature landscape of hills and castle turrets. Extracting the loupe from his bag of tools, he adjusted the double lenses for magnification and tilted it over the stone.

Under the lenses, the outer casing of granite formed a thick husk around the exquisite blue striations and crystals in a stone of excellent clarity. He angled it, and the crystalline cavity suddenly looked like a tiny cavern.

"What the devil," he murmured. Reminded of something he had seen recently, he carried the stone into the library and went straight to the painting over the mantel to compare the agate perched in his fingers to the landscape.

Aye, he thought. The cave rendered in the painting, under the profile of hills, looked identical in shape to the crystalline center of the stone. An odd coincidence, he told himself. Had the stone inspired Donal MacArthur's son, or was there an eerie, almost magical, reason for the similarity?

Or had Elspeth and Donal influenced his own opinion of this fairy business?

The hour was late, and he had work to do. He reached for his grandmother's manuscript again, remembering that his grandmother had mentioned an artist without naming Niall MacArthur. Where was that—flipping pages, he found it and sat back.

*A young artist went into the hills to sketch from nature,* Lady Struan had written. *Tired later, he lay down to rest on a hill at twilight. A shepherd saw him in passing, and the man's family said later it was the last that the artist was ever seen, for he never returned home. His father searched for his son, and one evening, as the father, a weaver, sat at his loom, the son appeared in a mist, and said that he had been lured inside the hill by a beautiful fairy woman. He loved her and wanted to stay with her. Begging his father to meet him in the hills in seven days, the son promised to give him a precious gift.*

Was that the stone? Astonished, James read on.

*When the weaver arrived at the agreed time and place, he met the fairy queen, a gorgeous creature he had loved in his own youth. And he saw his son and the fairy lass who had won his heart. The gift they presented to him was their infant daughter.*

*They made a bargain between them that the weaver would raise the girl until the fairies called her back to them on her twenty-first birthday. She was given the gift of the Sight so that she might see what cannot be seen and know what cannot be known.*

*The girl must return to her fairy kin to live in their realm forever. Only if she falls in love with a man who understands and respects the fairy ilk can she stay in the earthly realm. But her grandfather must forfeit his gifts for her happiness.*

Clutching the page, James read it again, heart pounding. Either his grandmother had a vivid imagination, or she knew more about the MacArthurs of Kilcrennan than James could imagine. He turned the page.

*The Fey posed another wicked bargain—all spells would break if the weaver could find and return a treasure stolen from the fairy ilk long ago and hidden in the wild hills. But, said the man who reported this tale, it may never be found.*

James set down the manuscript and sat staring at the blue agate.

# Chapter Twenty

"LOOK AT THE Highland natives!" Lady Rankin pointed as the open carriage rumbled along. Beside her, Elspeth saw two Highland men and a boy walking along the ridge of a hill, dressed in plaids. As the coach passed, they waved and doffed their caps.

"Please do not call them natives, Aunt," Fiona said.

"Well, they look like Hottentots," Lady Rankin said. "My gracious, your coachman drives fast!" She grabbed a strap by the half-door as MacKimmie took the carriage at a stiff pace up a curving slope in the road.

"Some coaches fly very fast through here," Elspeth said. "Grandda says you could set a tea-table on their coattails, flying out so straight." James and Fiona laughed.

"Is the Brig o' Turk mentioned in Sir Walter's poem the one in your glen, James?" Lady Rankin asked, pointing toward a stone bridge.

"That is another bridge, I believe. Ours was damaged in the recent rains," James answered.

"I enjoyed the passage you read to us from *The Lady of the Lake* this morning, Aunt," Fiona said. "Perhaps we will see other sights from the poem."

Elspeth smiled, remembering how the lady had droned on imperiously that morning as the group set out. She tugged at her gray bonnet and folded her gloved hands demurely in her lap, hoping her gray gown, green spencer, and plaid shawl were acceptable in this company, as she wanted to please James's family. Certainly her leather boots were well suited to hillwalking, and she was ready for an outing in cool autumn weather. She thought of Charlotte Sinclair, a vision in a pale blue walking dress and long pelisse with matching bonnet. Glancing at James, she was glad that Charlotte was riding in the second coach with Patrick, Sir Philip, and Donal MacArthur. Her grandfather would have scant patience with Charlotte's selfish ways.

As the countryside flew by with MacKimmie in command, Elspeth enjoyed the comfort of the open landau pulled by two sturdy horses. Lady Rankin had complained that a coach and four would be more comfortable until Angus MacKimmie had pointed out the larger vehicle would be a hindrance on Highland roads. "We will be lucky to even come near Loch Katrine in this carriage," he had said. "The ground is verra rocky."

Fiona sat close to James, discussing geology. Elspeth smiled, watching them, grateful to have found a friend in James's twin. Their engagement would be kept secret for a while, even from Grandda and Peggy. She trusted Fiona and Patrick, too, to keep the news to themselves. That they were pleased was enough for now, though she was eager to tell Grandda as soon as James agreed it was time.

"There is Loch Achray," she said, pointing as the coach rolled onward.

Lady Rankin consulted a small guidebook. "It looks scarcely more than a pool. How disappointing."

"It is a small one—a lochan. It is in a beautiful setting." Gold and russet trees, oak and birch, covered the hillsides, with clusters of evergreens.

Fiona consulted a page where she had written some notes for the tour. "I look forward to seeing the impressive Trossach Mountains, said to be the fringe of great Highland fastnesses, wildish and remote, to the north." She looked up. "It is noble and picturesque scenery. No wonder it is so popular, not just because of Sir Walter's poetry, but for its spectacular beauty."

"You must make some sketches of the scenery, dear," Lady Rankin told her. "I would like a visual memoir of what we see today."

"My skill is inadequate to the subject, madam, but I will try."

James looked out the other side of the coach. "Lord Eldin is opening a hotel near Loch Katrine. He called it Auchnashee."

"I know that area," Elspeth said. "Eldin has a good deal of work ahead of him if he thinks to open an establishment there."

"He has the funds for it," Fiona said.

"Does this road go all the way around Loch Katrine?" Lady Rankin asked.

"It ends near the loch," Elspeth said. "After a while, carriages can go no further and we will need to walk. There is a good mountain track and a wide heath."

"Walk! I had no idea the area was so rustic. I thought it was prepared for tourists." Sighing indignantly, Lady Rankin thrust her considerable bosom outward and fanned herself with a little book of poetry.

"We can walk or hire ponies," James suggested. "And there should be boats."

"There is a ferryman who lives in a cottage there. He has a little inn and hires out boats," Elspeth said. "He can take us around. We can have luncheon at the inn, though Mrs. MacKimmie sent baskets of food with us so we can explore on our own."

"I am looking forward to it," James said. Elspeth knew he was eager to hike up part of the mountain slope to look for a cave opening.

Fiona consulted her notes. "Ben Venue is a mountain that towers above the southwestern shore. There is a place called the Goblin's Cave. How intriguing!"

"Goblin's Cave?" James sat forward.

"Sir Walter mentions it in his poem." Lady Rankin thumbed through her well-worn copy of *The Lady of the Lake*. She began to read.

*By many a bard, in Celtic tongue / Has Coir-nan-Uriskin been
    sung:*

*A softer name the Saxons gave / And call'd the grot the Goblin-cave.*

"A grotto? There is one at Struan House," Elspeth said.

"My sister, Lady Struan, fancied herself an expert on fairies,"
Lady Rankin said. "She said the grotto in her garden was modeled
after one called a Goblin Cave."

"I did not know that," James said. "I would like to explore the
original." He exchanged a quick glance with Elspeth.

"Go looking for your little rocks, James," Lady Rankin said. "I
have no taste for hillwalking. A boat on the loch sounds just the
thing. Fiona, come with me. I think we can persuade the others
too. Miss MacArthur?"

"I would like to see the mountain and the cave," Elspeth said.

"Miss MacArthur can come with me," James said. "Perhaps
your grandfather will act as our guide, while Mr. MacKimmie
takes the others around."

"Charlotte will want to go with you too," Lady Rankin said.

"She is hardly dressed for hillwalking," Fiona pointed out.
"She will be safer and more comfortable in the boat."

Elspeth glanced at the sky to see gray clouds rolling overhead
and swirling around the peaks of the Trossachs. The wind was
brisk and cool, the view wide and awe-inspiring. Feeling its
elemental power, she drew a deep breath to take in that strength.

Fiona read aloud from the folded page. "Ben Venue has black
and towering sides with a certain rich gloss to them, and a craggy
dignity housing caves replete with legends. Why would the
mountain appear glossy, James?"

He glanced toward the black mountain with its multiple
peaks. "Deposits of mica, perhaps, or granite and crystal. I am
interested to examine it."

"I will leave that to you and Miss MacArthur as two brave
souls."

"You are no coward," James told his twin, "but luxury of a

boat would allow you to make sketches today."

"For your sake, dear brother," Fiona murmured, "I would be happy to do that."

"Let me read to you about Ellen's Isle, named for the heroine of Sir Walter's poem," Lady Rankin opened her book and began to read aloud again.

Elspeth listened and tried to quell her fears. Soon she would turn twenty-one, a birthday she dreaded. She sighed and glanced at James. He gave her a small, private smile, and she understood the silent message—*love, strength, passion, hope*—as his aunt's voice droned on.

BOTH COACHES DREW to a halt in the yard of the ferryman's house near the rounded foot of the loch. Mr. MacDuff and his wife emerged to greet them, soon serving the group hot tea in a small, pleasant parlor, along with warm oatcakes and rowan jelly. James gazed out the window at Ben Venue and other peaks, anxious to explore.

He gratefully accepted a dose of whisky in his tea, offered by Mr. MacDuff. "The best in the Highlands," the man said. "Made locally. You will not find better!"

James chuckled, expecting that every Highland man would claim his whisky to be the best, and with good reason. He had always found Highland whisky to be superior to the Lowland sort more commonly found in Edinburgh and the Lowlands.

"Who will sail over the water?" Mr. MacDuff asked, and arrangements began.

"Lord Struan will come in the boat with us," Charlotte said.

"Not this time. I am keen to look for rock samples," he said, giving his leather bag a little kick to demonstrate his intention to work.

She scowled. "What about your leg? Can you walk that far without trouble?"

"I do not mind the exercise," he said, while Elspeth and the others looked his way. The others would not have made so direct a reference to his lameness.

"I would be happy to accompany you, Miss Sinclair," Sir Philip said. "Struan can see all from his mountain top, though he will miss a sublime trip over smooth waters."

Patrick came back, having left to hire the boats. "We have two boats, enough for all. Though Struan and Mr. MacArthur are for the mountain."

"My granddaughter will accompany us," Donal said.

Charlotte whirled. "Miss MacArthur is going with Struan?"

"My dear," Fiona said, leaning toward her. "Miss MacArthur is used to Highland terrain, and she naturally would want to accompany her grandfather. You will be far more comfortable on the boat with us. I plan to sketch and be quite lazy as I take in the beautiful views."

"I thought today would be a coach tour," Charlotte complained.

Sir Philip smiled. "Miss Sinclair, allow me to escort." He offered his arm.

Soon they went down to the shore of the loch, where some boarded the boats, and James, Elspeth, and Donal set out on the track to the mountain slopes. The wind was brisk, and clouds glowered over the mountain peak. Donal produced gnarly, sturdy walking sticks, and James took one in lieu of his usual cane. Though his leg often ached in chilly or rainy weather, he had noticed lately that his knee had given him less complaint, perhaps due to the refreshing Highland air.

Patrick turned to James. "We will meet you here in the late afternoon for the return drive. Best of luck with your rock hunting."

"Bring back souvenirs," Philip called. "Diamonds and sapphires!"

James laughed. "A few crystals if we are lucky. Ready?" he asked Elspeth.

"Aye," she said. James heard a tremor in her lightsome voice.

THEY WALKED TOGETHER over heathery moors up into the foothills, then climbed steadily, saying little. Elspeth paused to rest her ankle, relying on the walking stick, and looked out at the magnificent view. The steely surface of the loch stretched below, fringed by heathery moorland with blazing autumn trees against the dark slopes of the mountain. Above towered the mountain peaks, obscured at the top by a thick cloud ring.

James shaded his eyes with a hand. "Mica and schist up there," he said. "That makes the slopes so dark and shiny. There is a good deal of that with shale scree in streaks down the sides. So much schist indicates massive heat early in the mountain's formation. A good sign for my research."

"We are here for more than your research," Elspeth said with a half-laugh.

"I know." Shouldering his leather pack, he walked ahead to catch up to Donal, who stood above them now.

"Why are we here, if not for the lad to find rocks?" Donal called.

"We are looking for the Goblin Cave," Elspeth said.

"Ah, Coire nan Uruiskin," Donal said. "Why do you want to go there?"

"We are looking for fairy treasure, Donal MacArthur."

"Are you! Well then!"

Elspeth looked at James, who seemed to immediately understand her question, for he nodded. "Grandda, we have something to tell you," she said then. "Lord Struan asked me to marry him, and I agreed."

Donal broke into a grin. "Excellent! When are you taking her to Edinburgh?"

"We have not decided on that yet," Elspeth said quickly.

"Elspeth accepted on one condition," James said. "We must find the fairy gold."

"Do you think it is here?" Donal asked. "Do you know what they call it Coire nan Uruiskin? The urisks are small goblin creatures who haunt rocky slopes and caves and cause great mischief. But they can be helpful to humans if they are treated politely."

"What about the Fey?" Elspeth asked.

"The ancient Sidhe are sometimes up here too, so they say. Caves can be portals to their realm in the Otherworld."

"It may be a good place to search for the treasure, Grandda," she said.

"Would their treasure be under their noses in their own parlor?" Donal huffed. "Then it would not be missing. It must be elsewhere."

"Grandda," she said. "Perhaps we should tell Struan why this is so important."

James held up a hand. "First let me tell you what I read in my grandmother's fairy manuscript. She writes of a weaver and his son and their meeting with the fairies. And she tells of the infant girl given into the weaver's care."

"Did she now," Donal said, and did not sound surprised.

Elspeth stared at him. "Tell me."

James explained quickly what he had read, and Elspeth looked at her grandfather, who was listening without comment. "Grandda, that is the story you told me."

"So Lady Struan wrote it in her book," Donal said. "I told her some of it. And it is true, Lord Struan. What do you think of that?"

"I am not sure," James said. "But I trust you. If you say it is so—then I will do my best to believe it."

"Aye, then," Donal said.

"So Elspeth's birthday is coming soon," James said.

"Aye, four days from now," she said.

"I think you will not be happy until you see the twenty-first of October and find yourself still in this realm, aye?" James asked.

"I would feel relieved, that is certain." She shivered and pulled her plaid closer against the chill wind. "Which way is the Goblin Cave?"

"There," Donal said. "But I tell you the treasure is not there."

"I would like to see it," James said. "Even if there is no treasure, there will be something of value for my work." He reached into the leather knapsack and drew out a stone. "We may find more stones like this one."

"The blue stone! You brought it!" Donal reached for it and turned it in the light.

"Keep it," James said. "You found it. Agate of that quality is rare, and finding a deposit of it could be important for the science of Scotland's past."

"To be truthful, I did not find it, exactly," Donal said. "It was given to me by a queen of the Fey years ago. It is a key to their realm."

"To the fairy world?" James asked.

"He tried to tell you at Kilcrennan, do you remember?" Elspeth asked.

"Aye. We were a bit fou, I think," James said.

"I have seen similar stones in this mountain and near Struan House," Donal said.

"Then let us proceed, sir."

As they went up the slope, Elspeth saw that James walked steadily but with the uneven gait common to him. Yet she noticed that he never complained even where the walking was strenuous. Her heart went out to him to see his steadfast courage.

The sky clouded over in a cool mist, and Elspeth felt raindrops on her cheeks. She looked up as they went higher, following a narrow dip between two slopes, a natural path like a tuck in a quilt. A slim runnel of water trickled downward, and ahead she saw a vast piling of rock and scree, tumbled eons ago from the mountain's massive black shoulders.

Now and then, James stopped to pick up rocks and examine them, sometimes dropping small chunks into his satchel, other times setting them back in place reverently. "Limestone with marine fossils are signs of the Old Red Sandstone layer," he said at one point, then later, "there are volcanic traces here." He made notes in a small journal, muttering to himself. "Granite and basalt. Fascinating."

Donal looked at Elspeth. "I do not understand why he loves old rocks." She laughed.

More than once, James picked up small stones and handed them to Elspeth. She gasped at the glitter of perfectly formed crystals, clear and peat-colored.

"Rock crystal and cairngorm," he explained. "For you." She tucked the crystals in her skirt pocket, delighted.

"The Goblin Cave is over here," Donal said, leading them across a slope covered with turf and broken rock, so that they went carefully, offering a helping hand as needed. Overhead, mist gathered and rain spattered their heads.

Cut into a cliff among the widespread scree was a dark, deep opening in a fold of rock. Elspeth went toward it.

"We cannot go inside. It is not safe," Donal said.

"Grandda, we came all this way. We have to go inside."

"The power of the Fey is strong here. We should stay away. But you two have more protection against them than I do."

"Why is that, sir?" James asked.

"Love," Donal said. "That bond guards you, and can break their hold. Though it would be stronger if—well." He stopped, shrugged. "You will think me mad."

"He thinks both of us a little mad already," Elspeth said. "What is it?"

"If you were wed already, and securely bound in love."

Elspeth glanced at James, who looked from one to the other soberly, silently. The rain began in earnest as she reached out to take his hand. "Grandda, come with us. We will search together for the fairy gold together."

"Mr. MacArthur, may I see the agate again?" Taking the rock, James held it up to the light and turned it. Then he held out the stone. "Look here. Do you see the resemblance to the slope and the cave?"

As Elspeth studied it, the shapes and points seemed to form an image. She gasped. "It looks like a miniature of the cave opening! How could that be?"

Donal frowned. "I have held this stone many times and never noticed that."

"Elspeth spotted the cave in your son's painting, and when I compared the agate geode to the picture, I saw the similarities. Perhaps this is the place to look, sir."

"Why would Niall paint this cave in the picture?" Donal was still frowning.

"Perhaps he wanted to leave a clue to lead you to the treasure."

"To break the spell! Oh, Grandda," Elspeth said. "What if James is right?"

"He left us a map? Huh," Donal said. "There is nothing in that cave but rock, and signs of the smugglers who come here now and then. And possibly a fairy portal, so we should stay away."

James shouldered his pack and grasped his walking stick. "I intend to go inside. I promised Elspeth I would search. You two can wait here."

"I am coming with you," Elspeth insisted.

"If there is any danger here," he said, "you should stay with your grandfather."

Elspeth grabbed his coat sleeve. "I am coming with you!"

"Aye then, go," Donal said. "Take the stone. I will wait here." He sat on a boulder, leaned his back against the cliffside, and tugged his flat bonnet low as if to sleep.

Elspeth could not bear to leave him, but knew he would not come inside. "Go back down, Grandda," she said. "Do not wait here alone. We will be fine. We will meet you at the ferryman's house."

"True, the *Daoine Sìth* might find me here. But you could be in danger too."

"I am safe with James. Go on." She hugged him and stepped back.

"Eilidh," Donal said. "You must guard yourself."

Surprised, she turned. Her grandfather rarely used her Gaelic name. "How so?"

"You should have married the man already. He is a good man, and love will protect you and lessen their hold. If only you had married him before this."

"That will come soon enough," she replied quietly.

Donal stood, took up his walking stick. "Marry him now, lass," he said. "Take his hands in yours and wed him now, here, in the old way, before you enter that cave. With or without a witness, you can make a marriage here and now. It is a custom in Scotland that is old and respected."

She stared at James, then at her grandfather. "We would want a wedding where all can celebrate with us."

"Do that later. Give him your forever pledge and forge your bond before you go in that place."

The wind whipped hard and cold at her back. "That is not necessary. But thank you. Go down the slope, Grandda. I am more concerned about you than me. We will meet you at the inn by the loch."

Donal looked at James. "You take care of her. You marry her. See to it."

"I will," James said quietly.

Elspeth hugged her grandfather and turned to go with James as they proceeded up the slope toward the cave entrance in the cliff. Her grandfather's odd insistence seemed to haunt her, and she glanced back to see the old man descending carefully.

Thunder grumbled overhead as they approached the cave opening, which loomed and looked foreboding. She stood listening to growls of thunder, seized with quick fear.

"James," she said. He knelt to examine some rocks and waved, unbothered.

She paused to wait, thoughts racing. When James came back, he pointed.

"Much of this is limestone with excellent patches of granite," he said. "There are traces of chalcedony and obsidian, with mica and quartz as well. Granite is a composite rock," he went on, "and the mix here indicates there could be agate here too."

"That's wonderful," she said. Her heart was beating strangely fast.

"There could be real geological significance in that cave. The limestone layer over a layer of granite hints at a marine era a long time ago. Well, I will not bore you, my lass. I am glad your grandfather agreed to go back down. It is better for him."

"Aye, there is no need for him to wait alone where he feels uneasy. He said that you and I would only be safe if—" She hesitated, watching him.

About to use his magnifying lens on a rock, he looked at her. "If we marry before we go inside there? I heard him."

"What do you think?"

"I think it is your decision, my dear lass. Whatever you want, I will do."

# Chapter Twenty-One

"I<sub></sub>F WE MARRY," she said, "we should do it now. Here. Grandda thought it best."

James set down the loupe and the hammer, nodding, frowning. He took her hand to pull her up to stand on a rock with him. "Marry now? Would you?"

She nodded. "I think so. Grandda said that bond will protect us inside the cave."

"I see." He nodded.

Her eyes flashed silver as they met his. "You think it a silly notion."

"I rather like the idea." He felt bewildered, charmed, excited all at once. Her innocent quality often disarmed him, and her secrets were intriguing. "I am determined to find the fairy treasure before I win the hand of my lady love, but if she will agree first, I am content, and still determined."

"I am content too. I know I have resisted, but if this is a worthy precaution, and we are agreed, we could do a handfasting."

He smiled. "You are a fickle and adorable creature, Elspeth MacArthur."

"That alone might prove the fairy blood in me." She smiled too. "I will pledge with you here and now, if you want. But I am sure you find this capricious nonsense."

"Not at all," he said. "Not anymore."

She nodded, eyes wide, earnest. "If we declare our commitment in this ancient spot, in the old Highland way, it would feel perfect. I think it is very much what I want."

An unexpected and powerful emotion seized him—love, he realized, the very feeling he had avoided for so long. Now he felt rinsed through, cleansed and strengthened and renewed by a love that felt full and deep and real, no matter how long or short a time it had been in him. He wanted to let go of his reserve and let her see that he believed in her, trusted her. Committing to marriage would be a long step on that path.

He took her shoulders, drew her close. "I am for it, lass. I love you."

"And I you, so very much." She lifted her face to his. "And so?"

"This seems the perfect spot for it."

"If we say vows in this powerful place, it is forever," she said.

He nodded. "Clergy and court can be done later."

"James, what if later, you want to live in the south while I want to be in the Highlands? We have not settled that."

"We will keep a house here and a house there, and wherever else you like. And the home of your heart will be in these hills, aye? Good, then. How do we do this thing?"

His heart hammered fast, though he did not want to show that to her. It was not uncertainty, but realization of the risk, the challenge of this. He was not an impulsive soul, but something within insisted that this was utterly right to do now, and quickly.

"We hold hands and say a vow of our own making. And we need—let me see." She looked about. "Over here!"

Tugging on his hand, she led him toward a narrow stream of water that cut down over the rock from the mountaintop. "By the water that carries rain and melted snow from the highest to the lowest point, so it joins mountain, sky, and earth. Step to that side and I shall stand on this side, so it flows eternally between us."

He stepped across the narrow runnel to face her and took her hands in his. He paused to slowly draw her gloves off, taking them again in his bare hands. He tucked her gloves into his pocket, keeping them safe.

She crossed her forearms, and he did as well, holding hands again. "This forms a love knot in a handfasting. A union forged with a knot and entwined with a blessing will last forever."

"You know a good deal about this."

"My friend Margaret was married in a handfasting. I learned what makes such ceremonies special and important. Now, the vows." She drew a breath, closed her eyes. "Say what is in your heart," she whispered. "Let the words come."

James closed his eyes. Whether it was the place, the air, the spontaneity of what they did here, a feeling swelled within him, heart and soul. Its gathering force filled him with humility and love. With solid earth and rock beneath him and the quiet power of water and the mountain and the infinite symbol of their crossed arms, he felt moved, reverent. And then it came to him.

"I, James Arthur MacCarran, take you, Elspeth—"

"*Eilidh*," she whispered. "My birth name."

"*Ay-lesh*," he repeated softly, gazing at her through misting rain. "Beautiful lass. I, James Arthur MacCarran, pledge my troth and my heart to you, Eilidh MacArthur. I bless the day we met, and I take you as my wife and my lover, in body and soul, forever and a day."

"I, Eilidh MacArthur," she murmured, "pledge my troth and heart to you, James Arthur MacCarran. I bless the day we met, I bless your strength and your kindness. And I take you as my husband and my lover, body and soul, forever and a day."

"Let none put this asunder," he murmured.

Leaning over the narrow water, he unclasped his arms and drew her toward him to kiss her. Water burbled between and beneath, soft rain fell upon them, and his heart thumped with the promise he had made. *Forever.* It was as solid as the rock beneath him.

She lifted on her toes and leaned to meet him, then gently drew back. James stepped over the water and took her into his arms.

"Lady Struan," he said. "We will be safe inside the cave and anywhere we go."

"Safe always. Lady Struan?"

"That is who you are now. Though we should make it completely legal."

"Oh, we will. Come, let us get on with it." She tugged at his hand.

"Get on with what, madam?" He chuckled.

"Not that," she said, laughing. "Later for that. The cave and the search."

"We will find gold if it is here."

"We have no choice," she said, wrapping her hand in the crook of his arm. "We have to save Donal MacArthur."


Elspeth shivered in the cool darkness of the cave. She took James's hand, gripping it tightly. Husband, she thought, feeling as if this were a dream and she would wake any moment to find life ordinary again.

The cave itself looked ordinary enough, irregularly shaped, not large, with rough arched walls and deep shadows. At the back she saw a second narrow opening.

No fairy halls glimmering with gold, no tall, ethereal fey creatures awaiting them. She breathed out in relief, not certain what she might find.

James reached out to brush his hand over part of the rock wall. "Metamorphic dolomitic limestone," he said. "Very large limestone deposits," he explained, "often contain caves and caverns, as if bubbles or pockets of air formed as the stone cooled."

"I see," she said, a little bemused by his focus. They walked deeper into it.

Elspeth waited, chilled and wary, while he moved around to examine the textures in the rock. He glanced back. "What is it?"

She wrapped her arms around herself with a recurring worry.

"I hope there are no others here."

"We are safe. Did we not ensure that just minutes ago?" He came back to take her in his arms and kiss her. "Do you want to wait here while I look around?"

She shook her head. "I want to stay with you." She took his hand as they walked on. At the back, he ducked his head, too tall for the ceiling's downward slope, and then peered ahead.

"There are at least two chambers here," he said. "I see a small inner cave, and it looks as if this outer cave has been used recently." He gestured toward a niche in the side wall. "There is an iron ring over there, do you see? And a dip in the stone has been used for a trough. Not fairy riders, my love," he said. "Smugglers."

"Ah." She half-laughed at her nervousness. "A fair amount of smuggling goes on in this region. They must come up here to stash their goods and hide from excise men and sheriffs. Our MacGregor cousin does indulge in the fair trade."

"Your smuggling kinsmen will be snug in their homes on this dreary day. Even if they come about at night, it is not a concern now." He went toward the inner chamber to peer into it, and Elspeth followed.

She was surprised, looking past him, to see shadowed objects—wooden boxes, blankets, a flat rock ledge holding bottles, bowls, and half-melted candles.

"Smugglers indeed, making themselves comfortable here," James said. "It is good to see a trace of human presence. That alone might chase the fairies away. And I would rather meet a smuggler than a vengeful member of the Fey."

Laughing softly, Elspeth stepped into the smaller cave, curiosity heightened. The narrow space was just tall enough for James to stand upright as he joined her.

"These wooden crates are empty," he said, examining them. Finding a tinderbox on the rock shelf, he flashed steel to flint to spark a little flame on a sliver of wood. Then he lit one of the candles and held it high, looking around.

Elspeth saw that the little cave was nest-like with blankets and notes of comfort that included a whisky jug and a cloth sack that held oats.

"The rock walls here are different than the outer cave," James said. "Those are mostly limestone. This one has more granite composition. Interesting."

"Does that mean the layers are of different ages? This cave is lower than the other. Would the granite layer have formed first?"

"Quicker than my students, I vow. I did not think you listened to my ramblings."

"I always listen to you. And I am curious about the rocks here. Oh, it is cold and damp!" She rubbed her arms.

"The whisky and blankets will help, if you like. What's in that wee chest over there? Fairy treasure?"

Seeing a small wooden chest in a corner, she knelt to open it. "Nothing so special. Just folded plaids and shirts."

"If there was any treasure here, the smugglers would have found it by now."

"You still do not believe this," she said.

"Some. But whatever can be explained rationally is good too. Though fairy treasure makes a far better legend than smugglers mucking about in a cave."

She shivered again and removed her bonnet, for its curvature obscured her vision in the dark little cave. As she set it down her hair slid free of its pins. When James picked up one of the plaid blankets and draped it around her shoulders, she smiled her thanks and sighed, leaning into his embrace as he pressed his cheek against her head.

*Married and in love.* She had declared it—but was it enough to ward off the Fey?

Holding the candle, James went to the shadows at the back of the sloping cave. "There is another space back here," he said, and ducked, then disappeared into the darkness, taking the glowing candlelight with him.

Elspeth hurried to follow, stooping to look. Her shivers were not entirely from cold, for the feeling of dread remained. Where he went, she would go too.

The cleft in the rock was narrow, but she slid through easily, following the light of the candle James held aloft.

"What is this?" She looked around. The space was like a narrow tunnel that dissolved into blackness beyond. She could hear the faint drip of water.

"A natural channel in the rock." James moved cautiously ahead, following the curving walls, and she followed slowly. As he ran his hands along the rock to explore its character, she noticed pools of shadow and deep recesses ahead.

He picked up a loose rock and tapped on the rock walls. The sound echoed, and something broke away. He extended his hand to show her a chunk of colored stone.

"What is that?"

He moved it into the candlelight and she saw a green glow. "Agate. Not your blue sort, but good agate nonetheless. An excellent find. I must come back up here to make detailed notes and get more samples. Caves and passages like this are sometimes clustered together, so there could be much to explore. I doubt the smugglers have been back here, for the rock looks undisturbed."

"It is a good place to hide something, though."

"Aye, but so far I wonder if we would find any treasure in here."

Elspeth sighed. "You may be right."

He put an arm around her shoulders. "It was worth coming in here. We are handfasted, my love. There is that."

"Worth more than agates and granite layers," she said with a small laugh.

"I know you are disappointed that we are not finding what you hoped for."

"A bit," she confessed. Her dread over her upcoming birthday and the possible trouble it might bring was not alleviated. "Well. Should we go back now?"

"But we are so nicely alone here." He pulled her closer,

skimming his hands downward, raising delicious shivers in her. Resting her hands on his chest, she felt a wonderful, tender pulsing inside as her heartbeat quickened.

"Very alone here," she said. "No treasure. No smugglers. No Lowland guests."

"And no fairies but the beautiful one in my arms," he whispered. She laughed quietly, pressing into his arms as he kissed her, deep and lingering.

He took her hand and led her back toward the small cave, and took one of the plaids stored there, spreading it on the floor, bringing her down to join him. He set the flaming candle on the rock ledge, its low light like a flow of gold.

As he knelt with her and took her full into his arms, she drew in a breath as he kissed her, his hands slipping over her jacket, the buttons there. She undid them quickly as he kissed her again, the chill air making her shiver. But his kiss warmed, and his touch teased the neckline of her gown where her lace-edged shift peeked. James traced his fingers over her collarbones and brushed lower.

Spreading a hand over his chest, she felt his heartbeat beneath her fingers, fast as thunder. Deep in his embrace, lost in rich kisses and caresses, she sighed as he nuzzled his lips over her cheek, her ear. She felt sultry, warmed, filling with heat.

"Did you know," she whispered, "that handfasting is legal in Scotland by the old laws, but no more binding than an engagement unless it is consummated?"

"I did not. We had best make this unquestionably legal," he said.

"Aye," she agreed as he took her lips again. She moaned, arched against him.

"Odd," he said. "It is as if time has slowed inside here, do you feel it?"

"I do feel that." She closed her eyes, breathed in the odd sense of magic, desire, a leisurely stretching of time, as if her dread had lifted and she had no need to leave the place now. With him, she could trust that all was well. Once she set foot outside again, it might return, but she would be changed. She was changing, beginning to expand beyond the girl she had been, becoming a woman with a stronger sense of power, of purpose.

He kissed her again and her thoughts vanished like shadows before light. She bent her head back, accepting, sighing, feeling good and safe, loved and cherished. Time dissolved and passion warmed the atmosphere.

As he kissed her again, lips tracing downward, she felt a tenderness burgeon in her, limbs gone buttery as she moaned and sank with him to the nest of blankets. As they stretched out together, as he pressed his muscled body against hers, hard to soft, yield to thrust, she knew he felt urgent with passion, as she did.

When he traced his fingers over her throat and upper chest, her heart leaped. She arched to ask for more, savoring the supple touch of fingertips that grazed over her skin, making her breath catch, heart pound. Where his hands moved, she breathed, moaned, encouraged him to more. His hands were compelling, gentle, raising desire in her like lightning, like magic. She pressed against him, her ache for him matching his hunger, and the surge of love that filled her started tears in her eyes.

She rounded hands over his shoulders, his back, sliding under his shirt, letting her hands, her lips, her body tell him what she felt and what she wanted. He worked at small buttons and rucked up fabric and she helped, she invited, she deeply wanted the exquisite feeling of his touch. Then he kissed her, rolling with her in the piled plaids.

"This is right," she whispered. "This was meant to be."

"Love," he said, and kissed her again, flaring his big hands over her hips, bringing her to him as she shifted, opened for him, arched. Circling her arms around his shoulders, she stretched back, then surged with him as he delved. A kind of honey and fire ran all through her as she went into a cadence with him, sweet and hard, body and soul, time vanishing as the promise they made quickened.

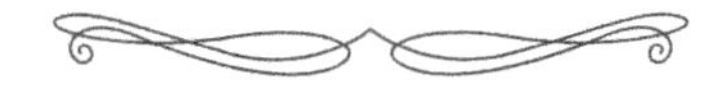

# Chapter Twenty-Two

"WE DIDN'T FIND a legendary treasure, but there is some significant geological evidence worth studying," James said later, extending a hand to help Elspeth enter the larger, outermost cave. "So we accomplished something."

"There was a wedding too," she reminded him with a laugh.

"Well worth the journey, my dear." He settled his arm around her and hefted the leather satchel on his shoulder. Even if the Goblin Cave only held signs of smugglers and interesting rock formations, he was deeply grateful they had come. And he planned to return as soon as he could, intrigued by what he could discover for his research.

"We should search the smuggler's things again before we leave," Elspeth said. "They might have found something that they hid away." She took the blue agate from her pocket to turn it in the low light. "Why would my father leave clues that led us to this cave if there is nothing here to help us?"

"We found a cache of rare gems again. But no more talk of geology," he said, holding up his hands as his bride slid him a glance. "And it is a good thought to take another look before we leave."

"Your siblings and the rest will worry if we do not meet them soon. At least we have some crystals and agates to show them," she added. "And we married ourselves." He looked at her quickly. "Should we tell them?"

"Perhaps not yet. Let's keep it to ourselves for now, and just tell Grandda."

James nodded agreement. He wanted her to be happy, wanted to see her smile like sunlight, but he was not sure yet what she most wanted. The rare blue agate was a puzzle to him, its map-like formation mirroring this cave. When next he came here, he intended to search for a pocket containing similar agate. He had a feeling it had originated here.

"I need to sit down and record some information before we go. Do you want to take a few moments to look in the smaller cave, Lady Struan? I can work here."

She nodded, looking pleased, and hurried to duck through the lower entrance. Sitting on a wide ledge, he rummaged for notebook and pencil and began to jot down his thoughts while Elspeth knelt to look at the wooden crates.

*Trap rock lies under all,* he wrote. *Interior walls primarily limestone with abundant evidence of shell fossils.* He glanced up to see Elspeth moving just on the other side of the secondary entrance.

"I should bring my sister here to examine the fossils," he called. "She is quite knowledgeable about such things. As long as no smugglers are about, it seems safe."

"Even the fairies are not here," she called back. "I am a bit disappointed."

He smiled and continued to scribble his observations. *There are traces of granite composite with rock quartz, feldspar, mica, basalt, flecks of crystal formations throughout. Great heat once occurred beneath the limestone layers...*

Elspeth stooped to come back, then turned. "Oh! I left my bonnet." She slipped back into the smaller chamber while James made a few more notes.

Putting his things in the satchel, he walked to the back to fetch Elspeth, bending the enter the smaller, more intimate space. At first he did not see her—then realized she was on her hands and knees in a dark corner.

"Did you find something?" he asked.

"Behind these crates I found some rocks hiding an opening to another wee cave!"

He joined her, dropping to his knees. Elspeth was attempting to remove some rocks that blocked a cleft in the wall. They were the size of bread loaves and puddings, easy enough to move.

"Here, let me," he said. "These ought to be limestone and shale," he noticed, shifting them aside. "But these look like mica, schist, and iron ore. Odd. This is not a natural rockfall. These were put here deliberately. Perhaps they hid their finest whisky or some French gold."

"Gold?" Elspeth looked up.

"Not fairy treasure. New-minted coin that smugglers sometimes carry. What in thunderation is that?" He peered into the crevice. "Where is the candle we had before?"

"We burned it through, husband," she said with a laugh.

"Lord, we did. There's an oil lamp tucked on that ledge over there. Light that, if you will, love." She hastened to do that, returning with the glowing lantern, holding the light high as James moved more rocks.

"Hold the lamp just there." He crouched on his knees to peer into the opening, which was wider than he expected. Though not high, it was accessible on all fours.

Shining the light ahead of him, he moved into the gap, inching through the rocky threshold. Then, as if the earth gave way beneath him, he nearly fell into blackness down a steep slope even as he managed to keep hold of the lantern.

Elspeth came through behind him, then gasped as she too tumbled downward. Sliding over rough, toothy stone, James reached a level surface and came to his feet. As Elspeth fell against him, he steadied her, holding the lantern high.

"What is this place?" she asked low, her voice echoing.

"A pocket cave. Larger than I thought." She rose beside him, brushing stone dust from her skirts. "My God," he said. "Look at that."

The walls were covered in prisms and points of sparkling

color. All around, studded in the curving walls and ceiling, crystals and gems glittered in the lamplight like rainbows and stars.

James walked carefully to one wall to run his hand along its glimmering curvature, sharp with crystal points. Taking the lantern from him, Elspeth held it high to look around with him.

"So many stones, so many colors," she breathed. "Incredible."

"Clear crystal, rose quartz—this yellow is citrine," he said in a hushed voice as he ran his hand over the walls. "Blue sodalite, red jasper—over here, green aventurine." A tiny crystal rod snapped off in his hand, whitish crystal. He handed to her. "And a beautiful cluster of amethyst crystals."

With an easy snap, a purple wand came away in his hand. That, too, he gave her.

"All these in one place?" she asked. "How can that be?"

"They are various forms of crystals created in bubbles in the earth, growing in the rock bed over eons. Here is beryl...aquamarine..." He named them as he found them, a range of colors and shapes gleaming and sparkling in the lantern light. "There could be emeralds, rubies, sapphires, veins of gold here too, if it were to be mined."

"But it is too beautiful to mine it or disturb it."

"I agree, though it should be examined for science. Just astonishing to find so many in such profusion, though theoretically it is possible." He moved along. "Watch the sharp points. The break off easily. We should not break or crush them if we can avoid it."

"They are scattered on the floor already broken away," she said, bending to pluck up more pretty stones. "It is like a jewel box."

"The whole cave gleams like a royal ransom."

"Like a treasure chest," she said. "James, could this be—"

"It could indeed. Perhaps it was never a treasure chest that was lost, but a chamber, a pocket cave filled with natural gems."

"Grandda said there is a portal to the Otherworld somewhere in these mountains, so if that is true, this would not be lost to them. I do not understand."

"This can be explained without fairies, love. It is an exciting geological discovery. And we might find some perfect gems for your wedding ring." He opened his hand to show her a few gleaming stones—amethyst, aquamarine, rose quartz.

She gasped at their delicate beauty, then looked up. "But this place was hidden deliberately so that no one could find it. I happened to see the rocks there, stacked like a cairn, hiding the entrance."

He frowned as something occurred to him. He walked up the ramp a little way to peer at the stack of rocks they had removed. Then he returned, holding one of the smaller rocks that had been shifted. "Iron," he said, holding it out. "A MacArthur ancestor of yours stole the treasure and hid it away, is it so?"

Elspeth nodded. "According to the legend, the Fey have been angry ever since. But it must have been here all along, under their very noses."

"Iron and iron ore were mixed in that cairn. I read something about it in my grandmother's manuscript." He hefted the rock thoughtfully. "Perhaps that MacArthur ancestor of yours was very deliberate indeed, long ago."

"Oh!" She stared up at him. "Fairies cannot cross over cold iron!"

"So they say. Iron in its natural form, or cold-forged iron, not exposed to heat, are thought to block the power of the Fey. This chunk is natural cold iron." He hefted it.

"Then they would not be able to come in here," she said.

"Even more, it might be rendered invisible to them until the iron was removed."

"Then it was not a treasure they lost. It was access they lost. It vanished, and they could not find it or enter it. And we found it!"

"If this fairy nonsense has any merit. Though anything is possible once we start believing about fairies. Or marrying them," he added.

"I am so glad you did." She came to him, wrapping her arm around him in a hug. He bent his head to hers, held her.

"Well, to return this treasure to the Fey and free you and your grandfather from their wicked spells," he drawled, "we had best move that iron away from the opening."

A WHILE LATER, James wiped the back of his forearm along his brow and stood back to survey their work. The entrance to the sparkling pocket mine was cleared now, and he had moved the smuggler's goods to the opposite wall. Then he had carried the iron-bearing stones outside the cave to roll them down the mountainside away from the cave.

Satisfied, he stood in the smaller chamber for a final look and went into the outer chamber where Elspeth stood by the entrance, looking out. The mist had cleared and twilight gathered in purples and pinks, reminding him of amethyst and rose quartz.

"We had best make our way back or they will come searching for us," he said.

She sighed and nodded. "I hope we have fulfilled the old bargain."

"If that cave is indeed the missing treasure, it is available again. And you fell in love," he reminded her. "That will protect you from harm—and so will I, my lass."

"And so be it." She turned into his embrace. "It is done."

"Let the proof of it be our long, happy marriage."

"And your belief in fairies," she said, muffled against his coat.

He chuckled as she stepped away to gather her things, and he gazed out at the twilight sky, marveling at the colors revealed as the mist receded. "Come ahead, love." He turned. "Elspeth?"

She was not there. Going to the inner cave, he did not see her there either. "Elspeth!" His voice echoed against the walls.

*Eilidh . . .* He heard it in the still air, an echo and yet not. *Eilidh . . .*

WHEN SHE HAD stepped into the inner chamber to fetch her

shawl, they stood there, as if the wall had opened. Three watched her, a man and two women, slim and tall and beautiful. She realized they stood by the entrance to the pocket mine, its opening taller and wider than before.

They beckoned, all three. Despite the natural darkness in the cave, their eyes shone like jewels. She felt drawn forward. When they moved back into the gem pocket, she followed.

Vaguely she realized she was not walking down a ramp of rock, but passing through a depth of stone, following them like a wraith.

*You can do this because you have fairy blood,* said the blonde woman. Her voice was soft, not to the ear, but as if inside her head.

*Who are you?* She thought the words, and they heard her, nodding.

*We three are your kin,* they said in unison.

A chill went through her. Pausing, she summoned calm and strength. They stood together in the jeweled cavern, the ceiling and walls larger now, the jeweled brilliance more expansive.

The flaxen-haired woman was beautiful, though her angled eyes and chin had a harshness. Her eyes were deep violet. The man was tall, handsome, dark-haired, oddly familiar. The other woman was small, delicate, with long ebony hair and eyes sheened like pale crystals.

*Eilidh,* the man said. Then she knew. "Niall?" she asked. Her pounding heart reminded her that she was flesh and blood. "Father?"

"Daughter." He reached out, and his hand was warm when she took it. He was flesh and blood, too, after all. "This is your mother, Riona."

The small dark-haired woman stretched out both hands, her crystalline eyes filled with tears. Then Elspeth was enfolded in an embrace that felt loving, comforting. She had never felt a mother's arms around her, and her eyes filled with tears too.

Curiously, she felt relief, wonder, and perfect ease in their company. She stepped back, trembling. "Mother," she said, a word she had never used for anyone in her life. "Mother. And Father."

They smiled, the one handsome, still a young man, for he had never aged. The other was as beautiful as a delicate jewel. "This is our queen," Niall said of the pale-haired lady. "Queen of the Fey in this region. There are many such rulers, and this part of the land is under her thrall."

"Eilidh." She held out a long, slim hand, milky pale, shining rings on her fingers. Her long hair was like spun gold and her creamy white gown, sewn with glittering threads, seemed to glow. She dazzled with an inner luminosity.

Elspeth stared, entranced, then dropped in a curtsey. "Am I... Have you taken me away?" she asked, straightening.

"We lured you here and we will take you farther," Niall said.

"I cannot go with you." Elspeth stepped backward.

Her fairy mother lifted her hands. "Stay with us, dearest."

"I cannot not. I am married. I will stay with my husband. Our souls are joined now. I love him. He loves me."

Her voice sounded odd, and all seemed strange, as if she were dreaming, and yet not. And she knew the risk of refusal. "I will not go with you."

"Eilidh," her father said, reaching out.

"Elspeth! Where are you?" At the sound of James's voice, she turned.


"Elspeth!" James called again. He had looked in both caves, had stepped outside, and returned, still looking. "Where are you?"

Going back into the smaller cave, he dropped to his knees to peer into the newly discovered pocket mine. It was utterly dark and silent inside. Concerned that she might have ventured in and fallen down the slope, he leaned into the. "Elspeth!"

After a moment, he heard her voice, sounding strange and faraway. *James! Here! I am in here!*

Puzzled, he began to crawl through restrictive opening, and

heard her voice again, soft, somewhere ahead of him. He called her name once more. Her answer seemed to come from within the little gem-filled cave. Making his way down the ramp, he stood in the semi-darkness. Then a light flared, an odd glow that came from above and made the walls shimmer and flash with color.

Elspeth stood there with three people who were strangely clothed, as if they were in some theatre play. Their eyes caught his attention, great, large, luminous eyes in narrow faces, gleaming like jewels. As Elspeth looked at him, her eyes took on that silvery sheen he had sometimes seen there.

"My God," he breathed, moving toward her—why did the room seem so large now, he wondered. "What is this?" He held out an arm and she went to him, tucked against his side, her arm on his back.

"Hush," she whispered.

He stared at the three standing there so calm and eerie. "Who—"

"This is—the queen. And here are Niall MacArthur—and my mother, Riona."

Astonished, frankly stunned, James wondered if he had fallen asleep, or had hit his head, or had taken too much whisky without recalling it. Niall moved forward and held out a hand. Tentatively, James grasped it, feeling a strong, firm, very human hand. But the man, handsome and fit, had an unearthly light in his gray eyes.

The small dark-haired woman came forward and extended her hand next. Her fingers were slim, cool. James suddenly realized he was holding a fairy's delicate hand.

Surely he had fallen and broken his head. This could not be real.

"Elspeth," he said. "Come with me. Our friends will be looking for us. Donal MacArthur will be looking for us," he added, and glanced at Niall.

"We will see Donal soon," the man said. "Seven years are

nearly up again."

"But the fairy spell is undone," Elspeth said. "We found your treasure. This very cave. And—I love this man," she said, holding tight to James. "You told Donal yourself that only love has magic strong enough to break a fairy spell." She faced them, lifted her chin. James gazed down at her, proud, adoring, waiting for her to speak.

"This is James, Lord Struan," she said. "I have married him for love. You have no hold over me or him or his lands any longer—if you ever had hold."

"She speaks true," the queen said then. "We cannot take her with us now. Love will pull her back. She has discovered it. But we will call Donal back to us again, and he may stay."

"He can decide to stay with us," Elspeth said. "He has that right now that you have the treasure. It was your bargain with him. It must be honored."

"Again she speaks truly." Niall had a compelling voice and a regal and ageless beauty. James could see a resemblance to Donal in features and sheer pride. "Eilidh, we owe you a great deal for finding the way back to our treasure room."

"Once again we are free to enter this place," the queen said. "Long ago the Fey mined the riches and magic of the earth. But we could no longer see it after the treachery of a thief of old."

"Thank you," Riona said.

"Of course," James said, feeling a wave of absurdity. Logic told him this could not be real, yet he was seeing them, hearing them, strongly aware of their power and presence just an arm's length away.

He reached out to touch Niall MacArthur's shoulder with a finger, pushing. He felt muscle flex, saw the man move.

Niall smiled. "I am human. Magic keeps me here."

"How is it I can see you?" James asked.

Niall smiled gently, sadly, and gathered his fairy-wife under his arm, much as James held Elspeth safe and close. "When you opened your mind to allow the impossible, all things, including our magic, became possible."

"James MacCarran may have fairy blood," the queen said then. She was a shining, lithe, gorgeous creature.

"It has long been said in my family. But it is just a legend."

"Legends are born of truth. Your fairy blood allows you to see us today."

Again he wondered if he had inadvertently sipped some wild Highland brew that day. But he had not. He had to accept that this was happening before him.

"Take my hands." The queen reached out. "Do not be afraid."

"We do not want to go into your land," Elspeth said quickly.

"Briefly. Let us show you something," Niall said. "I give you my word, daughter. No harm will come to either of you. We will bring you over and back again. I vow it."

"A moment there is a day here," James said, remembering his grandmother's writings. "A day can be a month. A year."

"Only if we cast a glamourie over you. Only if you eat or drink in our world," the queen said. "Only if you look back as you walk away."

"Come see what few have ever seen." Niall beckoned.

Frowning, James felt the queen's outstretched hand meet his, cool and soft. Beside him, he kept his arm, tight and protective, around Elspeth.

Riona reached out, and Elspeth touched her small, lovely hand.

The air went to mist and light, and James felt himself flowing forward as if on water. Then a glittering, gem-studded wall of solid rock turned to gray mist and he was through.

Awestruck, he saw rock walls of golden stone in the shape of arches and vaulted ceilings, stretching into a long corridor. Walking with Elspeth, holding her hand tightly, he followed the three. As he moved, he looked all around at a wonderland of subterranean passages, lit as if from within, tunneling into the heart of the earth.

And he realized then that he was walking easily without a cane or a limp.

Moments later, the queen slipped away, lifting a hand in farewell. Keeping Elspeth's hand in his, James followed Niall and his fairy wife along the hewn corridor toward a blaze of light. He heard a carillon of laughter, the strumming of harps, a steady drumbeat, voices raised in song, the skirl of pipes.

Niall turned. "Do not cross any threshold here. Follow only us. You will see food and drink, but do not partake. Speak to no one but us."

Chambers like cells and bubbles in the stone lined the corridor. James and Elspeth walked steadily past, following her parents. The rooms gleamed with light and crystal, gorgeous fabrics, polished furnishings. Though he heard voices, he saw few people, and those were either translucent or shadowy.

Tables along the hallway held dishes of fruits, cakes, breads, cheese. Wine trickled from silver fountains into crystal goblets. James felt intensely thirsty, desperately hungry. Wanting to pluck grapes from a golden bowl or take up a goblet, he moved on.

The tunnel split into three paths that channeled through the heart of the stone. To the right, he saw a lofty room filled with light, music, ghostly laughter. To the left, the rock walls flickered as if from fire, and he heard the sound of a hammer upon metal, as if from a forge. The center pathway was dim, dull. Niall led them that way.

The tunnel walls flickered with flash-fire colors that traced along veins of gold and silver, ruby and emerald. He touched the wall, his fingers coated with sparkling dust.

"Do not," Niall said. They walked on.

Now the floor sloped upward and they climbed its ramp. His leg, even after the climb up the mountain to the cave, did not hurt at all. He walked with more stability and ease than he had in the seven years since his injury.

He gathered Elspeth close again, and she braced her arm about his waist as they walked up the stone slope. Ahead, he saw sunlight, a cave opening, trees and sky.

Niall stopped near the top of the incline. "Here we will leave you. Go back to your world. We have no hold over you now. And we are in your debt."

"Father," Elspeth began, and threw herself into his arms. Then she turned to her mother, their delicate faces and shining dark hair so much alike. James swallowed hard, watching, aware that she might never see them again. She drew back, tears on her cheeks. Niall clasped James's hand. "Take care of her. She is precious to us."

"I will."

"She will bring much joy to your family. Riches and happiness will bless your family. We will see to that, in gratitude." Niall sighed, set his hand on his daughter's shoulder. "Eilidh, you were born to be with this man, not with us."

"Did you know that?"

"I see it now. Riona knew from the moment you were born that your destiny was tied to Lord Struan and his lands. You will have a family, responsibilities, joy."

"Grandda always said you would take me into your world one day."

"If you never found love," he replied. "But you two found each other."

"But the night we saw you riding through during the storm—what of that?"

"We saw that night that you had found your destined love, even if you did not know it. We could not take you. We had to wait, and hope the treasure would be found instead. I always wanted you free of that spell. And your Lord Struan is too firmly bound to the earth and this life. He would never have let you go."

James smiled. "I would have gone after her wherever she went."

"You would, I know." Niall smiled at Elspeth then. "Your grandfather loves you dearly and has done his best to protect you. He only knew we might take you. He wanted to send you away, but we changed our minds when we saw you had found this man."

"Before we go," James said, still feeling the strangeness of this interlude, and feeling dreamlike, as if it was real and not real. "Do you remember my grandmother? Your painting was precious to her."

"She was kind and dear," Niall replied. "We met before I went over to the Fey. She was so interested in the local legends, and I told her what I knew. We spoke of the future—what could happen if her grandson ever met a daughter of the Fey. Lady Struan would be very pleased that our plan turned out so well."

"Plan?" Elspeth asked.

Niall glanced at Riona. "Lady Struan told me her grandson James was not happy, that he would not allow himself happiness. That he felt responsible for a cousin's death."

Straightening his shoulders, James realized that his grand-mother had known more about him than he had realized. "She knew that?"

"She was concerned you might never wed, never let yourself love, never expand her family. Your siblings as well—she had a great desire to renew the fairy blood in the MacCarran line through her grandchildren. But she had to ensure that there would be great-grandchildren someday, and that meant making sure you and the others found the right matches."

"So she put that in her will?"

"She did. She wanted you and your siblings to have lives that changed for the better, that brought magic back to your line. Even after I had gone over to the Fey to be with Riona, I sometimes saw Lady Struan in the hills. And she saw me. Fairy blood," he said, "showed itself in her."

"I am not surprised," James said.

"She wanted to bring happiness to her family, and I wanted my daughter to find happiness too—either in her life, or in this realm if need be. Your mother and I have watched you grow from afar," Niall added, looking at Elspeth. James saw the sheen of tears in her eyes again, and he pulled her close.

"So you put your heads together, you and my grandmother," he said. "Have you made plans for sister and brothers too?"

"That is not for me to say. But I know Lady Struan wanted all of you to find something special in life and in love."

"Love makes its own magic," James murmured. "The motto of the MacCarrans."

Elspeth drew back, looked at him. "You know about the motto?"

"I did," he said with a little smile. "But I found it hard to believe in magic."

"There is never a guarantee of the outcome with love or fairy magic," Niall said. "Human free will can accept it and grow, or circumvent it and diminish. What happens to you is not up to us or our kind in the end. It is up to you."

"That," James said, "sounds very sensible to me." Niall smiled. He understood.

"What of the treasure?" Elspeth asked.

"That was the one condition that could change everything for good or ill."

"But love changes everything," Elspeth said.

"Love and treasure are sometimes one and the same."

Riona, quiet and gentle, stepped forward. "We can make no barters or manipulate humans where love is present. You had to find it and realize it. But if the treasure had not been found, we would have had to ride forever, seeking, demanding."

"And now we must let you go," Niall said, drawing Riona back to his side.

Riona nodded. "If you stay too long inside our magic, the glamourie will take you over, and you will not want to leave."

"Go," Niall said. Elspeth embraced them again, and James took their hands. Then they stepped back, and within the moment, turned to mist.

Taking Elspeth's hand, James guided her up the slope toward sky and sunlight.

They stood at the top of the garden overlooking Struan House.

WITH HER HAND in James's, Elspeth stared, stunned to find herself in the rocky grotto where water trickled and late-blooming heather flourished. Glancing back, she saw that the rock wall behind them was solid, with no portal to another world. They had not even needed the blue agate still tucked in her pocket.

"We came rather farther than expected," James said, looking about.

She laughed. "Magic. We may have to get used to it."

"I can only try," he drawled, and they walked downward. "Careful."

"Just here," she said, "I slipped and fell in the awful weather, and landed at your feet in the mud."

"And a better day there never was, my love."

"I wonder if the others are back yet," Elspeth said, peering at the house.

"We will have to explain how we came to be here rather than meeting them out in the hills far from here." He led her down the slope.

Hearing the dogs bark, hearing shouts, Elspeth saw the door at the back of the house open. Patrick and Fiona emerged, flying across the lawn, waving, calling.

"Where have you been?" Patrick asked.

"We were so worried!" Fiona embraced James and then Elspeth. "Thank God you are safe! I dreamed you were lost in a cave in the mountain, captured by the fairies—just as in the fairy tales Grandmother used to tell us."

"We waited, but you never met us," Patrick said. "We were frantic, and sent people to search for you. Someone suggested you had gotten lost and found another way back home."

"We did," James said. "I hope you did not wait long."

Patrick frowned. "James, you have been gone for three days! We were beside ourselves, and about to send out yet another search party. But it was Donal MacArthur who said we should wait, that you probably found another vehicle and took your time."

"Three days?" James asked. "Impossible."

"We lost our, ah, sense of time when we got lost," Elspeth said hastily.

"It is such a relief to see you, and I am just grateful you came to no harm," Fiona said. "Donal MacArthur will want to know. He was the least worried of all of us. He said he knew the mountain best, and knew you would find a way home if you missed us."

"He was right," Elspeth said.

"Even Cousin Nick met us out in the hills yesterday to continue looking."

"Eldin?" James asked.

"He said he was only interested in fairy gold, and made rather a sour jest of it, but I thought he seemed worried," Fiona said.

"What about Charlotte Sinclair? Is she still here?" James asked.

"Charlotte," Fiona said, "decided you are a useless cad who fell for a simple Highland lass. She has gone back to Edinburgh with Sir Patrick, her new interest."

"May she be happy," James said.

"Did you find anything of value while you were out there?" Patrick asked.

"No treasure chest," James said. "But we did find some excellent crystals." He reached into his pocket and brought some out. "A few lovely gems perfect for a ring."

"A ring?" Fiona asked. "How can you think about jewelry now? You must be exhausted and in need of food and rest. Come inside."

"How did you find your way back?" Patrick asked as they headed for the house.

"Subterranean caves and tunnels brought us this way," Elspeth said.

"Labyrinthine, really," James said. "I doubt we would ever try that again." He glanced down at Elspeth, smiling. For a moment, she felt as if only they two existed.

"It looks to me," Patrick said, "that you two found more than a few crystals."

"I suppose we each found what we were looking for. But we are back."

"Donal will be glad to know it," Patrick said.

"We were fine," Elspeth said. She looked up at James. "We—made a decision."

"We were married," James said. "Handfasted. Legal, you know."

"Handfasted!" Fiona broke into a bright smile. "How romantic!"

Elspeth smiled, feeling her heart lift, wanting to laugh, suddenly.

"Married?" Patrick stared. "Without a vicar?"

"We will take care of that part of it," James said.

Fiona shook her head, smiling still. "Aunt Rankin will have a conniption."

"Let her," James said.

"We could have a quiet little wedding here," Elspeth said.

"So you found yourself a Highland bride after all," Fiona told James.

"And one with fairy blood." James hugged Elspeth close under his arm.

Fiona laughed. "Grandmother Struan would be so pleased!"

"More than you know. Now it is your turn." James laughed. "You should read our grandmother's book."

"I would love to read her book of fairies," Fiona said.

"Then you can each discover for yourselves what this fairy nonsense is all about. Though I warn you, it could be an adventure." James twitched his lips in a smile.

"Come inside and freshen up, and have something to eat," Fiona said. "You will both feel human again."

"I feel quite human," James laughed, and reached for Elspeth's hand again.

"So do I," Elspeth said, and he lifted her hand to his lips and kissed it.

# Epilogue



*December, 1822*

"WE CANNOT FIT another blasted thing into that carriage," James said, surveying the shabby landau packed full of belongings, most of them not his own. His breath misted in the chilly air and his boot heels crunched on packed snow. "We may need a cart and another driver as well as MacKimmie with the carriage. Are you sure the loom is necessary?"

"Aye," Elspeth said beside him. "If we agree to spend the winter in Edinburgh so you can deliver your lecture series, then I must have my loom to keep me occupied or I die of boredom." She smiled impishly, beautifully, from under the brim of her dark green velvet bonnet, her gloved hands inside the ermine muff he had given her for Christmas just last week.

Inside her left-hand glove, he knew, she wore the amethyst ring he had commissioned for their wedding in November. She loved it for the joy it represented—and he knew she delighted in its fairy-gem sparkle.

"Please do not languish of boredom," he laughed. He felt good-natured despite the dismantled loom precariously strapped to the back of the landau. Lady Rankin would no doubt call them gypsies when they arrived at the Edinburgh townhouse. He would set about buying or renting another place as soon as possible. He drew Elspeth under one arm. "I can think of ways to keep you well occupied." He nuzzled her cheek, where pink bloomed from cold and a rising blush.

"I would like that," she murmured. "But you will be so busy

with lectures and writing and your beloved rocks. What will I do without my loom and my work?"

"Lucie Graham will be dragging you off to teas and parties to introduce her dear cousin, the lovely Lady Struan. You will have little time for your craft."

"I want time for my craft," she said. "When word goes round that the eccentric new Lady Struan would rather sit home and weave than attend parties, there will not be many invitations."

"Nonsense. The eccentric, unique, brilliant, beautiful Lady Struan will make weaving the new rage among the ladies of Edinburgh."

"We shall see. I also need the loom to finish a plaid for my husband. It is Highland custom. It should be woven in a Highland home, but we must make an exception."

"You are always the exception, my girl," he murmured.

"You promised we can be back at Struan House by spring. I hope the handsome, studious, dashing Lord Struan can find something to do until the university opens in fall."

"I will have more than enough to do on this estate. And Angus MacKimmie will do a fine job looking after things until then. He is already arranging to have that old bridge repaired." He nodded to Angus, who grunted, busy tying the last of the luggage to the back of the vehicle. "But I have been thinking. This may be my last semester of lectures for a little while."

"Is it so? Could we live year-round at Struan?"

"We still need to go south now and then. We must be pragmatic about that."

"You are always pragmatic." She pouted a bit, then smiled.

"Grandmother's fairy book is nearly complete and will soon be in Sir Walter's capable hands. And I must spend time in Edinburgh to work on my book about geognosy. After that, I want to write a new study of Scotland's ancient rock layers. That would mean exploring the Highlands."

Elspeth nodded. "Good. I want to be here for my grandfather."

"Of course. Nor would I mind the life of a Highland laird much of the year. I can act as visiting scholar at the university rather than resident lecturer. I will have a word with the dean about that."

"Thank you. With the fairy spell off his shoulders now, Grandda is slower at his weaving, and there is much weaving work at Kilcrennan, with the orders growing. I want to help him."

"Donal has more on his mind than weaving these days, with his new wife."

"Peggy will keep him happy. They both seem so content."

"It is as if they've been married fifty years rather than two weeks. I hope we will be as happy as those two in our later years."

"We will." She laughed. "And if we are here, we could perhaps visit the realm where my parents live again. Donal could come with us."

"Do not test my acceptance too far, wife," he drawled very low, so only she could hear. "I am still not sure what happened on that mountain. I wonder if I hit my head on a rock that day, and dreamed all of it."

"Perhaps you did." She tugged on his hat brim and made a face. "What we have now is the best of dreams. Oh, here they come," she said, turning. "They wanted to bid us farewell."

James glanced there, but saw only the empty lane leading to the house. "Odd."

"Coaches coming," Angus called then. "A gig and a barouche."

"Barouche?" James asked quickly.

"Black barouche, sir, very fine," Angus said. "The one that was here before."

"Nick," James muttered. "What the devil does he want?" He walked a little along the lane beside Elspeth just as the coaches came over a low hill. "I see Donal's gig, but why is Eldin here?"

"I cannot imagine. Since you refused to sell the property, I thought that might be the last we would see of him."

"Until my grandmother's will is finalized, after my siblings and I all meet the conditions, he has no need to come here."

Elspeth tucked her hand inside the crook of his elbow. "He did help search for us when they thought we were lost. Perhaps he cares and came to say farewell. He seems a lonely fellow, though he shows only a grumbly side."

"Do not let him fool your tender heart. He wanted the treasure, so he joined the search. But only Donal and we two know where that is. The gem mine will stay secret."

"It may be invisible to anyone else who enters those caves anyway."

"I am not convinced of that," he said.

She left his side to dash forward on the snow-packed road. James hurried along. His balance was much improved, and he managed without a cane most days. Highland air and exercise, he claimed. Fairy magic, Elspeth claimed. Whatever it was, his leg had nearly gained its original strength.

The gig carrying Donal and Peggy rolled to a halt, and they climbed down to wrap Elspeth in warm, loving embraces, and took James's hands in excited conversation. He was happy to see them, though distracted by the approaching barouche.

"We will see you in Edinburgh," Donal was saying. "I will be delivering new plaids there next month. What is that raven-hearted rascal doing here?" He turned.

"I do not know," James said. He went to meet Eldin's barouche as it rolled to a halt, wheels crunching on snow. A riderless, saddled horse was tied to the back of the carriage. He frowned, not sure what this was about.

"Eldin!" He waited as the coachman jumped down to open the door and his cousin stepped out. "Greetings. How may we help you this cold morning?"

Eldin doffed his tall hat in greeting. "It is I who has come to help *you*."

"How good to see you, Lord Eldin." Elspeth joined them and

set her gloved hand on James's arm. He did not take his gaze from his cousin.

"Lady Struan!" Eldin took her offered hand. "You look in fine health."

"We are about to leave for the south, but would be happy to offer you tea before we go," Elspeth said. "My grandfather and stepmother are just arrived too."

"I regret I cannot join you, as I must return to Auchnashee," Eldin said. "The castle refurbishments are going well, provided I am there to supervise. I came here today to ask you to convey my best to Fiona. Please extend my invitation to her to stay at Auchnashee when she comes north. Free of charge, of course. We are cousins."

James frowned, trying to discern a motive. "I did not know Fiona was going into the north."

"In spring, I believe," Eldin said with a tight little smile. James saw a flash in his cousins's dark eyes, a glimmer of something he had not seen before. Hope or even vulnerability. Did he care for Fiona? But it was gone.

"We will be sure to tell Fiona," Elspeth said.

"The other reason I came here," Eldin went on, "is to offer you the use of my barouche for your journey. It is larger and more comfortable than your landau. I brought a horse to return to Auchnashee. My driver can wait here and be of use until your man returns with the barouche. You must arrive in the city in style and comfort. It will not do for Viscount Struan and his bride to travel like gypsies."

"How did you know we were leaving today?" James asked.

"Lady Rankin mentioned in a letter that you might strap all your belongings to the old carriage like a pair of tinkers. She seems to think young Lady Struan is a simple Highland lass. But she does not know what a girl with fairy blood is capable of." He tipped his head to smile at Elspeth. "I assured her I would help."

"Thank you," Elspeth said. "We are honored by your offer."

"Grateful," James said. "But it is not necessary."

"Come have tea," Elspeth insisted. Eldin relented, promised to leave the barouche and take the horse. Then he walked into the house with Donal and Peggy.

James stared after him. "What the devil was that about," he muttered.

Elspeth slipped her arm around him. "We may never puzzle him out," she said. "Let us go inside and have tea with our unexpected guests. Then we will take our tinker parade across the Highlands into the city in our gypsy landau."

James laughed. "Honestly I would not mind the barouche. It is much more comfortable." He took her in his arms in the snowy lane, his breath fogging. Elspeth's nose was pink in the cold, and he kissed it. "I know you are in no hurry to leave here."

"I would like to stay, but I will go anywhere with you, Lord Struan. Anywhere at all, city or hills, even if all you want to do is look for silly old rocks."

He kissed her, taking time with it, tender and slow, and felt the heat rising in him, heart and body, despite the cold. "And I am grateful, truly," he whispered.

"Do you really want to take Eldin's barouche?" she asked, snuggling close.

"I would, though I would not put it past Cousin Nick to put some kind of spell on it. The fellow is a condundrum."

"The only spell inside our carriage," she whispered, "is the one we will set ourselves." She kissed him again, took his hand, and led him into the warmth of their house.

# Author's Note

*A Rogue in Twilight* is another of my revised, refreshed backlist books, and I'm delighted to offer it to readers in this beautiful new Dragonblade edition. One of the advantages of digital publishing is that authors can have the chance to revise, republish, and improve previous stories and bring them to a new group of readers or bring updated versions to readers who may enjoy a brighter, fresher version of a story they read once before. Time lets any writer develop stronger skills and storytelling wisdom, and it's a privilege to apply that to a story that I loved writing years ago.

This particular story gave me a chance to explore the wavy line that runs between historical romance and romantasy. I often include paranormal elements in my books, which is no surprise to many of my readers. When James and Elspeth's story took on fairytale elements, it was fun to see where that would lead. I'm a historian and a dreamer, so I had fun with fairies as well as research—here, I learned a lot as I played with Scottish fairy lore, the craft of weaving, and the geology of rocks and stones and such.

Whether you read this book in its original form (published by Avon as *To Wed A Highland Bride*) or you're new to the story in this incarnation, I hope you loved James and Elspeth's fairytale romance in the Scottish Highlands. And I hope you'll read the related books about the other MacCarran siblings and their whisky-distilling, whisky-smuggling, romantic-adventure loving

MacGregor and Graham cousins. More to come! Look for information about my books at www.susanfraserking.com, and please check out the group blog at www.wordwenches.com, where I post with some wonderful author friends. Happy reading!

# About the Author

Susan King is the bestselling, award-winning author of (so far) 28 historical novels and novellas, a hefty nonfiction history, and dozens of magazine and web articles on education and the craft of writing. Her books, including mainstream historicals Lady Macbeth: A Novel and Queen Hereafter: A Novel of Margaret of Scotland, have been published by Penguin, Random House, HarperCollins, Kensington, ePublishingWorks, and Dragonblade. Praised for historical accuracy, lyrical writing, and storytelling quality, she is a USA Today bestselling author with numerous awards, nominations, and career achievement awards as well as starred reviews from Publisher's Weekly, Booklist, and Library Journal. Most of her books are set in Scotland ranging from the 11th to the 19th centuries.

Susan is a former university lecturer in art history, a private school teacher, and a founding member of one of the longest-running author blogs, "Word Wenches" (wordwenches.com). She holds a Bachelor's in studio art and English literature, a Master's in art history, and completed most of her Ph.D./ABD in medieval art history. Raised in Upstate New York, she lives in Maryland with her husband and three sons in an ever-growing family.

Website – www.susanfraserking.com